THE BIG GRABOW$KI

Dari — thanks for all your support — CJ

Mike Nettleton

THE BIG GRABOW$KI

Carolyn J. Rose
Mike Nettleton

KRILL
KP
PRESS

www.krillpress.com

THE BIG GRABOW$KI

© 2009 by Carolyn J. Rose & Mike Nettleton

The Big Grabowski is a work of fiction. The characters, incidents, and dialogues are products of the author's imagination and are not to be construed as real. Any resemblance to actual events or persons, living or dead, is entirely coincidental.

Published by Krill Press LLC. All rights reserved.

ISBN 978-0-9821443-3-6

Printed in the United States of America

In fond memory of Michael Bailey
Writer, deejay, friend
Always in our hearts

ONE

"Nothing exciting ever happens in Devil's Harbor," Jennifer Daley groused as she trudged along the trail to the edge of the cliff overlooking Neptune's Grotto. "It's the most boring town in Oregon. Especially on Sundays."

And she couldn't even sleep in. No, she had to count the sea lions hanging out on the rocks in the tiny cove and post the number above the cash register in the gift shop up on the highway.

"Tourists have a right to know exactly how many Steller sea lions they'll see for their money," Phil McGenny had lectured her just moments ago, right before he drove off and left her in charge of the roadside attraction. "So don't go making up a number. And don't forget to say that the sea lions are protected by law. And if they have questions about mating season, tell them to read the brochure."

Guh-ross. Like she *wanted* to answer questions about how sea lions do it.

She glanced over her shoulder, saw nothing but the weathered gift shop, and wondered how he'd know whether she counted every single sea lion. He and his wife had gone to Lincoln City and, unless the slot machines ate all their money, they wouldn't be back until midnight. It would be way too dark then to check. And besides, it wasn't like the sea lions sat still while you counted. They were always jumping in the water. Except for the males. Phil McGenny said they didn't go anywhere or eat anything during mating season.

"And they still look fat!"

She kicked at a pebble, skidded on the wet asphalt, and clutched at the slick wooden railing. Yuck. Seagull poop.

She bent and wiped her fingers on the scruffy grass beside the trail, remembering how she'd overheard Latrice McGenny sticking up for her: "Yes, Phil, I know Jennifer's only seventeen. And I know she's a little flighty, but deep down she's responsible. She can handle it."

"Well, duh," Jennifer muttered, "it isn't brain surgery." You don't put too much oil or salt on the popcorn, you count out the correct change, and maybe you unload a few "genuine handmade" Devil's Harbor whirligigs.

"Not!"

Everyone in town knew they were all made in China, but Mr. Grabowski insisted it wasn't exactly lying to fool people from out of town. And Jennifer knew it was pointless to argue with adults. *So…whatever.*

The trail cornered and angled down into a wispy fog. Jennifer shivered and rubbed at the goose bumps on her arms. It was creepy out here all alone, kinda like being in one of those slasher or vampire movies where the girl screams and screams and no one hears.

She patted her highlighted ash-blond hair. She was cute enough to star in a movie like that, and her mother said her screams could peel paint. Maybe she'd try out a scream on those stinky sea lions.

The odor rolled up out of the fog and smacked her— dead fish and poop and sea lion morning breath that lasted all day long. Yuck. She'd have to shower twice when she got home, before she tried on her coronation dress again and maybe sewed more sequins on the hem.

Miss Whirligig! Yesss!

She *had* to win, *had* to be the one to wear that crown and get the scholarship check from Mr. Grabowski and pose looking all surprised while Molly Donovan took her picture for the newspaper.

She stretched her arms out and waltzed in a tight circle on the steep trail, imagining her victory dances—first with Mayor Deeds and then with the winner of the belly-bucking competition.

Okay, well, that part sucked. Big Billy Bohannon had won the last seven years, and he looked like a pregnant phone booth—danced like one, too. As for the mayor, he was short, fat, sweaty, and smelled like low tide.

Double yuck.

She stopped waltzing, made an O with her lips and raised her hands in surprise, practicing for the newspaper photo. Maybe Molly would interview her, too. After all, Molly had been the first-ever festival queen. And now she was a famous newspaper reporter.

Wondering if Molly would ask about her diet secrets— orange foods only on Wednesdays and never eat pizza crusts— Jennifer reached the viewing area at the base of the trail. Disregarding signs warning against climbing the railing, she hoisted herself to the third rung, held her nose, and peered into the cove.

A huge wave loomed and slammed against the rocky ledges with a boom like thunder, spraying frothy water across a huddle of sea lions a hundred feet below. The cove faced due west and no sunlight would strike the ledges for hours. In the fog-shrouded morning light, the sea lions appeared to be the same color as the rocks they lay on, and both were slick with spray.

Jennifer leveled a finger at the right side of the cove and counted: "One. Two. Three. Four."

No, that was a rock. Or was it?

A bull the size of a compact car cranked his head back, glared at her, and gronked out a roar.

"You don't scare me," she said. "Sea lions eat fish, not people."

The bull roared again, then lurched to the lip of the ledge, scattering a cluster of barking cows and almost squishing a pup. He thrust himself out over the edge, intent on something bobbing in a floating mat of kelp.

Jennifer squinted, wondering if the thing in the water was a bachelor come to challenge the older bull. A fight, even a fight between sea lions, would break the monotony. She hunched farther over the rail, wishing she hadn't been worried about smudging her mascara and had brought the binoculars.

Another towering wave broke against the ledges and for a few seconds the big bull disappeared beneath a blanket of foamy spray. When it cleared, he roared once more and launched himself at the thing in the kelp.

Jennifer knew next to nothing about marine biology, but she knew that thing wasn't a bachelor bull.

Sea lions didn't wear ties.

Sergeant Greg Erdman spun his cruiser onto the narrow road looping along Perdition Point north of Neptune's Grotto. Oblivious to the glittering blue ocean and the surf thundering on rocks far below, he grappled with how to explain to Molly Donovan why he'd stood her up last night.

A simple lie about being ordered out to investigate a robbery or handle a domestic violence call wouldn't wash with a reporter. Molly would check his alibi. No, he'd have to go with the truth: sprawled in his recliner, he'd drifted off in front of the Mariners' game. "Damn." He kneaded the kink in his neck. Dating at forty was complicated and confusing—almost more trouble than it was worth. *Almost.* He grinned, remembering that night last week when he and Molly had built a driftwood fire on the beach. After splitting a bottle of wine, he'd finally kissed her and had been working up the nerve to grope for the top button on her blouse when his pager erupted. Reaching for it, he'd slammed his elbow against a log, hit his damn funny bone, and jumped around squawking like a psychotic chicken. Molly had laughed her ass off and run for her car. Women! No matter how much daytime TV he watched, he'd never understand what they wanted. Except for his ex-wife, Patsy. She wanted every dime he made.

Wincing, he turned onto a narrow road leading to a viewpoint. The tires bit into thick gravel that rattled against the undercarriage. Ahead, two weathered picnic tables hunkered on a patch of weed-infested grass beside a six-car parking lot. Beyond them, Greg spotted a silver late-model Lincoln, its roof glistening with dew, wedged into the brush at the edge of the lot. The driver's door hung open; the window was down.

Damn joy-riders. Greg eased the cruiser up behind the car and left it idling. Why couldn't they abandon a car in town where someone else would find it? Where he wouldn't get stuck with the paperwork. He kicked a rear tire and then peered inside, catching a whiff of faux pine air freshener. The keys were in the ignition and the interior was immaculate. Strange. Joy-riders usually trashed a car.

Using the tip of his pen, he opened the glove box. Cleaned out. Not even an owner's manual. He was about to call the dispatcher to have her run the plate when she called him.

"We're almost home, Molly girl."

I nodded and waved to my father as the *Helen* rounded a rocky spit on the north side of Purgatory Bay. Devil's Harbor lay before us, spread along the lava shelf spewed by an ancient volcano, weathered buildings looking like they'd been cast up by a storm tide. Except for fresh paint and new shingles, the exteriors hadn't changed since I'd left for journalism school twenty years ago. Beyond them was evidence of so-called progress—a jagged oozing wound slicing across the ridge Vince Grabowski had leveled to build an up-scale development. In keeping with the town theme, he'd named it Devil's Acres. Then pounding winter rains arrived weeks ahead of schedule and six luxury homes had mud-surfed onto the seventh fairway of his newly turfed golf course.

"Progress." I shook my head as the *Helen* plowed toward the narrow curving channel leading to a tiny pocket in the lava. The anchorage sheltered a dock and a dozen boats the size of the one my father had named for the woman he'd loved, married, and lost to cancer the day I turned twelve.

"Smell that air," Dad ordered from the skimpy bridge rigged off the roof of the small cabin. "Nothing like it anywhere else on earth."

I waved again, but didn't answer. Yelling over the throb of the engine would only aggravate the pounding around my eyes. Tangy sea breezes couldn't clear sinuses clogged by assorted mold spores and the pollen from a wealth of spring blooms. I longed for Albuquerque, for dry air and the sharp aroma of roasting green chile. But more than that, I missed the crime beat and the action of a daily newspaper. Now I hammered out fluff for a paper I delivered myself.

They didn't even have a crime beat here.

"Don't need one," my editor insisted. And he had a point. Crime on this stretch of the coast consisted of a dismal round of fender-benders, drunken fistfights, and stop 'n' pop artists who cleaned out cars while tourists took in the sights. Of course there were also shady land-grabbers like Grabowski, but my editor called them 'shapers of the future.'

Reporting for *The North Coast Flotsam* beat shucking oysters. Just barely. As they say, necessity is a mother. But I'd be out of here soon.

My father bent to check the depth gauge. His crew-cut white hair was too short for the wind to riffle, his skin too mottled by years of hard weather for the sun to do more damage. At seventy-two, Mike Donovan didn't need glasses or false teeth or a hearing aid. What he needed was to take it easy to prevent another heart attack.

"Hey, Molly! Think he's ready to take her in?" Dad bellowed, nodding at the lanky man below him on the deck.

Jeffrey Wolfe turned for my answer and I saw a mix of eagerness and uncertainty on his face. He'd left a bad marriage and a high-stress job at a Chicago ad agency and drifted to the coast to write poetry and, as he put it, "learn to tell time by the tides." He'd won a regional award and been published in two national magazines, but he'd discovered that it's not called "free verse" for nothing. If Jeffrey couldn't pull his own weight and more, I'd stay and crew myself because the odds of keeping Dad off the water were on a par with my chances of capturing a Pulitzer Prize writing about crab molt for *The Flotsam*.

"What about it, Molly? Shall we let him try?"

I massaged the skin between my eyes. Maybe he'd surprise me.

"Go for it!"

Jeffrey shot me a smile, climbed to the narrow platform beside my father, and clutched the wheel, fingers white against the chrome. Dad stepped onto the top rung of the ladder. "Center up on the middle span of the highway bridge, back off on the power, gauge the wind, watch how the waves break, aim for the starboard piling, then gun her, cut hard to port, and we're in."

Jeffrey bobbed his head, but all three of us knew it wasn't that simple. With the tide nearly full and a strong wind from the south, this was like threading a needle while wearing mittens. His shoulders hunched beneath his bright red T-shirt as he death-gripped the throttle. He stood six feet four inches tall and I doubted he weighed more than a hundred and ninety pounds. Too stringy for my taste, but some women found his wry smile, faded blue eyes, and tousled graying hair attractive.

The bridge loomed above us and I heard the distant hum of tires on pavement. Dry land! In thirty-seven years of pitching and rolling, I'd never found my sea legs. My aunt claimed my red hair and stubborn streak were the only indications that Mike Donovan was my father.

Gulls circled the bow screeching, their black eyes checking for signs we had a catch on board. Forget it, I thought, this is a training mission. Besides, commercial fishing had nearly petered out a few years back. That's why Dad now cruised up and down the coast, searching for a puff of vapor or the flip of a fluke, and attempting to be pleasant to tourists wetting their lines.

Gripping the railing, I studied Jeffrey as he angled the *Helen* to starboard. Straight ahead, waves broke against pock-marked lava. Frothing white water streamed down jagged rock to be caught and tossed back by the next wave. On the highway bridge above, a gray-haired couple pointed at the splintered edges of the channel, then focused their cameras, ready to record our certain wreck. Above the thrumming of the twin diesels I heard Dad mutter an obscenity-laden invective against the channel, the Pacific Ocean, and the wind.

"Here we go!" Jeffrey gunned the engines. The *Helen* rocked and bucked, then shot forward.

The pager clipped to my belt vibrated. Hunkering over to block the sun, I squinted at the digital read-out. The first three numbers were the local prefix. The next four didn't look familiar. The last three were 666, code for a hot news flash. *Right.* The last so-called flash involved a grease fire at Grover's Clam and Ham out on Highway 101. Total damage: two dollars worth of rancid grease and Grover's eyebrows.

The *Helen* tilted and shuddered. I took three involuntary steps, clutched in vain at the ladder, and then rebounded against the starboard rail. Boat-crushing rocks loomed before me. Cringing, I shaded my eyes and peered at my father. His lips were sealed against each other. His eyes darted from the rocks to the bow, measuring distance. Jeffrey throttled down and spun the wheel to port, then jerked it back. I thudded against the side of the cabin.

"We're in, lad!" my father yelled. "You did it! Now aim for the Mark-up, bring her around beside the *Searchin' Urchin* and shut her down."

I staggered to my feet, dug the cell phone from my purse in the cramped cabin, and punched in the number from my pager.

"Neptune's Grotto," a breathless voice sang out. "Where sea lions come to play and you can see them if you pay."

"It's Molly Donovan. Someone paged me."

"Molly! Ohmigod. It's me, Jennifer."

I rolled my eyes. If you looked up space cadet in the dictionary, you'd find her picture. "What's up, Jennifer?"

"You gotta get down here. It's mega-nasty."

"What is?"

"That man."

I sighed. "What man?"

"Ohmigod, Molly, I don't know who he is. He's in with the sea lions."

My hand tightened on the phone. Could this be real news?

"Did you call the sheriff's office?"

"Well, duh. I almost called you first, but I didn't think that would be, like, you know, fair."

"Fair?"

"I mean, like, I thought they should have a head start. Because you're such a great reporter."

Jennifer-logic. Had I been that ditzy at seventeen? "Okaaay."

"And they told me not to let anyone in. But Mr. McGenny will fire me if I don't sell tickets, and I need this job to rescue my shoes from lay-away."

I opened my mouth to set her straight, but grinned instead. Tourists trampling evidence? Not my problem. Why should I help Sergeant Erdman?

"I'll be there in fifteen minutes."

"Okay. Ohmigod, Molly, I gotta bail. Here comes a tour bus."

I snapped the phone shut and stuffed it into my purse, scrabbling for my keys. "Gotta run, Dad."

"Hold on, Missy." He tossed a coil of rope to Jeffrey who wound it around a cleat on the dock. "What about lunch at the Devil's Food Cafe to celebrate?"

"Not today." I kissed his cheek and vaulted over the rail to the dock. "I've got a date with a dead man."

TWO

"... **brkkkk** ... Coast Guard helicopter ... grikkk ..
.. State Police, Fish and Wildlife ... brkkk ... coordinate ...
ffftttt ...."

Sergeant Greg Erdman had no problem deciphering the broken radio transmission. It meant everybody was getting into the body-in-the-grotto act and arguing about who had jurisdiction and how to recover the body without disturbing those protected sea lions.

"10-4. I'll be there in five and secure the scene."

He slapped the microphone into its slot and used both hands to wrestle the patrol car around one of the slick turns that made Highway 101 so treacherous. He bet the car he'd discovered belonged to the waterlogged John Doe. The current must have carried the body from Perdition Point to Neptune's Grotto.

He leaned into another turn and felt the rear end drift. The three-year-old cruiser, with ninety-two thousand plus miles on the odometer, needed new shock absorbers bad. Fat chance. The budget was "tight as a tick" Sheriff Archie Fletcher told him daily. That meant no raise, damn little overtime, and living on canned soup and fish sticks to scrape up child support and alimony payments. Like Patsy needed money now that she'd moved in with that smug corporate jerk in Salem. And like he ever had time to spend with the kids. Between this job and security work on his days off, he barely had time to eat and sleep, let alone drive two hours to the capital. He felt a pang of regret as he pictured his eight-year-old son and eleven-year-old daughter. He had to make more time for them.

"Damn!"

He pounded the wheel in frustration, then fed it between his hands and rocked around another curve.

"Neptune's Grotto. One Mile Ahead." The sign flashed by on his right and he pounded the wheel again. Sure as shit, Molly Donovan would turn up before he got the yellow tape out of his trunk. Greg again mulled his options—apologize, try the old "date, what date?" bluff, or act too busy to deal with it.

The rear of a battered tour bus loomed in his windshield.

Son of a b---!

He stomped the brake and skidded to a stop. Cars, trucks, recreational vehicles, and two buses clustered beside the bright yellow roadside attraction. Men, women, and children milled around the parking lot, some talking on cell phones, some looking pale and queasy. Head down, he lunged from the cruiser. Time to make himself unpopular with a pack of curiosity-seekers.

"Come on! Come on!" I pumped the gas pedal on my aging pickup. The starter clicked ominously then ground itself into a frenzy.

Varroommmm!

The engine caught, belching black smoke from the tailpipe. A bad sign.

Great!

Just what I didn't need, a big repair bill to push my credit card balance into the danger zone. Back in February I'd sunk my savings into a house in Albuquerque and had just started to hang my collection of flea-market art, when I got the bad-news phone call. Now my vacation and paid leave had dried up, and only a few hundred dollars stood between me and financial ruin.

I hadn't told Dad that the scrawny paychecks from my stopgap job at *The Flotsam* didn't cover my mortgage payments; that would increase a stress level my presence here was supposed to help reduce. Dad would loan me money in a minute—if he had any to spare. He never talked about his finances, but I figured moorage fees, repairs, and insurance ate up most of his income.

But if Jeffrey's skills improved in a hurry, I'd be back in New Mexico and solvent once more.

Shifting into second, I roared past the Slackwater Bed and Brew and the fish market that Prudence Deeds, the mayor's wife, had christened Harborside Morsels but which everyone called the Mark-up because of her husband's propensity to squeeze an extra dime out of every deal. I made a rolling stop at the intersection by the Belly Up Bar and Bait Shop and turned left onto what natives still called the Coast Road. Guide books referred to it as "a scenic loop off Highway 101 winding through an authentic fishing village, Devil's Harbor, home of the annual Whirligig Festival, a celebration of the colorful handcrafted wind-animated toys and lawn ornaments made by area residents." Lately, that last part drew a bitter laugh from Devil's Harbor natives—followed by an expletive sandwich with Vince Grabowski's name in the middle.

I sped across the bridge over the channel, past the Come On 'n' Get It convenience store and on toward Neptune's Grotto, half a mile south of where the Coast Road reconnected with Highway 101. The radio crackled to life, and I heard the off-key organ music Elspeth Hunsaker used to announce her daily talk show.

"Good morning, good morning, good morning." Elspeth's voice trilled from the speaker on my dusty dashboard. "And a beautiful morning it is. We have a glorious sun shining above us and, as always, the forecast is for a one hundred percent chance of salvation here on KYMR, which stands for, as you know, You Must Repent."

In a twisted kind of way, I admired Elspeth and her reckless pursuit of failure. When her father died two years ago, he'd left her the station and a house on Temptation Way. Elspeth had abandoned a teaching job at a Utah private academy and within a week changed KYMR's format from an eclectic mix of light rock, oldies, big band, blues, country, and zydeco to hymns, Christian rock, and a scripture-centered talk show. No other signal penetrated to this stretch of the coast and most formerly loyal local listeners chose silence instead of what Elspeth offered.

"Today, once again, the topic is the willful disregard some of your community leaders have toward sacrilege. I'm talking about the blasphemous name inflicted upon this wonderful community, the homage we pay to the prince of darkness whenever we write a return address on an envelope. The time has come to change the name of our community to Holy Waters."

The signal faded out as the road slid around another hill and dipped to run along a rocky beach. I glanced to my right, hoping to catch a glimpse of one of the whales Dad's future depended on, but as usual I saw nothing more than breaking waves, long blue-green swells, and the flash of sun off the windows of a trawler balanced on the faint line between sea and sky.

"Sadly, I can lead you to the river, but I cannot make you drink of the waters of salvation. I can show you— Ah, I see

14

we have a caller. Caller, you're on the air on KYMR, You Must Repent."

"Elspeth? Elspeth Hunsaker?" A quavering falsetto dribbled from the dashboard speaker as my truck climbed the headland to Perdition Point.

"Yes. You're on the air, caller."

"Am I really on the air?"

Was that a faint French accent beneath those words? I tweaked the radio dial.

"You're on the air."

"You're sure? I can't hear myself. Let me turn up my radio."

I reached for the volume knob. Not fast enough. The metallic squeal of feedback filled the cab and set my teeth on edge.

"Turn down your radio," Elspeth screeched.

The feedback subsided as I spun onto 101 and gunned the truck. "Oh, goody, I'm on the air. I'm really on the air."

"Yes," Elspeth said with all the warmth of dry ice. "You are."

"Well, I've been sitting here thinking about something you said that reminded me of my late husband, Merle. A fine man. And fine-looking, too. Except for that nose hair. You know, we lived here in Devil's Harbor—"

"Holy Waters!" Elspeth interjected. "Holy Waters."

"Holding water? How ever did you know? My ankles are bloated like week-old fish. But, like I was saying about Merle and his nose—"

"Click. Bwaaaaaaat."

"Oh, mercy sakes," Elspeth simpered. "I seem to have accidentally cut that caller off."

"Accidently on purpose," I chuckled. Given enough time, even Elspeth could recognize a prankster and decide not to turn the other cheek.

I switched off the radio and leaned into the final curve. Up ahead, Greg Erdman knotted yellow crime-scene tape around a chain-link fence. Across the highway, a string of cars and RVs lined the shoulder. A gaggle of tourists gawked and two gangsta wannabes in crack-of-the-butt baggy jeans gave him the finger.

I scraped the truck up against a thick stand of brambles, grabbed my purse and camera bag, and ran toward him, sneezing.

Greg planted his fists on his hips. "You can't come through here, Molly. This is a crime scene."

"The body's in the water, not the parking lot. Besides, these tourists have trampled all the evidence." Peering over his shoulder, I saw Jennifer open the front door and wave. I reached for the tape. "And you owe me for last night."

He winced. "I can't let you through."

A whumping sound thickened the southern sky. A Coast Guard chopper appeared over a stand of Douglas firs, tilted, and circled. I slid my right hand down to waist level and gave Jennifer a thumbs-up sign.

"Look!" I pointed over Greg's shoulder. "They're signaling for you to stop traffic so they can land on the highway."

Greg turned. I dodged under the tape and sprinted for the door. It was so easy I almost felt guilty. Almost.

"Thanks," I called to Jennifer as I hurtled past, bolted through the back door, and pounded down the asphalt trail, digging for the telephoto lens. Not that the paper would print a picture of the floater. *The Flotsam* enforced strict standards about blood, guts, and sensationalism, but I hoped the long lens would give me a clue to the victim's identity and a jump on my deadline. Of course, this might be a suicide. That meant no story—and pissing Greg off for nothing. Well, not nothing. There was that little matter of last night.

Stumbling to a stop, I dragged out the camera and snapped on the lens. I heard Greg's boots thudding on the asphalt as I climbed onto the creaking wooden railing and focused on the body bobbing in the foaming swells below. It floated face down, pink shirt hanging in tatters, gray slacks torn around bruised and broken flesh.

"Damn it, Molly, get off that railing and up to the road or I'll cuff you."

"Promise?" I braced myself, squinting. A whiff of week-old-tuna odor drifted up to me. I stifled a gag.

"You know Ben Galloway won't let you print those pictures." He grabbed the back of my T-shirt.

"I'm not shooting, I'm looking." I zoomed and focused. A wave flipped the body and I caught a flash of color, a paisley pattern of pink and purple only one man I knew would put on his feet willingly. "Whoa!"

"What?" He tugged at my shirt. "What is it?"

As another wave rolled the body, I spotted a matching tie.

"I feel sorry for you, Greg. You just caught yourself one hell of an investigation."

"What the hell are you talking about?"

I snapped off three quick shots: the body, sea lion cows huddled on the rocks, and a big bull with an expression of disgust.

"Two words: Vincent Grabowski."

"The developer guy? He's the floater?"

I climbed down, grinning.

"Afraid so."

I packed up my camera.

"But look on the bright side. You won't need to make a list of suspects. You can just copy the Devil's Harbor phone book."

THREE

Prudence Deeds tapped a perfectly sculpted lavender fingernail on her polished desk and moved the telephone, also lavender, to her left ear while she pretended to listen to her client's concerns about Devil's Acres. So what if a few homes had slid onto the golf course during the winter? There were more standing, most of them a good hundred feet from the landslide, and half still for sale.

"I can assure you Mr. Grabowski's geo-technical experts are confident last winter's unfortunate incident was a once-in-a-century weather pattern. We have total confidence in the integrity of the remaining homes." That was the script Vince had crafted.

Crossing her fingers, she ad-libbed. "If my husband, the mayor, and I didn't already have a spectacular ocean view, I'd buy a home up there myself. With a gated community like that, you can rest assured your neighbors will all be solid citizens." *Not like the riffraff here in town.*

Riffraff. Trailer trash. Labels her family had worn when she was growing up. She'd sworn that she'd get out of the wrong side of Medford and make something of herself, no matter what it took. Overweight and pasty-faced, she'd been slinging hash in a diner along I-5 and studying accounting when Brighton Deeds rolled in and ordered the "big boy special." Two weeks and twenty-eight orders of biscuits and gravy later, he'd offered to take her away with him. Sure, he was fourteen years older and an inch shorter, but beggars can't be choosers.

Gazing out at the harbor, she watched Mike Donovan polish the *Helen's* rail, and then looked past him to the younger man painting the trim around the boat's cabin. Jeffrey Wolfe had shucked his T-shirt in the afternoon sun and her breath caught at the sight of his well-toned pectoral muscles and flat stomach. Jeffrey radiated quiet animal magnetism. Not like her husband, who exuded the sex appeal of a flounder. A fat flounder. With bad breath. She longed to be more than the wife of a fishmonger, even if that fishmonger was the mayor.

Sighing, she turned her attention to the client, a Los Angeles businessman desperate to escape smog, fires, earthquakes, gang warfare, and crowded freeways. He'd move here, she knew, and then complain that he was bored. He'd sell within two years and she'd score a second commission.

Out on the *Helen*, Jeffrey Wolfe stood, arched his back, ran his fingers through his wavy hair, then smiled at something Mike Donovan said and went back to the trim. Prudence felt her breath catch. Why hadn't she noticed Jeffrey before? His clothing, she realized. All those grungy layers people on the coast wore to keep out the rain and incessant wind.

Getting out of the weather would be one of the benefits of Brighton being elected to Congress. Although skeptical that he could pull it off, she'd increased her cream and lotion regimen and her daily labors with the weights and treadmill she'd crammed into the guest room. After thirty-five you couldn't win the war against flab and wrinkles, you could only fight a holding action.

"Of course you can have some time to think it over," Prudence responded to the buyer's automatic hedge. She had him. Now to set the hook. "But these homes will go fast now that the summer season's starting." She tapped her nails impatiently as he rambled. "Certainly. Call me any time. Any time at all."

"Yes!" She exulted as she hung up. The buyer had the bucks, and he knew that by California standards he had a bargain. Vince Grabowski had slashed prices after the mud slide. He'd needed quick cash to fight the lawsuit brought by those whose million-dollar one-hundred-eighty-degree-ocean-view homes were rubble. And he needed more cash to excavate the seventh fairway and shore up the hillside above Lucifer's Links.

"No way he gets a dime from my commissions." She grinned at her reflection in a full-length mirror across from the desk in her living room, and then walked to the window. Vince had thought he'd squeeze her by threatening to tell Brighton everything. But she'd fixed him.

It was a shame he'd let money spoil things. In fine shape for his age, Vince had been focused and inventive. Cheating on Brighton had been wrong, but Vince had met needs she didn't know she had. "I'll miss you, Vince," she whispered.

Downstairs, Brighton Deeds the Third listened to his wife's footsteps and stared mournfully into the dull eyes of a pair of trout reclining on a bed of ice at the front of the display case. Maybe, with the congressional thing nearly locked up, Prudence would let him back into their bedroom.

God, how he hated the fold-out sofa in the living room. Not only did the lumps make his back hurt, but without a cross-breeze from the bedroom windows, the aroma from the store hung in the air like a fart in a phone booth.

"The smell of fish is the smell of money."

Deeds tried to console himself with a saying his father had repeated endlessly. It didn't work. He'd slaved in the fish market since he was old enough to make change and handle a knife—nearly forty years beheading and scaling, filleting and freezing, weighing and wrapping—and all on his own since his parents retired and moved to Florida. For twenty years he'd also maintained the coin-operated car wash they'd tacked onto the side of the building. He longed for a job where he could wear shoes instead of rubber boots; he longed to smell like something besides spray-on wax and the catch of the day.

Closing his eyes, he imagined himself in a custom-tailored three-piece suit that would camouflage some of the gut he'd accumulated. He hoped that once they got to Washington and he started dealing and wheeling, Prudence would forget about men like Vince Grabowski and come begging.

Upstairs a door slammed and he heard Prudence's high heels tapping down the outside stairway. Her car started and she drove away.

"Drat." She'd probably gone to meet a prospective buyer. He hoped it wasn't a man. For the sake of his political future, he'd pretended not to know about her affair with Vince Grabowski, but he could forgive only so much.

He soothed himself, imagining he stood at the center of a fancy reception, holding a tall glass of French champagne, nobbing and hobbing with the rest of the Oregon delegation. Whoever they were. He kept meaning to look that up.

Boots squeaking on the linoleum, he walked behind the counter and opened the freezer. He had to thaw the Alaskan halibut LaDonna wanted to feature on the Devil's Food Cafe menu tomorrow, and then cut it into steaks. The fish was nearly three feet long, a frosty silver slab. About twenty pounds, he guessed. Small for a halibut. He grabbed it by the tail and effortlessly swung it into a tray beside the counter. It connected with a solid clang. He'd miss that sound. And the cash register's cha-ching. But it was way past time for change.

"Who do you think it is?" Jeffrey Wolfe stood back to admire his paint job, then glanced out to sea. Not a cloud in the sky. No sign of a squall. If the weather held a few more hours, the paint would set up fine.

"Who do I think who is?" Mike Donovan spat on a rag and buffed out a dark patch on the underside of the rail.

"The man Molly went to check on." Jeffrey wished again that he'd asked if he could ride along, wished he had the guts to tell her she was the main reason he wanted to work for her father. "The man in Neptune's Grotto."

"Oh, him." Mike spat again and rubbed harder. "Probably some tourist who ignored the signs to stay back from the edge of the cliff. Or a beachcomber nailed by a sneaker wave. Not anyone who deserved to die."

Jeffrey pondered the last sentence as he pounded the paint can closed with his fist. "I don't think I've heard of anyone drowning since I've been here."

"True. But you haven't lived a full season with us yet, have you lad?"

"No. I came in September."

"It's the spring and summer when the sneaker waves pick off the tourists. Winter we mostly lose our own to the sea." Mike sighed and looked out at the bridge and channel. "A fella gets tired waiting for a calm day, tired of listening to the fog horn. He needs money to keep the bank from taking the boat. So he heads out, thinking he's smart enough and fast enough." He folded the rag and returned to the railing.

Jeffrey studied the ocean, imagining how it would feel to be swept from the deck by a winter squall, buried in watery darkness. He shivered, wondering if he had the guts for this job. Storms hit in summer, too.

"There. She's ready to go." Mike Donovan stuffed the rag and polish in a cabin locker. "All we need is tourists."

"We'll have a town full during the festival," Jeffrey offered.

"Don't talk to me about that." Mike grumbled under his breath, something about that frigging land-grabbing Grabowski and the lard-ass mayor, then climbed to the bridge and bent over the console, checking engine display dials.

Jeffrey scratched his head. "I thought everyone looked forward to the festival. I heard it brings the community together."

"Sure. And it used to be that way, lad, before that damned Grabowski. It used to be just townsfolk and friends and relatives from up and down the coast. And hand-made whirligigs twirling in all the yards. Now its tour buses, loudspeakers, and streets so packed you can't breathe." He slammed a fist on the console. "And the whirligigs! If they're authentic, I'm a cross-dressing walrus! We've become a damn theme park with bulldozers. Look at what he did to the creek." He spat over the side, as if trying to purge himself of a bad taste.

Jeffrey didn't have to ask what Mike meant. Locals at the Belly Up carped endlessly about how Grabowski had leveled the ridges for his development. The tons of earth he had bulldozed into the creek during the salmon migration caused what marine biologists called a "major setback" to endangered fish. By the time state and county officials stopped him, the earth-moving was finished. Grabowski hired a team of lawyers who stalled and stonewalled, gambling that the fines he'd pay when it all shook out would cost less than if county planners had denied the project and left him with a chunk of land he couldn't develop. "It would be ironic if that's him."

"Who?" Mike squinted at him.

"The guy in Neptune's Grotto. Vince Grabowski."

"No such luck. He's too mean to die." Mike climbed down and headed for the dock, mumbling. "I wish I had my hands around his neck again."

Jeffrey stared after him. *Again?* Had he heard that right?

FOUR

Shading my eyes, I squinted at the orange and white chopper circling above.

"Grabowski! Great. Just f-ing great!" Greg Erdman yelled in my ear as the whumping blades tilted closer. Kicking one of the thick wooden posts supporting the railing, he glared at the body in the water. "The state boys will get the case now for sure."

"Maybe not," I consoled him. "You're first on the scene." And I could pry a lot more from Greg than from state information officer.

"Won't matter. We're talking a big case. Major headlines." He transferred the glare to me.

The chopper lifted and whirled sideways toward the highway. "But Grabowski lived in Devil's Harbor. That's in the county, your jurisdiction. So is Neptune's Grotto."

He rubbed the stubble on his chin. "Yeah. Maybe."

I watched a wave lift the body and drop it just short of the rocks. "Well, it's probably suicide. He's a prominent person and he washed up in a public place, so the papers will give it a few inches, but that's it."

The corner of his mouth twitched and he glanced away. The hair on my arms prickled. "What?"

"Nothing." He studied the ground at his feet.

"It's not suicide, is it? You know something, don't you?"

He smiled. Then torqued his lips into a frown.

"Tell me, Greg. After last night, you owe me." I slathered on a layer of guilt. "My ego may never recover."

He flinched. "I can't, Molly."

I tried wheedling. "Come on. Just between you and me. Off the record."

"No."

"I won't use it in the paper. Tell me."

His smile turned into a grin and I felt anger tightening my throat, acidic words on my tongue. Swallowing them, I turned to the railing, raised the camera, focused on the body again and clicked off a picture. Below me, a gargantuan bull sea lion hauled himself off a ledge at the waterline and ordered a dozen females to make way. The cows barked and shuffled, then returned to their original positions. I absorbed the lesson: being pushy and demanding wouldn't work. I'd try reverse psychology.

I pasted a "good loser" expression on my face. "Well, it sure looks like suicide to me. Grabowski would have known better than to climb over a guard rail or take a midnight stroll in the surf. And he'd tunneled himself into deep financial doo-doo."

I shook my head, careful not to catch his eye. "Nope. Definitely suicide. Not the big case that would get the state boys to notice you." I patted his arm. "Sorry, Greg. Better luck with the next body."

I got three steps up the trail before he snagged the back of my T-shirt. "It's not suicide."

I patted his arm again. "You believe what you want. The medical examiner will set you straight."

"Damn it, Molly. I'm right about this one. The car will prove it."

"The car?"

"Yeah. Big silver Lincoln. I found it dumped at the Perdition Point wayside this morning."

My heart jumped, but I stayed cool. "Sounds like his car. But if I were planning my final belly flop, that's the place I'd pick. Steep cliff. Jagged rocks. Odds about five hundred to one the impact will kill you."

"Same odds if someone pushed him, don't you think?"

I offered only a casual shrug. My strategy had worked so far. Why mess with success?

He hoisted himself up on the railing. "Let me borrow that camera."

I did as he asked and he snapped off a string of shots. "I'll need some pictures of the scene. Before the Coast Guard cutter gets here." He pointed toward an orange and white boat plowing through a wispy, swirling fog.

"Sure, take all you need." I thought about asking if this gave me a free pass inside the yellow tape, but why screw things up just to be a smart ass?

"Thanks." He snapped off a few more shots and climbed down. "I'll return the camera after I transfer the shots to my computer."

"I can e-mail them to you."

He shook his head.

"Let me at least take the lens."

He nodded an okay, planted his elbows on the railing, cupped his chin in his hands, and stared out at the ocean. I wondered if he was about to say something like "the game's afoot." We'd watched two Sherlock Holmes television mysteries recently. Both times he'd guessed the killer after the third commercial. Both times he'd been wrong.

"I found the car wedged up against a big clump of Scotch broom, the door hanging open. Your average Lincoln owner doesn't risk scratching that glossy finish and he'd close the door so the next squall won't soak the seat. I figured joyriders dumped it."

I nodded. Thieves wouldn't care whether the upholstery got moist enough to grow mushrooms. But somebody intent on air-walking wouldn't either.

"The keys were in the ignition. That's not exactly the MO for your average joyrider—to have a key in the first place, and then leave it in the car. But I thought it had to be kids—the seat was right up against the wheel."

My lips unzipped. "Did you run the plate?"

"I know my job, Molly," he snarled. "The computer was down. And there was no registration, no credit card slips, not even an owner's manual. No suicide note either."

"They don't all leave notes." But Grabowski probably would have. He'd want us to realize exactly what we'd lost. "Maybe it's at his house. Or his office. Maybe it's in his pocket."

"There's no note. I'll bet a six pack."

"You're on," I goaded him. "Maybe Grabowski dropped it in the mail, but there's a note." I heard the Coast Guard cutter's engine rumble as it idled about a hundred yards beyond the heavy surf breaking around the narrow inlet to Neptune's Grotto. "Still, it makes for a good story. It always does when the mighty fall from grace. Or from Perdition Point." I zipped the lens into the camera bag. "Guess I'll be going. We've got file pictures of Grabowski. No point in waiting for the body shot if it's not a homicide."

Behind and above us, footsteps thudded along the trail. I shaded my eyes and saw Jennifer leading two Coast Guard officers. Behind them sunlight glinted off the gold insignias pinned to the shirt of State Police Lieutenant Pete Grimes.

"Joyriders didn't leave that car on Perdition Point," Greg insisted.

Jennifer waved, a finger-tip flip. Her high-heeled pink plastic sandals skidded on the steep incline. I waved back, ignoring Greg.

"Listen, Molly, most joyriders trash cars. I find them full of beer cans, butts and cigarette burns." Greg lowered his voice as Pete Grimes drew closer. "That car is clean as my wallet before payday. I'll bet the lab techs don't find a single fingerprint. Somebody sanitized that car and drove it to Perdition Point, before or after he tossed Vincent Grabowski off the cliff."

"Oh, no! Not Mr. Grabowski!" Jennifer slid the last ten feet, arms flailing. She crashed against one of the coin-operated viewers that allowed close-up looks at flippered grotto residents.

"Ohmigod! That can't be Mr. Grabowski," she wailed. Flinging herself at the railing, she peered over, and then collapsed into a sobbing heap. "What about the contest? And my scholarship money? How will I get out of Devil's Harbor?"

"Grabowski, huh?" Pete Grimes pushed back his hat and scratched a barely visible crew cut. "Get the kid up the hill," he advised me. "Get her a soda. See if she can get hold of Phil and Latrice and get them back here. But don't let her make any other calls and don't let her tell anyone who that is."

He leaned on the last few words meaning the same went for me. I felt a quick flash of anger. I'd been covering crime scenes half my life. I knew the rules.

Grimes smiled. "You'll probably get better pictures from up there, anyway. It's too risky to try to get into the grotto. I bet they winch him up. Just like him to make trouble for us."

I glanced at Greg and saw the warning in his eyes. Nodding at Grimes, I helped Jennifer to her feet, dug a tissue out of my camera bag, and steered her up the trail. "It's just not fair," she sobbed. "I had my dress almost ready and everything." She sulked as I fed quarters into the soft drink machine, popped open a can and forced it into her fingers while I pushed her down on a wooden bench outside the ladies' room. "I've waited my whole life for this year's festival," she gurgled. "My whole life. What am I supposed to do?"

There were a dozen answers, but none that she'd want to hear.

"I mean. The entire summer is trashed." She drained half the can, sneezed, then began to hiccup. "It's no big deal to you if they—hic—cancel the festival. You've already got a crown. Hic. You scored the first year."

Yeah, I thought, and thanks to Vince Grabowski's plans for a twenty-year commemoration of that horror and two months of badgering by organizers, I'd agreed to wedge myself into the world's ugliest dress and be trundled through town wearing the Wally-the-whirling-walrus crown in a car driven by His Slobbiness, the mayor.

Thrusting my hands deep into my pockets, I walked to a window in the west wall and looked down at the viewing area. Pete leaned against the railing, picking his teeth with a fingernail while the coasties gestured toward the boat, then back to the highway. Greg nodded, grinned, and hitched at his belt, practicing the fine art of macho posturing.

"I wanted to look as beautiful as you—hic—Molly." Jennifer chugged more soda and held her breath for half a minute, then started sobbing again. "And now they'll cancel the festival and I'll never be queen. And next year I won't be able to enter because I'll be too old." She kicked at a wind-up sea lion toy that had fallen from its rack and sent it clattering into a corner. "It's just not fair."

The coasties started back up the trail and I guessed that Pete had been right about the recovery operation. Jennifer took a deep sobbing breath and broke ten seconds of silence.

"Why does everything bad always have to happen to me? Why did I get that totally enormous zit the first time Bart asked me out? And how come I get my period and get all bloated whenever we go someplace where I want to wear that rad white dress? And why—"

She floored it into self-pity overdrive, but I tromped on the brake. "I don't think the mayor will cancel the festival."

She gaped. "You don't?"

"No."

"But Mr. Grabowski's dead. And he was like, the guy who ran it."

I sighed. Three years ago, Vince Grabowski got the mayor to appoint him chairman of the festival and took Devil's Harbor hostage with grandiose schemes. He transformed a small town's spring party into a crass commercial event most townspeople wished they could avoid. Yeah, he ran it. Into the ground.

"The festival went on years before Vince Grabowski came to town."

She sighed and fluffed her hair. "Oh. He was really nice, huh Molly?"

Nice and oily. I nodded to the coasties as they came in through the screen door. They nodded back, unlocked the front and headed for the chopper hunkering in the parking lot.

"Wasn't he?"

Her voice had the plaintive quality of a child asking for confirmation that Santa exists. I grubbed another tissue from the camera bag, wishing I could leave her and get started on the pictures Pete was hounding me for.

"People said some really mean things about him, but he tried to do good things for the town. And he built the whirligig factory and lots of people come to see that."

"Yes, they do."

I reminded myself that for a teenager, having more people around meant excitement, a chance to dream of where you'd go when you got out of a town where everybody knew your name, who you went out with on Saturday night, and where you parked before you went home. I remembered the rush I'd felt at seventeen when the quiet streets boiled with people who'd come to see a hundred types of wind-paddling whirligigs and cheer on the belly buckers. Then people became addicted to tourist dollars, and Vince Grabowski capitalized on that greed.

"I never believed a lot of the bad things people said about him. Like the rumors about him and Mrs. Deeds." Jennifer snuffled into her tissue. "I mean, he was married and all. So is she."

Married to a slug. I made another noncommittal noise in my throat as I watched the coasties clamber into the chopper. The blades turned with whooshing thumps. A wave of dust and grit rolled along the ground, spattering against the window.

"And I didn't believe that Shelley went with him to that motel in Lincoln City and did all that stuff."

Shelley? I spun to face her. "Shelley Perkins? Why she's only—"

Jennifer held up two fingers. "Two years older than I am."

And Grabowski was as old as Shelley's mother. LaDonna Perkins had a hot temper. Had she tossed him off Perdition Point?

"But Shelley's always been, well, you know," Jennifer lowered her voice, an unnecessary precaution given the whumping helicopter, "boy crazy. Mom says I shouldn't hang with her, but it's not like there's mondo selection. And anyway, I'm not going to flirt with everything with a hairy chest like Shelley does. I have way more respect for myself."

She sat up straight and pushed her hair away from her face, then slumped again. "But it sounded soooo romantic: room service and flowers and champagne in the Jacuzzi and dinner at a fancy restaurant. Not like guys my age who buy you a burger then paw you in the back seat. Not that Bart's like that." She blushed. "He's totally cool about waiting."

I pondered this tidbit and LaDonna's relative strength while Jennifer sipped the rest of her soda. "Shelley was so not happy when Mr. Grabowski called it off. She'd never been dumped before. She told me she was going to get even with him. Big time."

Her face whitened under her makeup. "Ohmigod, Molly! If he didn't like, you know," she pointed toward the grotto, "get there by himself, then somebody—" The can clattered to the floor. "You don't think Shelley killed him, do you?"

"Of course not," I lied as I patted her shoulder. My joke about using the phone book as a suspect list was becoming too true to be funny.

FIVE

Henri Trevelle whistled an aria from *Madame Butterfly* as he swished a feather duster over boxes of bullets and shotgun shells stacked neatly on glass shelves behind the counter of the Gilded Puffin Gift and Gun Shoppe. Once again, he thought about moving the ammunition to the back room for the summer. That would make more space for tourist claptrap—postcards and pennants, T-shirts, and those horrible squatty creatures made from rocks and pipe cleaners with beady little rolling eyes that reminded him of his third grade teacher back in Canada. He could create more space at the rear of the store, too: shove the sagging easy chairs into the storage shed, set a philodendron on the pot-bellied stove, and stick the hunting jackets and vests on a small rack in the corner. Just until after Labor Day.

"I hang on the horns of a dilemma, *ma petite,*" he told the three-legged Balinese-mix sleeping on an embroidered cushion in the display window. Should he preserve the Shoppe as it was when he bought it, and lose business to others with fewer scruples? Or should he give in to Grabowski-style creeping commercialism and risk driving off the regulars?

He mulled that over. Could he survive without the audience that allowed him to relive his exploits as a hard-skating, stick-wielding professional hockey center? Locals who stopped to check out new rifle sights or pick up ammunition usually stayed to talk, prodding Henri to tell them how it felt to take a body check against the glass or catch the puck with his teeth.

No, it wouldn't do to alienate them. Lord knew it had taken them long enough to accept him. But now, after five years of hard work, he was vice president of the chamber of commerce—permed and highlighted hair, diamond eyebrow stud, sexual preference, and all.

"What to do, what to do, what to do," he muttered, locking the cabinet and moving on to flick imaginary dust motes from a display of gnome-faced ceramic mugs a woman in Netarts swore would go like hot cakes this summer. He'd use the profits to buy something he could look at without retching. He'd found he had to sell trash so he could afford to sell treasure—and continue to divert his pension to his mother's condo mortgage in San Juan Capistrano.

"But it's all just so tacky, isn't it, Angel?"

The cat yawned; curling her tongue, then licked a front paw, stretched, and found a more comfortable position.

"Are you bored, my little sugar plum, suffering from ennui? Daddy understands. He wanted quiet when he moved here. Not sensory deprivation."

The cat yawned again and tucked her head, twitching her tail over her eyes. A truck on the highway in front of Henri's shop had claimed her leg four years ago; he'd been pampering her ever since.

"Say no more, *ma petite*." Henri checked the jeweled watch on his wrist. He'd close early. No one had been in for an hour. "In ten minutes, at the very stroke of three, I shall bolt the doors on all those nasty people who disrupt your rest and whisk away to the Mark-up and procure a perfect salmon steak for your dinner."

The word "salmon" brought a soft meow from the pocket of a camouflage jacket on the rear wall. A tiny tabby peeked out, then jumped to the floor, raced to Henri, and threaded herself between his ankles.

"So, Margaret, you'd like salmon, too."

The tabby meowed again and another cat answered from the back room with a yowl like a hungry baby's cry. The tabby ran to greet a rusty black tom with tattered ears, a broad head, and a bent tail.

"Margaret, you little slut," Henri chided the tabby. "It's bad enough you go slumming in the alley like a common trollop. Now you bring rabble home."

The tom sat, slanting yellow eyes sizing up Henri, showing no fear. The tabby licked his face.

"Disgusting." Henri moved to the window and petted the Balinese. "Let some hairy beast with a you-know-what come through town and she's all over him. Thank God Daddy had her fixed or we'd be knee deep in kitties."

The chimes above the door sounded seven notes from *A Chorus Line*. Henri pivoted and spotted Adam Quarles' dirty-blond dreadlocked hair and sunburned face. Really, that unkempt hippie look didn't do a thing for Adam. He needed to surrender to a decent stylist. Not that you could find a true artiste within a hundred miles. But Shelley Perkins had developed a flair for trimming. He glanced at his hands. And she gave a nice manicure, too.

"Yo. How's it hanging?"

Henri cringed. He'd had his fill of men belching, farting, fighting, and bragging about their sexual prowess during his hockey years. But in the interest of being accepted, he tolerated testosterone-soaked locker-room language and even displayed some himself. "They are, as you say, hanging quite nicely, Adam. And your own?"

"Like billiard balls in a rack, Henri. Solid." Adam stalked to the rear of the store, and then returned. "Are we alone?"

"Except for the girls." Henri glanced at the tom. "And Margaret's latest flame."

Grinning, Adam surveyed the locked cabinet of guns behind the counter. "When will you stop enabling the decimation of the local wildlife?"

"When you develop a birth control pill for rabbits."

Adam threw his head back and released a deep baritone laugh. "That's what I love about you Henri. You don't take any crap."

"And you do?"

"Hell, no." Adam barked out another laugh, then frowned. "Except from that bastard Grabowski. But he craps on the whole town."

"What's he done now?"

"Now? Nothing that I know of. Except use up air that could support an actual human being. And step up his efforts to transform this into Fresno-by-the-sea." Adam strode to the rear of the store and returned to sneer at the gnome mugs. "I've had it. We've got to take this town back. We've got pollution, landslides, lawsuits, genuine fake whirligigs, and—"

"Don't forget that marvelous seventeen-hole golf course," Henri reminded him as he glanced at his watch. Three minutes to three. Adam must have shut down the kite and health-food store early. Or perhaps he'd left Bart Yamamoto behind the counter of Passing Wind. The week before the Memorial Day weekend festival was as quiet as a testimonial dinner for pension-fund rip-off artists. And almost no one flew kites in the early spring—the wind ripped them to tatters or carried them off to Idaho.

Pondering that, Henri realized he hadn't seen Adam all weekend. Maybe he'd been off on what he referred to as "a buying trip." Although if all you brought back was tofu and millet, why bother? No, Adam had been doing something else. With a woman, he'd bet. *Cherchez la femme*. Henri suppressed a shiver of excitement. A secret affair. Delicious. He'd find out, and then tease Molly about knowing something she didn't.

"Yeah. Lucifer's Links!" Adam finger-punched a gnome's nose.

"You did all you could to stop him. Chaining yourself to that bulldozer, picketing, splattering ketchup on his wife's mink coat. Ah *mon dieu!*"

Adam spit out a harsh laugh. "That was worth putting up with His Sliminess trying to organize a boycott of my business. The pompous little jerk is second on my list of people to throw off a cliff as part of a civic improvement project."

"Perhaps if he goes to Washington—"

"Puh-lease!" Adam kicked at a plastic bucket of sea shells imported from the tropics and pasted with Devil's Harbor labels. The bucket swayed and thumped over. The tabby and the tom yowled and ran; Angel merely yawned and tucked her head back under her tail. "The man's a moron. Were you here when he painted the center line and the curbs hot pink?"

"No." Henri righted the bucket and pulled his favorite chair from the corner: the oak rocker with the fringed purple shawl. "But it's a local legend."

"Pissed off the highway department something awful. It was colorful though. You might have liked it."

Henri shrugged. "Not neon pink. Now, a nice fuchsia, perhaps . . ."

"Definitely neon, trust me. And then he blew the city budget on that second-hand ice resurfacer machine."

Henri raised an eyebrow. "But there is no ice rin—"

"Thought he could convert it to a street sweeper. The blockhead."

"But he's been re-elected since then." Checking his watch, Henri smiled at the cats, walked to the door, shot the bolt, and flipped the closed sign down.

"Because no one else—" Adam paused, mouth open, eyes widening. "Hey! Why don't you run?"

Henri put a hand over his heart. "Me? Mayor?"

"Sure. I'll manage your campaign. And you know Molly will write some great pieces about you."

"And Elspeth Hunsaker will call for lightning to strike me." He picked up Angel and carried her to his chair.

"It would drive her into a frenzy," Adam conceded. "But think about it, okay?"

Henri shrugged. It was an amusing premise.

Adam got to his feet. "Time to get back and close up. You going to the Belly Up later?"

"*Oui.*" Henri settled Angel on the shawl. "To meet with the festival committee. I must review the rules for the belly-bucking competition. I am the judge and referee."

Adam cocked his head. "What about Mike Donovan? He's been in charge since the event started."

"*C'est vrai,* but he won't do it this year. Absolutely refuses. And in a moment of weakness I agreed to oversee that barbaric spectacle."

"Barbaric?" Adam roared with laughter and pointed at the framed pictures above the gun cabinet. "Henri Trevelle, the 'Assassin on Ice,' thinks a little belly-bucking is barbaric? The man who performed nose jobs with his skates balks at the idea of a few fat guys bumping guts?"

"That was then," Henri lifted his double chin proudly. "This is now."

Gus Custer rubbed sandpaper along the belly of a whirligig French poodle, snapped a one-second smile at the children pressing their fingers against the glass panel, and then turned his back and cursed Vince Grabowski and all his ancestors.

Time was when he was an artist, when he'd dream a design, and then carve it from a block of wood or chip it into stone. Time was when he crafted otters and dolphins and leaping whales, works of fancy that flew, ran, or paddled on the wind.

He surveyed the shelves of finished whirligigs surrounding his workbench. Woodpeckers, cartoon roadrunners, and rabbits posed alongside rock guitarists thrashing their instruments. Not one bit of it hand-carved at the Waterside Whirligig Factory and Store like signs and brochures claimed. Vince Grabowski's scam. Devil's Harbor's dirty little secret. One of many.

He waved at the kids, one brief flip of his hand, then twirled the poodle's ears and went back to sanding its belly— rubbing away the stamped-on red letters reading "Made in Taiwan." When he finished, he'd toss it into the back room where some pimply kid with a couple of spray paint cans would "painstakingly apply a lustrous finish to creatures lovingly whittled from wood hand-picked by our team of craftsmen." *Bull!*

He checked his watch and waved again. Right on time. Just like his contract specified. Gus cursed the day he'd signed that. But what else could he do? Grabowski had had him by the throat.

At first Gus had thought tourists would catch on. But at most they spent two minutes gazing at him and returning his cursory smiles and waves. Then they ambled off to the gift and snack shop to buy overpriced hot dogs and agonize over whether Aunt Beulah would prefer a twirling hamster or a flapping turkey. Yeah, those really captured the "true spirit of the coast wind." More like the true spirit of greed, Grabowski style.

He dropped his sandpaper, bent and cut two farts—the first by accident, the second, a much longer one, on purpose. Not that the tourists could hear. Or smell. Grabowski had taken pains to soundproof this little room and vent it to the outside— probably suspecting Gus would try to sabotage the illusion.

He would, too, he thought, if he could stomach the idea of living on cat food in his golden years. At seventy-one, thanks to Grabowski, his retirement consisted of meager Social Security checks and a job working eleven to five, seven days a week through tourist season, decked out in a plaid flannel shirt, and a pair of overalls. He'd even had to bleach his hair— Grabowski didn't think his own was white enough. And he had to rub pink blush on his cheeks every morning. He looked like something an undertaker's intern screwed up.

His own fault. Bad enough he let Grabowski con him into selling most of his property with that story about a "wilderness development" the whole town would be proud of. It wasn't a bit of that. It was a just a big land grab by the big Grabowski. Still, if he'd quit then, just left the money in the bank, he'd have been okay. But Grabowski kept after him, talking about Social Security crashing, property taxes going up, and the art market going soft. Scared, stupid, and greedy, Gus had handed over the money from the sale. And more. Every penny went into the scheme. And now he was stuck. An animated mannequin.

His own fault, once again. The world had changed and he hadn't. He had no other skills, was frightened to death of computers, and refused to live anywhere else. One of these days he wouldn't be able to take it anymore. He'd grab that giant smiling sperm whale whirligig and run amok through Devil's Harbor, flailing away. Like he'd flailed at Grabowski last night. He paused, treasuring the memory. It had felt good when old Grab-ass went down. Gus smiled and favored the tourists with an extra wave. Maybe later he'd wander over to the Belly Up. Heck, maybe he'd buy a round for the house.

SIX

When I got home after watching them winch Grabowski out of the grotto, I found a note from Dad on the kitchen table. "6:27. Just heard about Grabowski's misfortune. Gone to the Belly Up to celebrate. See you there?"

Not for a nanosecond had I thought the story wouldn't leak out once Greg Erdman had opened his big mouth in front of Jennifer. He might as well have stood on the corner of Brimstone Boulevard with a megaphone. By morning a squadron of hair-sprayed TV reporters would arrive just in time to check their makeup before their live reports. Maybe Greg would get some TV face time. Then he could tape the interviews and replay them while he was spending tomorrow evening alone.

"No you won't see me there," I told the note before I wadded it up, tossed it in the wastebasket, and popped open a can of grapefruit soda. Dad had a half-hour head start. By now the whole town would be crammed into the bar. The air would be close and steamy.

I took a long swallow. Close and steamy. That didn't define my relationship with Greg. He was fun to hang out with, but he was pushing me toward the point where I'd have to say yes or no. "Yes" was a word I hadn't used since a marriage shorter than the Christmas-shopping season.

I studied the refrigerator shelves, searching for something more substantial than the two bags of stale Grotto Corn I'd eaten over the course of the afternoon. Three limp pancakes lounged in a plastic bag beside no-fat mayonnaise, half a head of lettuce browned slowly in the crisper, and the meat drawer held reduced fat cheeses and turkey.

"No fat, no flavor," I told the healthy-eating brochures stuck to the side of the refrigerator with magnets shaped like Oregon's renowned slugs.

When I'd come back in February to take care of Dad, I'd decided it wouldn't hurt me to stick to his prescribed diet. I'd picked up a couple of cook books, bought a load of fruits and vegetables, and learned to bake and grill and substitute. Our meals were as exciting as your average political debate. Sure, I'd lost six pounds and I had more energy, but recently I'd started dreaming about fry bread and enchiladas, bowls of blue cheese dressing, chili dogs and nachos, cheesecake and pecan pie with vanilla ice cream.

The Belly Up would be packed with people who knew and loathed Grabowski—all of them with multiple motives to shove him off Perdition Point. The floor would be covered with peanut shells, the bar sticky with spilled drinks. Chuck Yamamoto would be frying quarter-pound burgers, topping them with slabs of sharp cheddar cheese, scooping them onto buns slathered with real mayonnaise, and setting them on plates groaning under mounds of greasy fries. Fat. Cholesterol. Alcohol. All the things my father shouldn't have.

I held out for a full minute before I caved and ran for the bar.

"—and good riddance," Maybelline Yamamoto told Ichabod Ferris as he slouched on a bar stool toying with the tiny paper parasol in his Mai Tai. Icky sipped frequently, blew bubbles, and swirled ice cubes, but he never finished a drink. Maybelline suspected he got high another way. He had that look—dark T-shirt and jeans, clunky boots, silver skull nose ring, and a beret. A walking black hole. Sullen, too. Not just quiet. She was used to that, living with Hiroshi all these years. And Bart, too. Quiet. Never cried, even on the day he was born.

"LaDonna says it might be a robbery, but I think somebody finally got mad enough to say to hell with the consequences." She drew a pint of Belly Up Brew and poured a glass of house wine. Icky's business did all right despite his outfit, but that wasn't the way she'd dress if she ran the ice cream shop. She fingered the pin curls in front of her ears, patted the mound of orange hair sprayed into an obedient crouch on top of her head, and straightened the pink and purple flowered top she wore over beige stretch pants. Buying ice cream should be like going to a party, not like shopping for a coffin.

Coffin? The word reminded her of her grandmother's advice: "never speak ill of the dead."

"Lean forward a bit, hon."

Icky obeyed and she reached over his shoulder, handing the drinks to Adam Quarles and Henri Trevelle. What happened if you spoke ill of the dead? Would a ghost rise up? She shivered, wrestled briefly with her conscience as she wrung out a rag to mop the bar, and decided to let the facts speak for themselves. Holding all this in wasn't healthy.

"Could be somebody in this room right now did it. There were times I wanted to strangle him myself. The last time that sorry excuse for a man came in here, must have been Wednesday—no, Tuesday, and—couldn't have been Monday because I took off, and Chuck closed early business was so slow. Anyway, he comes in with the mayor and they take that table right over there." Maybelline pointed at one of five round tables set beneath the disco ball on the parquet floor where the belly-buckers would square off Friday night. "And then he walks up to the bar, big as you please, and orders a Hell Fire. 'Make it a double,' he says. 'And give me a martini for His Dishonor. Put it on my tab.' His tab? Fooey! Two hundred over the limit, and owes us for putting his lawyers up at the Slackwater last winter."

Icky nodded, his muddy brown eyes following the swirling design he'd created from a small puddle of beer Maybelline had missed with the last swipe of the bar rag.

"Treated the whole town like his personal servants."

Ding.

Maybelline spun toward the high counter than separated the bar from the kitchen. "Got it," she called, grabbing two plates of burgers and fries before Chuck's finger left the bell. Pulling a couple of pints of Belly Up Blond, she tossed napkins and silverware and a bottle of ketchup on a tray with the plates and slid around the end of the bar, threading her way through the crowd toward the last booth, the one with the best view of the harbor, the one she reserved for guests at the Slackwater Bed and Brew.

She unloaded the tray, smiling and winking at the California couple who claimed they were just married. Maybelline recognized adultery when she saw it. After all, she knew Prudence Deeds, didn't she? But what did it matter, as long as these folks paid their bill and didn't steal her towels.

"Grabowski was a menace," she muttered as she returned to the bar. He had some nerve, sashaying in here just a few hours after he'd threatened to go after her liquor license if she didn't get Hiroshi to stop a class action lawsuit against his corporation. Of course, Grabowski called him "Chuck," like everyone else, but she preferred Hiroshi. It sounded still and mysterious. Chuck sounded like somebody stacking cordwood.

But Hiroshi didn't mind. In fact, he'd picked the nickname himself.

She sighed picturing the night they'd met at a dance at Wright Army Air Field just ten months before Bart was born. No point in playing coy when you know what you want, Maybelline thought. And she'd wanted Hiroshi and his calm silence, even if marrying him did scandalize everyone in Crossroads, Georgia. Well, he got her out of there and she didn't miss the south at all, especially the humidity that made her feel like she lived in Mother Nature's armpit.

Flipping open an order pad, she hustled over to Molly Donovan who'd just slid into a booth with her father, two local charter operators and that poet. Molly had watched them pull Grab-Ass up out of ocean and stuff him in a big old plastic bag. Like scooping a dog turd off the sidewalk. Sure as hell everyone at that table was speaking double-ill of the dead. That meant safety in numbers. In case Vince's ghost came calling.

"So we're all agreed." Mayor Brighton Deeds looked around the table at Henri Trevelle, Adam Quarles, and LaDonna Perkins. He smiled at Prudence, who sat beside him studying Jeffrey Wolfe across the crowded barroom. Remembering how she'd betrayed him with Grabowski, Deeds swallowed a lump of anger and humiliation and willed his fingers to uncurl before they snapped the stem of his martini glass.

"Our official position is that we're extremely sad one of our leading citizens is no longer with us." He quoted himself, reciting the statement he intended to give to Molly Donovan when she finally got around to asking him for a comment like any decent reporter would have done an hour ago. "But as far as the Whirligig Festival is concerned, everything will proceed as planned. We're sure Vincent Grabowski," he nearly choked on the name, "would have wanted it that way."

"Right," LaDonna agreed. "It's not like we didn't do this for years before Grabowski blew in." She extracted a piece of paper from her purse and unfolded it. "Maybelline and I will handle the cocktail party Friday night as usual, and line up the parade Saturday morning. We put the mounted patrol at the back this time. You all remember that, um, incident we had last year when someone fed the horses a bunch of green apples and laxative. I always suspected Gus Custer, but . . ." She shrugged.

Deeds nodded. He'd suspected Gus, too. But without proof the town got stuck with the bill for dry-cleaning thirty-seven marching band uniforms. "What about the parade of ships Saturday night?"

"Looking good," Adam informed him. "I heard from two more boat owners this afternoon. Since word got out Grabowski took the big leap, they're scrambling to get their decorations up and blinking. The Come On 'n' Get It is out of light strings and extension cords."

Deeds turned to Henri and suppressed a gasp. *Was he wearing lip gloss?* "And the belly-bucking competition?"

Henri sighed. "I'm ready, I suppose."

You suppose? Deeds made no attempt to keep testiness out of his voice. "Didn't Mike Donovan go over the rules with you?"

"*Oui.*"

"And you understand them?"

"*Oui.*"

"Then what's the problem?"

"No problem, really, just . . ."

Damn it. This was like dragging an anvil. "Just what?"

"I think Henri's trying to say that there's no nuance to the competition," Adam supplied. "No style or grace."

Henri crooked his little finger and sipped his wine. "No panache."

Panache? Deeds gritted his teeth. "It's not ballet. It's belly-bucking. Can you referee it or not?"

"Yes," Henri hissed. "I just won't like it."

"You don't have to like it," Deeds snarled.

"Calm down. Both of you." Adam put a hand on Henri's arm. "It's a tradition, Henri. A stupid one, but you can't mess with tradition. It would be like replacing the puck with a basketball. Like Las Vegas without Elvis impersonators."

Henri shuddered in mock horror. "I see what you mean, *mon ami*: a tragedy of epic proportions. Then I am prepared. And there are," he settled a pair of rhinestone-studded reading glasses on his nose and consulted the list Mike Donovan had handed him earlier, "fifteen competitors registered."

"Including Big Billy Bohannon?" Adam peered at the list. "Yeah, well that will make judging easy. The man's got a gut the size of a mutant watermelon."

"I will treasure the experience of being close to such a colossus." Henri folded the paper and tucked it back in his pocket as Chuck Yamamoto walked over, drying his hands on a spotless white apron.

"We are ready for the Sunday morning pancake breakfast, Mr. Mayor."

"Good, good." Deeds rubbed his hands together. He could always count on Chuck to do what was best for the town. He frowned. Except for that lawsuit. He drained his martini. Could Chuck file suit against Grabowski's estate, his corporation? And if so, did that mean he could still lose his shirt?

"We received a butter and milk donation from the dairy farmers. Sixty dozen eggs free. Paper plates. Plenty of volunteers. No problems." Chuck nodded at the others and hurried back to the kitchen.

Deeds signaled Maybelline for another drink. Prudence had informed him the developer had a fat insurance policy, that Grabowski was worth more to the town dead than alive. But if Chuck Yamamoto tied it up in court, Deeds might as well have taped his fifty-thousand dollars to a crab and tossed it into Purgatory Bay.

Prudence jabbed his wrist with a pointed nail. "You don't care about the dance?"

Deeds rubbed at the gouge. "Of course I do. It's the pinnacle of the festival."

"Then why haven't you asked me about it?" She blew on the nail and polished it against her green satin blouse. Deeds noted that she kept her eyes on Jeffrey Wolfe who in turn watched Molly Donovan devour a cheeseburger.

Deeds tried to placate her without whining. "I was saving the best for last. We're all eager to hear your plans."

LaDonna rolled her eyes and Adam snorted into his beer, but Deeds plunged on. "I'm sure the gym will be lovely."

"Lovely?" Prudence spoke the word as if it were a synonym for "putrid." "Yes, it will be as lovely as fraying paper lanterns, a hundred feet of crepe paper, and a wad of tinsel can make it. Yes, Brighton, the gym will be perfectly lovely for that magical moment when the Whirligig Festival Queen kicks off the shoes she dyed to match a discount-store gown and waltzes into your flabby arms in her ridiculous crown." She favored them all with an icy smile and walked from the bar, her hips swinging as she passed Jeffrey Wolfe.

Deeds moaned and clamped his thighs together, then gulped down half the martini Maybelline set in front of him, patted his lips with a napkin, and forced a smile. "Well, then, it looks like we're all set for a lovely weekend."

I pounded the pillow and flopped onto my back. The pool of grease in my stomach released another bubble of gas. Dad's snores echoed from across the hall. He'd had grilled chicken on a bun with lettuce and tomato. No mayo. No extra salt.

I smothered a belch, but let the next one loose.

"Aahhh."

Why were women so uptight about belching? Men just let it rip. Even Jeffrey Wolfe, although he said "excuse me" afterward and spoiled the effect.

Tomorrow I'd pitch Ben Galloway my plans for a front-page story on Grabowski's murder. Ben would back-burner it for sure. Just like he'd circular-filed my proposal for a series on coastal development and urban sprawl centered on Grabowski. "Paradise Looted," I'd wanted to call it.

"*The Flotsam* has a long tradition here. We're the good neighbor newspaper," he'd told me. "We don't throw stones. We don't editorialize. We write stories grandparents can read to their kids."

That's why your circulation numbers are smaller than my paycheck. "But we cover robberies," I'd pointed out, "and car theft and arson."

"Yes, but we don't scare people to death about crime. We put those stories in the back, by the want ads. And we make it clear," he'd pointed a finger at my nose and repeated himself, "we make it *very* clear that those crimes are committed by criminals."

I'd almost laughed. "Who else commits crimes?"

He'd shaken his head in disgust. "Criminals, Molly, are people who . . . well, they're people who *intentionally* go out and do bad things. They're not pillars of the community who *occasionally* take action that may be, um, occasionally unpopular with others."

"You're saying Grabowski's illegal bulldozing and the landslide were merely unpopular?" I'd argued in my defense. "You're saying it's just a minor public relations problem?"

He'd pointed the finger again. "I'm saying that if you want to work for *The Flotsam* you'll do things my way."

I flopped and burped and flopped once more. Okay, I'd lost that round. But surely even Ben Galloway would see this story deserved front page play.

SEVEN

LaDonna Perkins yanked the laces on her running shoes a little tighter, tied double bows, stood, and tugged the sheet and blanket over the pillows as she glanced at the clock. Late again. She couldn't remember the last time she'd had two extra minutes in the morning to make the bed the way her mother had taught her, smoothing out the sheets, turning hospital corners, plumping the pillows, and tweaking the spread into place. But her mother, she consoled herself, hadn't been a single parent running a seven-day-a-week business.

LaDonna straightened her shoulders, ran her fingers through her short graying brown hair, tucked her white blouse into her khaki slacks, and started down the hall, rapping on the door her daughter always kept locked. "Rise and shine, Shelley. Doors open in fifteen minutes."

Not waiting for an answer, LaDonna hustled down the stairs, grateful she'd cleaned the restrooms right after she'd closed Sunday afternoon instead of leaving them for later. She left too many things for later. Like that talk she'd meant to have with Shelley about the birds and the bees. Before she'd gotten around to it, Shelley had gone from being a pigtailed pre-teen to someone who'd lie about staying overnight with Jennifer and then check into a motel with a man old enough to be her father, a man who'd probably bragged about that to anyone who would listen.

Her throat tightened with rage. Well, things would be different between them from now on. She'd see to that. Just like she'd seen to Vince Grabowski.

LaDonna poured water and measured coffee, then fired up the grill, popped the plastic top off the can of grease, and got a bowl of eggs and a sack of pre-cooked shredded hash-brown potatoes from the refrigerator. There had to be a way to keep investigators from questioning Shelley.

She shivered in spite of the heat rising from the cooking surface. Clutching the edge of the counter, she stared at the loaves of bread lined up beside the six-slice toaster: sourdough, white, rye and whole wheat. She kept the croissants, bagels, and English muffins in the freezer. Only tourists asked for those. Folks in Devil's Harbor liked their bread without pretensions.

Shelley had gone ballistic when Grabowski broke off their affair. If that's what you called a one-weekend fling. But Shelley wouldn't kill anyone. Shelley couldn't—

LaDonna shuddered, remembering the tall man with white-blond hair who had made a living extinguishing human lives.

She remembered the day she'd discovered that. She'd still gone by the name of Marilee Reed then. She'd been cleaning the utility room when she'd found the collection of guns and wallets stashed in the back of the cabinet above the washer. Dave must have thought she'd never look there. After all, she stood barely five feet tall and had to climb on a chair just to see the shelf, let alone haul out the old gardening gloves and boxes of nails he'd used to hide the tools of his trade. She remembered opening those wallets and staring at the passports and licenses in amazement. Each one had a picture of Dave, and each one had someone else's name and address. Someone named Sam Watson, someone named Peter Skordahl, and someone named Tom Danelli. The wallets were stuffed with money, thousands in old bills, some with foreign writing. Three of the guns had what she'd guessed were silencers.

She'd wilted to the floor, head spinning, and that's where Dave found her when he came home from his imaginary sales job. He said only, "I'm sorry you found those. But it was time to go, anyway." Then he packed the car, put her in the passenger seat, and picked up Shelley from pre-school. They left White Plains in the rear-view mirror and drove west for three days. She had cried all the way, thinking he'd kill her, wondering how she could still love him.

When they had dead-ended against the Pacific Ocean, LaDonna saw the "for sale" sign in the window of the Devil's Food Cafe and stopped crying. Dave bought the restaurant by selling property she hadn't known was in her name. Then he disappeared.

She'd become LaDonna Perkins, learned to fry a dozen eggs at a time and balance a tray full of dishes on one hand. For each of the next ten years, on her birthday, she'd received a card containing a cashier's check for twenty thousand dollars. The money paid for her car and Shelley's clothes and a new roof and updated equipment for the restaurant. When the cards stopped, she guessed another hired killer had drawn Dave's name.

The front doorknob rattled and someone tapped on the double-paned window. She glanced at the clock over the refrigerator. Two minutes after six. The regulars stuck to a tight schedule. They made sure she stuck to it, too.

She raced to the foot of the stairs. "Shelley, come on! It's opening time!" She cocked her head, heard nothing. "Shelley! I need you now, honey!"

I need to look at you, she thought, at the part of you that comes from me. I need to convince myself no one will find out what I did, that we're going to be all right.

Upstairs, Shelley sniffed the aroma of brewing coffee, marked her spot in a worn book, crossed to the mirror, and made an "O" with her lips so she could outline them with "Daring Desire," her latest color. Not that anyone would appreciate it at this ungodly hour. Only the regulars ate breakfast at six—tired millworkers and charter captains who smelled like fish. The others—tourists and salesmen—came in around eight. Still, you never knew. Maybe Mr. Right would walk in and sweep her off her feet before the morning rush ended. She dabbed perfume on her wrists and the pulse points under her jaw the way the magazines said to do. The tiny glass vial Vince Grabowski had given her was nearly empty and, at seventy dollars for a quarter ounce, no way could she afford more.

She pouted and blotted her lips. Damn him anyway, dumping her just before she could ditch him. She sighed. Being with him had been exciting, but not like Christmas or the Fourth of July. Not like she'd hoped.

Still, it pissed her off when he'd told her he wouldn't call again. Nobody had ever dumped Shelley Perkins. She'd warned him he'd be sorry. He'd smirked and told her she'd been fun, but now she should be a good girl and play with kids her own age.

Well, she'd fixed him. And now he was dead.

She fluffed her bangs and left her bedroom, locking the door behind her and tucking the key into her bra.

Claire Grabowski rolled over, picked up the television remote and clicked it at the small set perched on the bureau across the room. Then she clicked it again. Vince's death wouldn't make the news here in Chicago.

The police chaplain they'd sent to break the news had cloaked it in euphemisms, describing the demise of Vince Grabowski as an "unfortunate accident," and an "untimely passing, even "misadventure." He'd offered to call someone to help her bear up under her grief. As if she hadn't had tons of practice at doing just that while Vince had been alive.

She realized she'd been gritting her teeth and forced herself to take deep breaths. The aggravations and embarrassments were over. Yes, he'd sunk her inheritance into that slippery-sloped development. Yes, after she'd left him, she'd had to scrabble for jobs as a substitute teacher and live on boxed macaroni and cheese. And yes, she was still waiting for a decision on whether her sham of a marriage could be annulled. But now that was all past.

For a short moment she felt a twinge of wistful sadness. The early years with Vince had been good. Before he decided he had to be a big shot, the big Grabowski. Before he viewed every woman as a conquest.

She shook her head. That Vince was long gone. Now the other was, too. Swinging her feet from beneath the sheet, she crossed the room, opened the blinds and looked out the window.

"Goodbye, Chicago," she told the sullen building across the street. "I'm going to Oregon."

She glanced at the clock again. If she hurried, she could be in Portland before five, and be in Devil's Harbor two hours later with the man who'd made her life worth living. Should she call, or surprise him?

Surprise, she decided as she yanked a suitcase from the coat closet and stripped the luggage ticket from its handle. Good thing she'd stuck it there when she got home last night. Otherwise the chaplain might have spotted it and been suspicious enough to call the police in Devil's Harbor.

Elspeth Hunsaker tossed a brown square-toed, low-heeled shoe behind her and crawled deeper into the closet looking for the mate to the bone-colored pump on her left foot.

"If Papa could see this, he'd be livid," she muttered, rummaging beneath a tumble of wool skirts and long-sleeved blouses. "He'd make me stay in here until this room passed inspection. Until he'd checked the tops of the doors and the bedsprings for dust and looked in the back of every drawer." Papa had had high standards and a low tolerance for clutter. And children were clutter. Even children like Elspeth who tried so hard to please, to be neither seen nor heard. But now Papa was gone and she was on the radio. Everyone heard her.

She unearthed a black hat that looked like a pot lid with a veil, and found the shoe beneath it. Crab-like, she scuttled out of the closet, stood, and wedged her size eleven foot into it. Catching her reflection in an age-flecked mirror, she drew herself up even straighter than usual and smoothed her dress down over barely-visible breasts and meager hips. She checked to make sure her mousy hair was pinned firmly in place. One must look professional.

No, Papa had never approved of her, no matter how hard she'd tried to be good, to be an example to others. Maybe if she'd gone the other way, been a flighty creature who laughed all the time like her cousin Phoebe.

She glared at the mirror, and then turned away. She didn't need a reflection to tell her she was nearly six feet tall and thin as a whippet. Phoebe was short and soft and had a voice like a little girl, not like a bassoon.

"But I'm smarter," Elspeth told the picture of her father in the hall. "And better. I follow the golden rule. I honored you. Even though you didn't deserve it." She flicked dust from the frame and clattered down the stairs. "And I never broke a commandment."

She paused on the landing. That wasn't strictly true. She didn't love her neighbors. But they didn't seem to have a lot of affection for her. And then there was the little matter of what she'd done to Vince Grabowski.

She shrugged, clacked through the living room and out the front door. Surely there had to be some wiggle room in the commandments. If Moses had met Vince Grabowski before the encounter with the burning bush, he might have asked for stone tablets etched with ten suggestions instead.

Picking her way across her overgrown lawn, she folded herself into a fossilized Corvair and listened for the gerbil-on-a-treadmill engine to turn over. She'd been forced to take action when Grabowski threatened to file a complaint with the Federal Communications Commission. She couldn't stand by and let him take her radio station away, could she? The salvation of the community she called Holy Waters depended on her.

EIGHT

As I pulled onto 101 a Portland television news van whizzed by heading south. It belonged to the station with enough helicopters to mount a respectable air strike on a third-world country. I wished I had time to follow it to Neptune's Grotto and watch the public relations flak from the county's development board put a positive spin on yesterday's discovery.

Not that he needed to try. Any fool knew this wouldn't drive tourists away. Just the opposite. People would trek a hundred miles to gawk over the railing and wonder if the sea lions had actually munched on Vince. (For the record, I'd looked it up. Sea lions are carnivorous and they have sharp teeth, but allegedly they eat only fish they catch themselves.) Heck, I bet some of the locals had rushed down there this morning pretending they'd stopped by to commiserate with Phil and Latrice.

There's a little ghoul in all of us. And a lot of ghoul in me, I admitted. Why else would I have begged for the crime beat back in Albuquerque? I craved the stories with "legs," the ones people read before the comics, the sports section, or the obituaries.

Downshifting and goosing the gas, I swerved around a motor home taking its half of the road out of the middle. My truck fishtailed onto the shoulder and I cursed the balding tires that spewed gravel back at the Californian checking a map and arguing with his wife as he drove. I made a face at their images in my rearview mirror as I crested the hill. The medical examiner would have Vince Grabowski's liver on the scale about now and I should be lurking in the lobby of the sheriff's department, or questioning my friends and neighbors. Instead Ben Galloway had ordered me to do yet another article on the effects of the winter weather patterns.

At least this story seemed legitimate. Not like last week's interview with a woman who called herself Elinor Nino and claimed responsibility for everything from warmer ocean currents to a heat wave in Houston to those hideous polyester retro fashions at department stores. Today's story, a piece on seabirds dying because their food supply had dwindled, needed to be told and maybe I could feed it to the wire service and gain some name recognition. Still, this trip could wait. The first few days of a murder investigation are critical. For reporters as well as detectives.

"If he didn't jump. Or slip. If. If. If." I mimicked my boss.

"We don't publish based on ifs," he'd told me. "We publish based on facts. What I want is the weather story, a short piece on Grabowski's untimely death, and a longer sidebar— how Devil's Harbor reacted to the loss of its leading citizen, the funeral arrangements and blah blah blah. No ifs. No surmises. No possibilities. Just facts. And get your stories in on time this week. Tuesday morning at ten. Not one minute later."

"Ten?" I'd squawked. "The deadline is noon."

"Not this week," he'd informed me. "We sold extra advertising. I want your stories at ten. Or else."

I slowed for a railroad crossing near Garibaldi. Ben Galloway preached like I'd just arrived from J school with a dull pencil behind each ear. But he gave the same to everyone, even his wife, Cynthia. She wrote one of the few remaining society columns in the country for the Wednesday edition, cranked out "Gertrude's Garden" for Sunday, kept the books, designed ads, and maintained the obituary files. "Ignore him, dear," she often told me. "That's what I've done for forty-seven years. It's the secret to our happy marriage."

So, I'd hung up without bringing up the glaring lack of facts in the Elinor Nino story he'd sent me on last week, cleaned the kitchen, made my bed, stopped at the post office, checked the horizon for squalls, went back to the house for my slicker, pulled into the Come On 'n' Get It for some snacks, and then got right on my urgent quest for factual news.

Chuckling, I swung into a roadside espresso stand to order a tall skinny double shot latte. We'd banned caffeine at home since Dad's heart attack, so I got my coffee fixes on the run. I paid, popped the lid and slurped at the froth, mentally conceding one point to Ben Galloway—this wasn't murder until the medical examiner found something: bruises and brain damage not consistent with the fall, wounds not consistent with rocks or sea creatures, needle or ligature marks, or something more subtle but just as suspicious.

I took another sip, secured the lid, and considered what I'd learned over the years about the myriad ways people committed murder. Sometimes the cause of death wasn't an obvious wound. We might have to wait weeks for results of toxicology tests. The medical examiner believed in caution; he wouldn't issue a statement on what *might* have happened until he eliminated what *hadn't* happened.

"Damn." I pulled back onto the highway, nursing my coffee through a tiny hole in the lid. I'd bet he wouldn't go out on a limb about time of death, either. He'd probably just guestimate something within a couple of hours. But I might get closer by backtracking through Grabowski's final day; I might even find the last person to see him alive. As a bonus, I could do that while I prepared the reaction piece Galloway wanted. Not that I couldn't scribble that story on the back of my gasoline credit card receipt right now based on what I'd heard last night. "He had it coming. Devil's Harbor breathes a sigh of relief."

Slowing to watch an eagle soaring near Twin Rocks, I wondered what leads Greg was pursuing and whether I could find the killer before he did. Wouldn't that frost him? Yeah, and it would make Ben Galloway realize he was wasting my talents. Crime *could* pay. By selling newspapers.

Sergeant Greg Erdman snatched a book of tickets from the dashboard, hauled himself from his cruiser, slammed the door, and stomped up the potholed shoulder toward the motor home, cursing tourists, the sheriff, and life in general.

The day had started with a call from Patsy. The support check hadn't arrived. No way would she believe he'd mailed it Thursday. He took it like a man, without saying a word, and without listening. Same way he took the lecture the sheriff delivered after he'd protested being assigned patrol duty instead of devoting the day to the Grabowski case.

"It's not a *case*, you idiot! It's a goddamn suicide!" The sheriff thundered. "Now leave. Get your butt out on the asphalt. Write some damn tickets. But don't ticket any locals. It's an election year."

As Greg left, he'd passed Barbara Sue, the dispatcher, arriving with a sack of doughnuts and a bag of fresh-ground coffee. "For the television reporters," she'd bubbled. "The sheriff's holding a news conference about the Grabowski case at eleven-thirty. All the Portland stations are coming. Could you help me set up more chairs in the conference room?"

"No way," Greg had snarled and then banged out of the building.

He kicked at the tire of the motor home and growled, "Fat-assed headline-grabber."

"Excuse me?" The jowly man leaned from the driver's window of the motor home, offering his license and registration.

"Not you." Greg snatched the license and started filling in the blanks on the last ticket in the book—number twenty for the day and it wasn't even noon. "Do you know you were going twenty-seven in a fifty-five zone?"

"Um, yes. But that's all this thing will do uphill." The driver took off the hat that read "ask me about tax shelters," and scratched the bald spot it covered. "Surely that's not against the law, is it?"

"No. But not pulling over to let other vehicles by is. You passed a turn-out a mile back. I counted fifteen cars behind you coming up that last hill." The ballpoint pen stuttered and Greg shook it, tapped it against the pad, and jabbed it at the paper. "Slower vehicles are required to make way. You passed two signs stating that while I followed you."

"That's ridiculous," the woman in the passenger seat carped. "Why would we want to pull over and let other people get ahead when we're in a hurry?"

"Now, Beatrice, I'm sure—"

She shot him a glare that could freeze molten lava and leaned across the console, cheeks puffing. "We have just as much right to the road as anyone. We pay our taxes and we're for less government and less interference in our lives. You can bet someone will hear about this."

Greg offered a snake's smile and went on writing the ticket.

She glowered. "Don't give me that look, young man. I'll call my congressman."

"I doubt he'd have much clout up this way."

"For your information, we've bought a piece of property here, *with* an ocean view. We'll be voting here in the fall." She whipped a small notebook from the glove compartment. "Who represents this district?"

Greg filled in the final blank. "We're in between congressmen right now."

She tapped a pencil on the notebook. "That's absurd."

"It's a fact ma'am. Nothing but a fact." Greg grinned and handed the ticket to George who squirmed like a netted eel. "Nathan Sedgewick died ten days ago. He was for less government, too. I think they're doing some kind of a study on how being videotaped accepting a briefcase crammed full of cash can trigger a heart attack. Next week the parties are picking candidates to run for his seat." Greg tipped his hat. "You have a nice day. Remember to check your mirrors and pull over if you're leading a parade."

As Greg strode back to his car, he heard the motor home door clunk open.

"Hey! Deputy!"

Greg spun, right hand on the butt of his holstered gun.

"Whoa!" The driver halted and lifted his hands. "I just had a question."

"If it's about the ticket, they'll answer it when you go to court."

"Oh, I don't care about the ticket. I'll pay it tomorrow." He stuffed the paper in the pocket of his plaid Bermuda shorts and shuffled a little closer. "It's about a place called Devil's Harbor, I can't seem to find it. I drove by the turn-off heading north, and didn't realize it until I was all the way to Tillamook. Now I think I might have missed it again coming back south." He wiped sweat from his forehead with the back of his hand and glanced at the motor home. "Beatrice is about ready to skin me and make a seat cover out of my hide. We're two hours late for our appointment at Devil's Acres."

Grabowski's development. Greg suppressed a smile.

"That's where we bought the property. Haven't seen it yet, but we fell in love with the pictures in the brochure. Hundred-eighty degree view of the ocean. Right on a golf course. They're going to have our house up before fall."

And the rains will bring it down before spring, Greg thought as he shook his head. "You folks don't read the papers much, do you?"

"Well, no, I guess we don't. Is there something we should know?"

Greg smothered a grin. "Well, the developer had what he called a few minor problems. But as of a few days ago his problems are over." He pointed down the road. "I'm heading to Devil's Harbor now. Why don't you just follow me?"

Maybe he'd run into Molly. Drop a few hints about the investigation and see if she'd agree to another date. Tonight.

Icky Ferris switched on the exhaust fan in the small bathroom at the back of the Sweete Temptations Ice Creame Shoppe and fished a roach from his back pocket. Clamping it into the alligator clip that hung on a chain dangling from the towel bar, he lit up, sucking thick marijuana smoke deep into his lungs and holding it for the count of ten.

"Aaaahhh." He exhaled, flexed his shoulders, rolled his head, and took another toke. Two more hours and he'd lock the door and retreat to his studio apartment to unwind. This would help him make it through.

"Yesssss." He pushed smoke out through his nose as he flushed the remaining scrap of the joint, then spritzed the tiny room and his black sweatshirt with vanilla air freshener. Fascinated by his reflection in the mirror, he checked the silver skull ring in his nose and the black pearl in his left ear, pulled his dark hair tighter into the ponytail at the base of his neck, and washed his hands.

Two sullen teenaged tourists bent over the counter, finishing up bags of caramel corn and leaving greasy fingerprints on the glass. Icky's teeth chattered as he approached the case containing twenty varieties of ice cream and frozen yogurt. Behind it, three shelves displayed a dozen varieties of chocolate candy. He walked to the center of the counter and stood, thinking about creation, decay, and the wakened dream he inhabited.

"Hey, dude." T
he shorter teen, the one with the two-tone blue hair, put both hands on the glass and stared at Icky. "Is this all you got? Just this weird shit?"

"Yeah," the larger one with the bleached-blond double Mohawk and eyebrow ring chimed in. "Where's the chocolate chip?"

Icky said nothing. He took a sliding step to his right and pointed at a tub labeled Beelzebub Bits.

"Get real, dude," Shorty sneered. "If that's what you call chocolate chip, what the hell do you call vanilla?"

Icky's lips curved up into a cherub's smile. Last year's crop of marijuana delivered one powerful high, and delivered pronto. This year's would improve on perfection. He took two sliding steps to his left, past Brimstone Berry, Celestial Caramel Crunch, Purgatory Pistachio, Limbo Lemon and Sell Your Soul Strawberry and pointed at a tub labeled Original Sin.

"What kind of cones you got?"

Icky twirled, his boots feeling as light as the clouds through which his mind sailed, and pointed to an array of waffle and sugar cones and a dozen toppings.

"Don't you talk none?"

Icky smiled and grooved on the colors in the display case and the bright yellow stripes his mother had painted on the walls. Not long after that, she and his father grew tired of rain and dark winters and returned to Oklahoma City. Icky never tired of rain. He loved the grays in the sky, the mist, the fog, the clouds and the dripping and drumming and splashing, the sloshing and bubbling of water running across the roof, through the gutters and along the streets. In the winter, he could close the shop for days at a time and groove on that. But when the sun came out, so did customers. Bummer.

He stared at the yellow stripes again. How long since his parents left? Five years? Four? He wondered when he'd talked to them last. Months ago, probably. They phoned now and then to make parental noises and ask if might be home for one holiday or another. He never went. Never had much to say to them. Or anybody. All the best words had already been spoken. How could anything compare with Keats and Shelley, Emerson and Whitman?

"You gonna serve us or not?"

Icky shrugged and went right on smiling.

"Yo. You are one bizzaro dude."

"Yeah. Spooky. I like that ring in your nose, though."

Icky smiled on, humming a snatch from Mozart's *Requiem*, thinking about the mega-joint he'd torch after he locked up, and fantasizing about that jar of chunky peanut butter in the refrigerator. A vanilla shake would feel good on his tongue, too. Then, after the sun slid into the ocean, he'd check on the five hundred spindly young plants in that hidden hollow up behind Devil's Acres. His little green friends.

"I'll have a double scoop of Pitchfork Passion, in a waffle cone."

"And gimme one scoop of Eternal Agony Mocha and one of Deal with the Devil, in a dish, with chocolate sprinkles and whipped cream."

Icky filled their orders, passed over the ice cream and took a ten-dollar bill. He stared at it, then opened the cash drawer and began counting on his fingers. He'd never been much good at addition and subtraction. Customers always told him when he gave them too little, but there were times when he knew by the way their eyeballs shifted that he'd given them too much.

He dug a few bills and some coins out of the cash register and handed them across the counter, sensing he'd given the kids a deal.

"Hey, thanks, dude." Blue-hair tossed his empty caramel corn package on the floor and pocketed the money. "You rock."

Icky's smile broadened to a grin as they went out, making the bell over the door jingle. What did it matter? It was only money, after all. Jeffrey Wolfe's rent paid for his groceries. And if the ice cream shop didn't show a profit Icky wouldn't starve. He'd make plenty on the harvest later in the summer and, since Vince Grabowski took his swan dive off Perdition Point, the money was all his. Icky closed his eyes and visualized Grabowski sailing onto the rocks. Far out. No more Vince. No more blackmail.

A small, fuzzy fear uncurled in the pit of his stomach. What if Vince had kept notes on their deal? What if someone found out?

He gripped the countertop until his dizziness passed. If anyone could screw him from beyond the grave, it was Vince Grabowski.

NINE

"Molly! Jeff's here!"

Dad's voice finally penetrated my consciousness. I peeled one eyelid up and saw a familiar pillowcase—white with blue and green stripes.

He bellowed again. "We're leaving for the boat!"

I grunted through puffy lips and felt the sound reverberate within my skull—a series of sharp hollow impacts, like a golf ball bouncing down an escalator in an empty building.

"Molly? Did you hear me?"

I lifted my head and focused one throbbing eyeball on the clock before a wave of nausea slammed me back into the pillow. Seven-thirty. And I had three stories due by ten. Ben Galloway would crap cabbages if I didn't make the deadline. I separated my tongue from the roof of my mouth and ran it over my teeth. They felt furry and tasted like the gunk stuck to the bottom of the bleachers in the high school gym.

"Molly! Are you all right? You've got to get up, lass." My father's feet clomped up the stairs and he tapped on the door. "Molly?"

"Morning, Dad," I muttered into the pillow. "Come on in."

The door squeaked open. "Are you okay?"

"I'm fine," I lied to the pillow.

He crossed to the bed and laid a gnarled hand on my forehead. It felt like a ten-pound sack of flour. "What's the matter, honey? Got the flu?"

"Nuh-uh."

"Should I get you some aspirin and a glass of juice?"

"Uhhhh."

"I can't understand you, sweetheart."

"Sorry to intrude, but I think this is what she needs."

I turned my head a fraction, opened one eye and saw Jeffrey Wolfe crossing my bedroom, a round cardboard container in one hand, something wrapped in foil in the other.

"A double tall latte and a bacon, egg, and cheese sandwich on a buttered English muffin." He smiled and set his offering on the table beside the bed. "I made them myself. Grease and caffeine always work for me." He turned to my father. "And a couple of aspirin couldn't hurt. I'll wait downstairs."

"Nice lad," my father said as he puttered across the hall to the bathroom. "Smart. Hard-working. I like him more all the time." I heard the cabinet creak open, heard him rattle the aspirin bottle and curse at the child-proof lid. In a moment I felt him press two pills into my palm. "I think he likes you, too." He pried the plastic top off the coffee and handed it to me, then walked to the window and zipped up the shade.

"He's not my type." Seizing the cup, I slupped down coffee, trying to drown the annoying little voice in the back of my head. "If he's not your type," the voice trilled, "why are you worried about your bloodshot eyes and egg-beater hair?"

I gritted my teeth and informed the pillow, "I don't care if he sees me looking like week-old roadkill." What did it matter if my breath smelled like Neptune's Grotto, and my room was strewn with a week's worth of dirty clothes? What did it matter if he wrote cerebral poetry about sunsets and the meaning of life while I wrote about sand dune erosion and the Friday evening fish fry at the Grange hall? Irrelevant. Jeffrey Wolfe wasn't my type. Period. End of discussion.

"Your mother wasn't my type, either." My father stroked my hair, his rough skin catching some of the strands, sending pain pogo-sticking across my scalp. "Too short, for one thing, and I'd never gone for women with dark hair. I thought I liked them blond and quiet, but when I met her, why it was like a rogue wave slapped me broadside. She was the exciting woman I'd ever met—and the most alive. Until . . ."

I grabbed his hand and squeezed. "I miss her too, Dad."

He rubbed at his eyes. "I wish you could have known her better."

"I know her through you." I sipped coffee and glanced at the clock. Seven forty-five. "And you'd better get going. Don't you have a charter at eight?"

He didn't answer, just stroked my hair again and gazed out the window.

"Dad? Jeffrey's waiting for you."

"Oh. Yeah. We got a charter at eight. Will you be okay?"

"Sure." Nothing that brain surgery won't fix. Or maybe hair of the dog. "You go on."

He started for the door, then stopped and spoke without looking at me. "You've not taken to drinking too much, have you Molly?"

"No Dad." I unwrapped the muffin, then shoved it aside as the aroma launched another wave of nausea. Maybe I'd stick to liquids.

"Are you sure?"

"I'm sure, Dad. I swear I only had a couple of drinks." Or maybe three. Possibly four. I usually didn't drink anything stronger than beer or wine, and not much of that, but after a day on the road, the first cold gin and tonic slid down my throat too fast. I used the second to wash down my cheeseburger. Greg bought me the third. It would have been rude to refuse. Then came the fries and Maybelline's secret dipping sauce. And another drink courtesy of Jeffrey. Also rude to refuse.

"I don't want to pry, Molly. I promised myself I would never do that. But I know there isn't much for you here. Not like in Albuquerque."

"There's plenty to do here, Dad," I lied.

"But there aren't a lot of people your age to do it with." He paused, fingering the light switch beside the door. "People who aren't married and don't have families to take up all their time."

Ah, now we cut to the chase; when would Molly find a man and settle down? "I'm fine, Dad. Really. I've met some men out here." Two, actually: Greg Erdman and Jeffrey Wolfe. Not counting Big Billy Bohannon and Henri Trevelle (for obvious reasons), Greg and Jeffrey were about the only unattached men in my age bracket on this stretch of the coast.

Greg, with broad shoulders and soft lips, resembled all the other men I dated over the past few years. Like them, he was both fascinated and repulsed by strong-minded women, had limited interests outside of his job, and had racked up a lousy track record at relationships.

Jeffrey, on the other hand, was an anomaly. Witty, interesting, introspective—but not my type. Okay by me. Given the way my heart got mangled the last time I'd handed it over to a man, I'd decided to wait at least a decade before I made another emotional commitment.

"I don't want you missing out on life because of me, Molly."

I tossed back the sheet and blanket, noticed I still wore the T-shirt, jeans and socks from yesterday, and wobbled across the room to hug him. "I'm not missing out on anything, Dad. I'd rather be right here with you. Thousands of people would cut off a finger to live in a house with this view of the coastline, and here I am, squatting in one rent-free."

"And it's falling down around us." He shrugged out of my hug and pointed to a brown spot on the ceiling and another on the flowered wallpaper above the window in the room that had been mine as long as I could remember. "We need a new roof and a paint job and I'm worried about the foundation. I never was much good at making money, Molly."

"That's okay, Dad. Nobody's perfect at everything." I squeezed back tears and wrapped my arms around his neck. "You took good care of Mom and me, that's what matters." And it cost him a fortune. He'd sold his share in a commercial trawler to pay for doctors and nurses and medicine that didn't work. Then the funeral took the last of it and he worked odd jobs so he'd be home to make breakfast and dinner and help with homework, and get me through college. And he never let me pay back a single dime.

I couldn't hold the tears in any more. What I'd given up for him was nothing. "I love you, Dad," I choked.

He patted my back, then untangled my arms. "I've got six tourists waiting and no clue where the fish are biting. You sure you're okay?"

"I'm fine," I sniffed. "See you later. I'll make dinner. How about pasta and salad? Maybe I can find a low-fat dressing with some kind of taste. Okay?"

"It's a deal." He touched my hair once more, and then tromped down the stairs.

The bed called my name and the pillow invited me to go another round, but I brushed my teeth and threw water on my face instead, then grabbed the coffee and muffin and headed for the corner of the cluttered living room I'd turned into my office. Flipping open the laptop, I dug my notebook and tape recorder from the bag I'd tossed on the chair last night and took a bite of muffin. I'd crank out the weather piece first, then the sanitized story on Vince Grabowski's demise. By then I might be able to remember some of what Greg Erdman told me last night. Finally, I'd sort through the mayor's bombast and a blizzard of "good riddance to bad rubbish" comments I'd collected in the bar, and extract something to use in the other story Galloway wanted, a heart-warming piece about a small town struggling to cope with the loss of a visionary leader. If my hangover didn't make me spew breakfast, writing that would.

"Damn. Fifteen minutes late already." Greg Erdman tossed the clock on the bed, rubbed a towel over his hair, and tore open the top drawer.

"Awwww, man! No clean T-shirts."

He dropped to his knees, clutched his head until it stopped throbbing, and fished under the bed, pulling out an assortment of dust bunnies and dirty clothes. He shook out a couple of T-shirts, picked the one with the fewest holes and stains and carried it into the bathroom to spray it with air freshener. How the hell was he supposed to hold down two jobs, visit his kids, clean the apartment, and keep up with his laundry too?

"Aaaa-chooo!"

"Crap!"

"Aaaa-choo!"

Tossing the T-shirt onto an overflowing clothes hamper in the closet, he plucked another from the floor. He'd forgotten that damn lemon-scented spray raised hell with his sinuses. Just like he'd forgotten his intention to pry information from Molly and ended up spilling his guts. One minute he'd been pumping her about which Devil's Harbor citizens she'd vote most likely to toss Vince Grabowski into the drink, and the next he'd been ordering another round and quoting verbatim from the medical examiner's report.

"Damn!"

The sheriff would skin him alive if any of that privileged information showed up in *The Flotsam* tomorrow. Especially the part about how the way the blood had settled could mean Grabowski had been dead and lying on his back for maybe a couple of hours before he hit the rocks. Or the bit about how the injuries on the back of his head and neck looked more like something done by a blunt instrument than by the fall. He tried to remember if he'd blabbed about the shiner around Grabowski's left eye or the marks on his neck that suggested someone had strangled him manually as well as with something that might have been a thin chain. It was all a blur.

He buttoned his uniform shirt and tucked it into his pants, then dug out a pair of clean socks and sat on the bed to pull them on and tie his shoes.

"Argghhh!" A ball peen hammer pounded on the inside of his skull. Had he mentioned he'd be checking into rumors of a big insurance policy, payable to Grabowski's estranged wife?

"God. The sheriff will fry my ass." He had to call Molly, convince her it was all off the record.

He reached for the phone, then drew his hand back. Reporters were like sharks. They could sense fear, smell blood. He was screwed. Even if she attributed the information to an anonymous source, the sheriff would know.

Greg took his gun from the bedside table. Might as well go into the office and pretend nothing happened. Grind out his paperwork, then cruise up the coast to Devil's Harbor, start checking alibis for Saturday night, nail down the identity of the last person to see Grabowski alive.

He crossed the living room his ex-wife sneeringly referred to as a litter box with chairs and slammed the door behind him as he headed for his car. Maybe he'd send Molly flowers, then call her later in the afternoon, see if they could get together for dinner. Someplace besides the Belly Up where that tall poet dude wouldn't horn into the conversation. Not that anyone could find much to talk about with a bookworm who didn't own a television, who never watched baseball. Probably thought a drag bunt had something to do with cross-dressing. No competition. Who wanted a man who couldn't even say good night without quoting from Shakespeare?

"Ummmm." Claire Grabowski inhaled cool salt air, stretched, and swung her feet to the floor. Standing, she looked out across the living room and through windows soaring nearly twenty feet to the raftered ceiling. She'd helped the architect design this house with its bedroom loft and the sweeping ocean view that aggravated Vince's fear of heights. Now it was all hers: state-of-the-art kitchen, wine cellar, guest suite, library, deck, and hot tub.

And hellacious mortgage. She shivered. Would she lose the house? Or could she find a way to save it?

A second thought triggered another shiver. She should call the sheriff's department and tell them she was in town. Offer to claim the body for burial. *The body.* She hoped she wouldn't need to make an official identification.

Vowing not to think about that until she had to, she walked to the railing. Today she'd concentrate on beautiful things, like the way the sun gilded grains of sand tumbling in the surf, the way that blue and white boat sliced through the swells, and the way a cup of coffee would taste and a croissant would melt on her tongue.

Her stomach rumbled. She'd had nothing except a cardboard airport meal and a couple of glasses of wine since yesterday morning. Hurrying back to the bed, she draped herself across the man sprawled on his stomach, and snarled her fingers in his long, knotted hair.

"Wake up, sleepy head."

"No. Can't," he mumbled.

"I need breakfast. And you've got to open the shop in less than an hour."

"Can't move. I'm on empty." He shook off her hand and slapped a pillow over his head. "You wore me out last night, woman."

Claire smiled. "I did, didn't I?" She'd let go of years of rules and inhibitions and felt no trace of the guilt she'd believed would be inevitable. "I'll make coffee. Then let's shower together."

"Just bring me coffee, Claire, please. I can't shower with you," he groaned. "I'm dead meat. Beached. Drained. Wiped out. Roadkill on the highway of love. Nothing left."

She slid her hands along his back, and then drew her fingernails in small circles at the base of his spine. "Nothing?"

"Nothing." His voice climbed half an octave on the second syllable.

"You're such a liar, Adam."

"It's my best quality, Claire."

She grinned and squeezed a portion of his anatomy. "Next to this."

"Come on, Jen. Pick up the pace now or I'll be late for work."

"Ohmigod, you are such a whiner," Jennifer Daley gasped as she struggled to keep up with Bart Yamamoto on the steep road to the uppermost cul-de-sac in the Devil's Acres subdivision. If she didn't lose two more pounds, she'd pop the zipper on her coronation dress when she sat. She'd begged Bart to take her with him this morning, but no way did she know running would be this hard. Her cute outfit was all sweaty and smelly. Yuck. "It's not like Adam would fire you."

"Yeah, but—"

"Ohmigod, Bart. You like completely ran the shop all weekend."

"Yeah, but, my father says—"

Jennifer stopped running, turned her back on Bart and the bull dozed vacant lots, locked her eyes on the ocean, and jammed her fingers in her ears. Sometimes Bart could be such a dweeb. Quoting his father's prehistoric advice. "Boooorrrrring. I am so not listening."

She should totally break up with him right now. Well…maybe not. Devil's Harbor was like so end-of-the-earth she'd have to import a date for the festival, like from Mars. And Bart was major good-looking. For a dweeb. Maybe she'd just sulk until he bought her a present.

As she pulled her fingers from her ears, she heard a car engine sputter and then clatter to life. She stuck out her lower lip in the pout she practiced daily before the bathroom mirror and turned to accept Bart's apology. But Bart was a hundred feet ahead of her, jogging in place and staring at an old Volkswagen as it chugged out of the cul-de-sac. Adam Quarles flashed a peace sign as the car clanked by her in a cloud of exhaust.

"Gross." Now she smelled like a car fart.

Grinning, Bart jogged down to join her. "Did you see that?"

"Yeah. Adam. So?" Jennifer adjusted her headband.

"Did you see who was with him?"

"No one was with him. Ohmigod, you are, like, such a loser. You can't even see straight."

"Not in the car, Jen. Up there!" He pointed toward the only house in the cul-de-sac: a big one with enormous windows. "Mrs. Grabowski. She was wearing just a towel. She kissed him goodbye. Like this." He grabbed Jennifer's arm, swung her around and planted an inch of tongue between her lips.

"Ooooh," Jennifer gasped. "You are such a liar."

"If I'm lyin', I'm dyin'."

Jennifer squinted at the house. "But Mrs. Grabowski left town like virtual centuries ago. What's she doing back?"

Bart smirked. "Something you get naked to do."

Jennifer felt herself flush. "With Adam? No way."

"Way."

Jennifer stared at him for a moment, and then plucked her cell phone from her pocket. "I've got to call Molly."

TEN

I stared at the phone after Jennifer hung up. Adam Quarles and Claire Grabowski? Talk about off-the-wall. I'd never met the widow Grabowski, but she must be in her mid-forties, at least. And Adam was . . . Well, who knew? With his cocky save-the-earth swagger, dreadlocked hair, and hemp-woven clothing he seemed ageless. Had Vince Grabowski known?

Chewing on a huge bite of cold muffin, egg, and cheese, I reviewed what I knew about Grabowski. For sure Vince's alpha male ego would have gone to condition red if he'd found his wife boinking anyone, especially the eco-freak who'd picketed his construction sites. Had he tried to end the affair? Had they, in turn, put an end to him?

I added that question to a string of notes: find out more about Grabowski's corporation and its investors and officers, check out the rumor about a big insurance payoff, and call my contact with an organized crime task force to see if any of Vince's investors were on the shady side.

I swallowed and took another bite, feeling invigorated. The Grabowski story was getting bigger all the time. A whole lot went on in Devil's Harbor that Dad hadn't shared during our weekly phone calls. Fortunately, there was someone who knew which skeletons hung in which closets. And usually couldn't wait to tell.

I finished the muffin, drained the coffee, and headed out to my truck. Ben Galloway would have to stretch the deadline.

Maybelline Yamamoto shot another glance over her shoulder at the two men in dark suits hunkered over coffee cups at a corner table in the Devil's Food Cafe. "IRS."

"You think?" LaDonna Perkins topped off Maybelline's cup, put the coffee pot back on the burner and came around the end of the counter to sit beside her friend. Maybelline stopped by every morning on her way to the Belly Up to check the beer vats and sweep peanut shells and fries off the floor. That tradition went back to the first day LaDonna opened the doors. "Not FBI?"

She didn't say what she really thought—that the two men were contract killers, like her husband, and they'd come to erase her. Feeling her hands shake, she clutched the edge of the counter. Her mind wound in tight circles. Would contract killers be so obvious? Or would they blend with the tourist crowd, check out her routine, then ease in after dark, kill her, and leave. What did she really know about how they worked? She wished she could tell Maybelline about her past. But silence had kept her safe so far.

"Could be FBI." Maybelline stirred a packet of artificial sweetener into her coffee. "Could be drug enforcement agents, here to check on what Icky's smoking. Or ATF checking on whether Henri is supplying guns to some militia group. They're government, definitely. They must starch those shirts with one of those get-it-up drugs. What did they order?"

"The number three breakfast. Both of them."

"Ham and eggs, hash browns, toast, and coffee," Maybelline recited, checking the blackboard behind the counter.

"Not as spendy as the crab omelet. Or eggs Benedict. Is that all they had? No side orders?"

"They asked for extra jelly." LaDonna shot another glance at the men, one of whom was writing something on a napkin. "Except . . ."

"Except what?" Maybelline narrowed her eyes.

"Well, one of them—the short one with the big nose—he wanted everything on separate plates."

"Separate plates?"

"Right. He specified that none of the food touch any other kind of food, even back in the kitchen. Wanted his toast cut into fingers, too, not crosswise. And when he ate, he'd take a bite of egg, then a bite of ham, then a bite of potatoes and a bite of toast and a sip of coffee. Just like that. In that order, every time."

"Weird." Maybelline spun on her stool and studied the men.

"Don't look right at them," LaDonna hissed.

"Oh, don't be such a nervous Nellie. They're not after us."

LaDonna wished she had Maybelline's confidence. "You sure?"

"Sure I'm sure." Maybelline spun back, grabbed her coffee cup, and took a long drink. "Unless they're egg-suckers checking on my liquor license."

"You don't have anything to worry about, do you?"

"Shit, no. But they'll waste my time and make my customers edgy. I've followed their regulations to the letter, no matter what Vince Grabowski told them. Whoever bounced him off the boulders did a million dollars worth of improvements to this town."

LaDonna snuck another glance at the two men, one of whom thumbed through a thick wallet as he studied the check she'd delivered with their last round of coffee. "You don't think they're investigating his death, do you?" She felt her hands start to shake again and wove her fingers together. They'd find out right away he'd been seeing Shelley. But only two people knew she'd threatened to castrate Grabowski if he didn't end it. They'd been alone in the kitchen when she got the point across with a carving knife. And she bet he would never have told anyone a woman scared him so bad his voice cracked.

Maybelline snorted. "Don't be silly. Why would the feds be interested in Vince Grabowski's death?"

"Well, he was a pretty important man."

"Yeah, the big Grabowski, a legend in his own mind. Hell, LaDonna, he was just a big frog in a small puddle. A big frog whose tacky ties matched his tacky socks. The FBI wouldn't give a rat's ass about him. And the sheriff wouldn't call in the feds unless someone held a gun to his head." Maybelline turned to watch the two men walk out. "More likely they're with some organized crime family Grabowski borrowed money from."

LaDonna's fingers felt like icicles. "You're kidding."

Maybelline stood, patted her hair, and tucked her shirt into the waistband of her jeans. "Don't know if I am or not. Old Vince got way behind the eight ball. He'd tapped out all the locals. Maybe he found somebody to bail him out and these guys are here to make sure that somebody gets his money from the other investors." She turned at the door and waved. "See ya later."

LaDonna managed a sickly two-finger flutter. Before she learned about Vince and Shelley, she'd invested in his development, invested all she had in the bank. She had nothing left except the café.

"Hold that thought, Molly, *ma petite amie.*" Henri Trevelle pressed a flowered teacup and matching wafer-thin saucer into my hand and trotted to the door of his shop. "This is just too delicious. I cannot bear to be interrupted." He snapped down the shade and danced toward me, fingers fluttering. "Adam and the wife of the spawn of Satan? I must know more!"

"Sorry, Henri." I fought back a giggle. "That's all I've got. Bart Yamamoto saw them at Grabowski's house in Devil's Acres this morning laying a lip-lock on each other. I thought you'd have the dirt."

"*Moi?*" Henri feigned surprise, spreading his hands, palms out, and opening his eyes wide.

"Yes, you." I sniffed tea that smelled like petunias. "If there's a bigger gossip on the coast, I don't know who it is." I sipped. Plastic petunias. Give me coffee any day.

"It takes one to know one." His voice rumbled with anger. "You should check the mirror before you disparage my conversational habits."

I started to apologize, and then spotted the sparkle in his eyes. In a moment he chuckled. "I almost had you, *oui?* Oh, I am such a tease."

I laughed, set my cup on top of the cold stove, and checked my watch. 9:30. "So you didn't have a clue about this?"

"Well, I wouldn't say I didn't suspect Adam was engaged in an affair of passion." Henri drank, then blotted his lips with an embroidered napkin. "He tended to disappear now and then, the sly dog. Buying trips. But honestly, my dear, I didn't believe that for a minute. He's stocked the same brands of tofu, nuts, and grains since he opened Passing Wind."

"So you were suspicious?"

Henri nodded. "But you know I never pry."

"Yeah, right. And I never ask for extra dip with my fries at the Belly Up."

He sipped tea again, playing coy. "Okay. So maybe I asked him. And he stuck to that story, except once when he swore he'd been visiting family. But Adam's relatives are rabid right-wingers who disowned him years ago. Like much of my family." He smiled sadly. "So he must have been seeing her."

I finished the tea and studied the fragile cup. "Could Adam have killed Vince Grabowski?"

He leaned forward. "Are you implying he died of causes unnatural?"

"Well, the medical examiner won't commit to an official cause of death yet, but someone punched Grabowski in the face, choked him, and clubbed him with a blunt instrument."

He smiled. "Sounds like an ordinary hockey game."

"Yeah," I chuckled. "Except Grabowski's in the morgue and no one's in the penalty box. What about it? Could Adam have killed him?"

"That's like asking if I could shave off my eyebrows. Of course I could." Henri ran a finger along the ridges above his eyes. "But I wouldn't."

I shoved that image aside, concentrating on Adam. "But he hated Grabowski."

"Naturally. And I despise all those pass-the-loot club guys. But I wouldn't kill them."

"That's not the same. Maybe he thought Claire would collect a fat insurance policy."

"Money? Adam?" Henri threw his head back and roared. "Money would be the last reason he'd kill anyone."

True. He was a minimalist "Maybe Claire decided that with one quick shove she and Adam could live happily ever after."

While Henri mulled that over, I pulled a narrow reporter's notebook from my purse. "And then there's the rest of the town, right? Elspeth Hunsaker called him the bodily incarnation of the devil."

Henri grinned. "Elspeth does not—how do you say it?—mince the words. And she is on a mission. I would not rule her out."

"What about a woman scorned?"

He nodded. "Like Prudence Deeds? A woman scorned who loves money. That has possibilities."

I nodded, making a mental note to probe Prudence's financial agreement with the Devil's Acres development. "And Shelley Perkins? She and Grabowski had a fling and word is he dumped her. You must talk about lots of things while she does your hair."

Henri waved me off. "What does it matter who killed him? He's gone. And Devil's Harbor is a better place."

I fought the little voice in my brain that agreed and gave him doctrine. "We can't make an exception because we didn't like the victim. If you get away with murder, it seems an easy solution. You kill again because someone flips you off in traffic, gives your kid a D in math, smiles at your wife."

Henri waggled his fingers at my moralistic tirade, then brought the teapot, filled our cups, and settled back in his rocker. "What's the weather forecast for the festival?"

I knew evasion when I saw it. Henri didn't want to talk about Shelley as a suspect. "Let's get back to Shelley. Off the record. Could she have killed him?" I slipped my notebook into my purse and clicked in the point of my pen.

He sighed. "Shelley suffers from small-town syndrome. A sameness to every day. No adventure. *Je comprends.* I can relate. I didn't realize how far away from it all I'd gotten when I bought this shop. I'm nearly off the map." He tweaked the crease in his trousers. "The poor bored little dear was simply swept off her feet. Then LaDonna—" He gasped and shut up like a clam.

I smelled blood, clicked the pen. "Then LaDonna what?"

"Tch." Henri wrung his hands. "Shelley doesn't know. She'd be so angry with her mother" He wagged an index finger in my face. "But I would have done the same."

My heart pounded. "Done what?"

"A mother protects her young."

I clicked the pen faster. "Protects how?"

Henri stared into his teacup, then set it aside. "I popped over to get a trim one day." He ran his fingers through his hair. "Just a little off the top and behind the ears. As I came down the stairs, I happened to notice my shoelace flapping. As I stopped to tie it, I heard LaDonna and Grabowski arguing in the kitchen. Well, I decided to check the breakfast special for the next day— to see if the crab was still on special—and I heard LaDonna tell him to kiss his family jewels goodbye if he didn't leave Shelley alone."

And I'd always pegged LaDonna for the shy and silent type. "Do you think she meant it?"

"*Oui*. She said she'd use a chef's knife." Henri clamped his thighs together.

"What did he say?"

"Nothing. Just a squeak. But the next day Shelley came to me crying so hard she looked just like a raccoon, mascara everywhere. I let her sob her little eyes out, and then I got her a hot fudge sundae and set her in the rocker with Angel and filled her with the usual crapola about how she was just a child, and she'd fall in love again." He sipped tea, patted his mouth with the napkin, then smoothed it over his thigh. "Shelley was distraught, but she would never kill."

Henri studied my attempt at a poker face. "You don't agree."

"You and Shelley have a special relationship." I picked my words carefully. "You might not see what others do."

He puffed out his chest. "I'm not blind, if that's what you mean. Shelley seems self-centered and trivial, but underneath she's bright and clever."

Clever enough to kill Vince Grabowski? I shrugged.

"Oh, like you were perfect when you were nineteen!" He leaped from the chair, cheeks flushing, and loomed over me. "You—the town's Miss First-Ever-Whirligig-Queen. Miss Big-City-Investigative-Reporter."

I cringed. Was he teasing again? "Hey, Henri. I'm sorry. I just meant—"

"Take that ugly purse and get out. I know what you meant; you meant to throw Shelley to the wolves so the police don't ask your father why *he* threatened to kill Vince Grabowski Saturday night!"

Something cold and greasy twisted in my gut. "What? What are you talking about?"

"Don't pull that 'I'm so surprised' act on me. Grabowski mentioned your name right before your father went ballistic."

I peered up into his eyes. He had to be kidding. "Henri, I don't know what you're talking about. I swear I'm not trying to cast blame on Shelley. Honest."

He drew in a ragged breath and his eyes shifted away. "I'm sorry, Molly." He felt for the arm of the rocker. "I lost it. Snapped. Like when someone would high-stick me on the ice." He took a deep breath and sat. "I feel so sorry for that kid. No father to love her. That's why she flirts with every man around."

I released the breath I'd been holding.

"You don't know her like I do. Sometimes I think that if I were a few years younger and—" He snorted, and then

90

sputtered into hearty laughter. "And a whole hell of a lot straighter." He wiped his eyes. "A most comical thought, no?"

I nodded and forced a chuckle, my mind swirling over what he'd said.

"You'll still dance with me Friday night, won't you? You're the only one who can do the Macarena without looking like you've stepped in dog doo-doo."

I patted his knee. "I'll dance with you. Now tell me about my father." Knitting my clammy fingers, I focused on breathing. I didn't want to know, but I had to.

"You won't think I'm a snoop and a busybody, will you?"

"Of course not," I lied.

"I won't tell anybody else," he promised. Tweaking that crease again, he leaned forward. "I was trying to find Margaret, the little slut," he nodded at the tabby sleeping beside the cash register. "She didn't come home for dinner on Saturday. It doesn't do any good to call her, so I don't bother. I walk along and listen until I hear tomcats growling. Except I didn't hear that, I heard your father bellowing at Vince Grabowski."

A frigid finger touched my spine. "Did you see them?"

"No. They must have been between another boat and the *Helen*."

"But you're sure it was Grabowski? And my father?"

"Molly, no one swears like your father. It was definitely him. And that imbecile Grabowski. Grab-ass. I couldn't hear what he said about you, only your name, but your father flew into an absolute fury. He called Grab-ass a slime-bucket scum-sucking piss-ball. Then Grab-ass yelled and I heard a crash and your father bellowed, 'I'm going to kill you.' And Grab-ass begged him to stop and then I heard something that sounded like a gargle.

91

My chest tightened, but I squeezed out the words, "and then what?"

"And then Margaret came sashaying out from behind the mayor's fish palace and I took her home." He shrugged. "Who was I to interfere with a civic improvement project? Besides, I didn't think your father would kill him."

I closed my eyes, felt my heart throbbing in my trembling hands as I remembered that my father had gone to the boat Saturday evening to stow some new life vests in the cabin. Or so he'd said. I'd stayed home, waiting for Greg, and fallen asleep. I hadn't heard Dad return. At three I'd staggered out to deliver *The Flotsam*. I hadn't checked on Dad as I often did in the night. Had he killed Vince Grabowski and trucked the body to Perdition Point?

ELEVEN

Elspeth Hunsaker plugged in her electric teapot and selected the tea to match her mood—Earl Grey, somber, yet forceful. And no sugar—she planned to deliver an unsweetened lecture when she went on the air in twenty minutes. The residents of this town were in peril. Sugarcoating her message would only lead them farther down the road to damnation. The Lord had struck down Vincent Grabowski and that same swift sword would continue to cull the flock until they recognized their sins, repented, and renamed the town Holy Waters. That black-garbed youth with the blasphemous ice cream flavors would be taken next. She was sure of it.

Sitting at the cluttered desk, she tugged down her skirt and smoothed out a page from a yellow legal pad on which she'd made notes. She'd warned Vincent Grabowski. Every time he named another street in that subdivision, she'd tried to show him the light. It was bad enough the town already had streets like Brimstone Boulevard, Damnation Alley, and Temptation Way. Bad enough she lived on that one.

Well, Vincent Grabowski had learned what happens to those who consort with Satan and the dark forces in this world. He'd felt that terrible swift sword.

The kettle whistled and she hunted for the mug that should have been beside the sugar, the one with the handle in the shape of praying hands and the crown of thorns around the bottom. She'd won that for her high game at the Bowling for Souls Tournament in Coos Bay. Wondering if the engineer who read the meters and kept KYMR on the air had borrowed it, she searched around his console and in the musty-smelling commercial production booth—a room unused since before Christmas.

"Well, I hope whoever took it will be enlightened by it." She returned to her cramped office, took a ring of keys from her purse and opened a listing metal supply cabinet. Shoving aside copy paper, pens, pencils, a box of sanitary napkins, and a tin of ginger snaps, she seized a mug she'd collected as evidence of the depravity of the Whirligig Festival. It featured a red devil clutching a whirligig pitchfork as he rode a spouting whale. "Devil's Harbor," the slogan on the cup read, "you'll be tempted to stay."

"That's disgusting," Elspeth muttered. "Utterly sinful." She'd intercepted the cup from a shipment delivered last week, and confronted Vincent Grabowski about it Saturday afternoon. He'd taunted her, calling her a crazed religious nut job. A fanatic. A fruitcake. Told her that unless she got behind his plans for the future of Devil's Harbor, he'd file a complaint with the Federal Communications Commission.

"He deserved to suffer."

She glanced at the rusted can of insecticide she'd found in the shed behind her house. Had she used enough in the cup of sweet tea she'd fixed for Vincent Grabowski? She didn't know. The directions were for killing bugs, not two-legged cockroaches. And he didn't drink much of it—just a few sips before he made his threats and left.

But it must have been enough. Vincent Grabowski had died, hadn't he? She clapped her hands together. And now she must pray that he went to meet his maker before he'd mailed his complaint to the government.

"Beautiful morning, isn't it? And how can I help you, Sergeant?"

Marveling at the political system, Greg Erdman studied the stumpy man behind the counter of the fish market. Brighton Deeds had squeaked out a two-vote victory over an opponent who'd drawn a ninety day sentence for drunk driving just before the election. Despite the street-painting incident, no one ran against Deeds the second time. Greg decided that was because the job didn't come with a salary.

Deeds smiled, pooching out cheeks criss-crossed with tiny capillaries and revealing teeth too small for his jaw. "I've got nice, fresh rock cod. Put it on the grill with a little oil and cilantro and you've got yourself some fine eating. Or maybe some of those prawns?"

Greg shook his head. "Neither. I need to talk with you a few minutes."

Deeds rubbed his hands together. "I always have time for my constituents. You do vote in this district, don't you, son?"

Not for you, I don't, Greg thought. "It's my duty as a citizen."

"Fine. Fine. That's the spirit." Deeds waddled around the counter, used a corner of his stained white apron to wipe a smudge from the glass case, then offered Greg a card. "I'm running for Congress. Well, I will be as soon as the party puts my hat in the ring next Tuesday. Special election's in a few weeks. Now what can I do to help you?"

Greg kept his thumbs hooked in his belt, ignoring the card. "I have a few questions about Vincent Grabowski's death."

Deeds scowled like a baby passing gas and set the card on the counter. "I thought he committed suicide."

"I can't comment on that." Greg wished he'd stuck to that line the other night. On the way to Devil's Harbor he'd remembered exactly what he'd told Molly while that poet guy went to the bar for another round. The sheriff would crap a watermelon when *The Flotsam* hit his desk.

"Surely you're not treating it as a murder, are you?"

"I can't comment on that, either." He was starting to sound like a politician himself. "I'm looking into what Mr. Grabowski did just before he died, how he seemed, what he said. I understand you worked on the Whirligig Festival planning committee with him."

"Yes. Yes. Vince was a fine man. He had ideas for expanding the festival, bringing in more tourists." Deeds squeezed his eyes shut and wiped at them with his apron. "He was the heart and soul of this community. A visionary. And a hard worker. The kind of man this country needs more of."

Sounds like he memorized that, Greg thought. Wonder how he really felt? "He raised some hackles when he bulldozed the land for his subdivision. Didn't someone threaten a lawsuit?"

Deeds waved that off, a smile pasted to his face, his eyes as flat and dark as those on the salmon in the display case. "There are always those in the way of progress, Sergeant, those who don't look to the future and the greater good."

"And Devil's Acres was for the greater good?"

"Certainly. Environmentalists have practically shut down the logging and fishing industries. If we don't promote growth and development, Devil's Harbor will become a ghost town. Vince Grabowski recognized that. He turned a roadside stand into the Waterside Whirligig Factory and put literally hundreds of hours into planning the festival. Any other

96

developer might have taken his money and run. But not Vince."
He scrubbed at his eyes again.

Greg didn't buy it. "There's speculation the landslide
would throw him into bankruptcy. Do you know anything about
that?"

Deeds shook his head violently. "No."

"You hadn't heard any rumors?"

"No. No. Can't say I have."

"Did you invest in Devil's Acres?"

"What is this?" Deeds daubed sweat from a deep furrow
in his forehead. "What do my investments have to do with
Vince Grabowski's death?"

I struck a nerve! "Maybe nothing."

"You're damn right, nothing. Yes, I put some money
into that project, and yes, it made me nervous when that hillside
caved in. But Vincent Grabowski was a man of his word, and he
promised everyone that we'd make solid profits. I'm a
businessman myself," Deeds patted the top of the display case
and tweaked the apron over his gut. "I know things don't
always run smoothly."

"So you were on good terms with Grabowski?"

"Excellent. Excellent terms. I loved that man like a
brother."

"When did you see him last?"

"Saturday evening."

The night Grabowski died. "Where?"

Deeds pointed to a door in the corner. "Back in my
office, having a glass of brandy."

"How did he seem? Was he angry, upset, depressed?"

"He seemed fine. Just fine."

"Did you see any signs he'd been in a fight?"

Something glinted deep in Deeds' eyes, and then
disappeared. "Vince was fine. Just fine."

Greg drew himself up, looming. "You're sure?"

Deeds held his ground. "I'd know, wouldn't I?"

"You'd think so." Greg peered into Deeds' eyes and spotted the cold metal flash again. "I hope you're not covering for somebody. Like your wife, maybe. There's talk that she and Grabowski were more than just friends." He smiled. It felt good to twist the knife in another man's guts. The way Patsy had twisted it into his. "A lot more than just friends."

"You leave Prudence out of this!" Deeds' pudgy hands curled into fists. "That's malicious gossip! She and Vince worked together. That's all!"

Was he really that naive? Greg scratched his head, then remembered his own denial. Deeds might truly be unaware of his wife's infidelity—or be choosing to ignore it. "All right. But you're sure Grabowski hadn't been in a scuffle?"

"Damn it!" Deeds pounded the counter again. "Can't this wait until after the festival? We've got thousands of people coming. We don't need bad publicity." He headed for the back room. "We'll see what the sheriff has to say about this inquisition."

"Go ahead," Greg bluffed. "He's the one who sent me up here. Listen. I know somebody clobbered Grabowski. I'm just trying to find out when."

Deeds stopped and turned, rubbing his chin. He compressed his lips, glanced at the row of dead fish and sighed. "Okay. Okay. When Vince came in, he had one eye puffed shut, and a split lip. I got him some ice. Got him a brandy, too. He didn't drink but a sip. Said his stomach felt queasy."

"Did he say who hit him?"

Deeds communed with the fish again. "Yeah. Gus Custer."

Now we're getting someplace. "The old guy at the whirligig factory?"

"Yeah, Gus hated Vince. Tells everyone Vince cheated him out of his land. Of course, there isn't a bit of truth to that. Except for jumping the gun on the bulldozing, Vince did everything by the book. Why, he even insisted Gus get the best job at the factory—out there in the display room—even though lots of others wanted it and would put on a better show than Gus does." Deeds nodded to the fish and then to Greg. "Vince stopped by the factory at closing time Saturday and Gus went crazy. Hit him in the eye with a whirligig sperm whale. The super-sized flagpole model with the rotating flippers and the weather vane attached."

Greg fished out a notebook. "And Grabowski fought back?"

"No. Well, he started to, but Gus shoved a toolbox at him and Vince fell against the workbench and cut his lip. By the time he got up, Gus had disappeared."

Had the old man hid until Grabowski left, found him later, whacked him with the whirligig again, strangled him, and tossed him into the ocean? Greg scratched his head. Gus looked pretty frail. Could he haul a bigger man in and out of a car and toss him over a railing? Nah. But, just to be on the safe side, he'd better talk to him.

"Did Grabowski tell you anything else?"

"No." Deeds' eyes quickly shifted toward the window. "Not much."

Greg's nerve endings tingled. He gave Deeds the law-enforcement stare.

Deeds wiped sweat from his brow with the corner of his apron "Uh, Vince was upset that some people weren't behind the festival, weren't doing their part."

"Who?"

"Uh, Mike Donovan. But Vince said he knew a way to get him back on the team."

The tingle turned into a sizzle. "Mike Donovan? Molly Donovan's father?"

"Yes. He has quite a temper, you know." Deeds nodded toward the harbor. "He took a charter out a couple of hours ago. He'll be back around six."

Greg nodded and walked out. Molly would go nuclear if she found he'd put her father on the suspect list. Not that Greg could see Mike Donovan—even given his temper—as a killer. And not wanting to get behind the whirligig festival didn't seem like much of a motive. But, the sheriff would roast him alive if he gave anyone preferential treatment. He groaned and knew that when six o'clock came he'd be waiting at the dock.

TWELVE

"Crud." I stared at the flying squirrel images spinning up from the depths of my computer screen then tapped the space bar. The screen-saver blinked off and I faced the few skimpy sentences I'd managed to write since I left the Gilded Puffin. Fortunately, I'd dictated the dying birds story into my tape recorder as I drove back from Nehalem Bay yesterday. More fortunately, Ben Galloway had pushed the deadline back when he'd chartered a boat to check out reports of a huge school of tuna just off the coast.

Ben took along his rod to try to catch one and his cell phone to dictate the story to his wife. Cynthia had reserved space on the front page. "But not much space," she'd snorted. "Ben couldn't catch his pants on a nail."

Cynthia hadn't been fazed by the change in direction of the Grabowski stories, either. "You're the reporter. And we're lucky to have you. Forget that tragic-accident/loss-to-the-community stuff and go with what you've got. I'll handle Ben." Cynthia was quickly becoming my idol.

"And what have I got?" I asked the twirling squirrels as they invaded the screen again. "A dead man with a pile of enemies and Dad's name on the suspect list. If I believe Henri's story about the fight."

It sounded almost comical. My father, a killer? I rocked back in the chair, surveying the spider-webbing on the ceiling. The man who'd put his own life on hold to give mine a running start couldn't be a murderer.

I rocked forward and hit the space bar again, blitzing the squirrels. What the hell had he and Grabowski argued about? The belly-bucking contest? No, they'd settled that. The parade of ships? No, Dad had agreed to decorate the *Helen*, more because his business needed the publicity than out of civic obligation. Money? I shivered and looked across the room at the battered desk weighed down with stacks of paper Dad had shuffled around last month as he figured his taxes. Surely he hadn't invested in Devil's Acres?

I stood and took three steps toward the desk. Did I really want to know? I took another step. Yes. I stopped and scowled at something that looked like grape jelly on the white trim around the door to the kitchen. I had no right to sift through his papers. And if he'd been conned? Well, it was his money; he could do what he wanted with it.

I glanced at the desk again. I didn't want to believe he'd been that stupid. And why had my name come up? What would send Dad into such a rage?

I went to the kitchen, put a filter in the basket of the coffeemaker, ground a handful of beans, and started a pot of decaf. Then I scrubbed at a spot on the counter top, rearranged the magnets on the refrigerator, ate two no-fat cookies, tightened the laces on my running shoes, stirred milk into a cup of coffee, and tried not to think about my father's temper. Growing up, I'd heard stories from my friends whose parents had told them about barroom brawls, a man pitched through a window and another who'd needed thirty stitches. I'd also heard about the six months Dad had served for assault.

"But that was when he was young," I informed the coffee cup. "That was before he met Mom. People change."

But life on the crime beat had taught me that often they didn't. Dad had controlled his anger, channeled it into a series of small verbal eruptions. But the pressure might have been building. And then Grabowski—

"Dad didn't kill Grabowski."

Saying it out loud made me certain. If he had killed Grabowski accidentally in a fit of rage, my father would have stepped up, admitted what he'd done, and taken his punishment. That was how he'd lived his life. With honesty and honor.

Relieved, I squared the chair up to the table and put my fingers on the keys. "Now write your articles. Stick to the facts and keep things simple." I flexed my fingers. By rehashing the disaster at Devil's Acres and the financial impact, I could imply that Grabowski wouldn't be universally mourned. Without naming names, detailing specific incidents or even mentioning Grabowski's marital problems, I could imply that investigators were keeping their options open. I'd keep information about Grabowski's injuries vague enough to give Greg some deniability.

Once I got rolling, the story would write itself. Then I'd clean the house, take a shower and work on finding out who'd sunk money into Devil's Acres, and how much commission Prudence made on each sale. Checking Grabowski's insurance and bank balance would be tougher, but there were ways. Then, after Dad returned, we'd have a long talk.

Gus Custer hoisted a log, set it upright on the stump behind his cabin, seized the axe, and swung it. It struck with a solid thunk. Right on target. Chips flew and the log split in half, splinters pattering around the stump. He set up another log.

Muscles in his bare arms and shoulders rippled as he swung the axe; beads of sweat sparkled like a silver chain around his neck.

Mornings like this were the best. Enough sun so he could strip off his shirt, enough fog so he couldn't look across the ravine and see the ravaged ridge and start seething about the day he had signed it over to Grabowski. Mornings like this he could split wood for hours, listening to the axe whistling through the air, hearing it thud and rip down the grain, feeling the jolt in his arms and chest, and making conversation with the jays and fat robins that hopped about, picking at bugs scattered from the broken bark. It was a relief to be himself, not that doddering old fool who worked at the factory. Gus checked his wristwatch. Damn. Almost time to get down there and put on his show.

He leaned the axe against the stump, picked up half a dozen split logs, and strode to the woodpile. With Grabowski dead, who'd take over the factory? Maybe Grabowski's wife. No one seemed to know much about her, but Gus expected the worst: she would enforce his contract and institute the stiff production goals Grabowski had mentioned right before Gus whomped him with the whirligig.

Gus jogged back to the stump, picked up another armload, and carried it to the woodpile. Extra work didn't bother him. Real physical exertion beat the hell out of pretending. But Grabowski had demanded Gus recreate some of his original works—reproduce them in poor-quality wood with plastic wings and flippers. He'd claimed the small print in Gus' original contract gave him exclusive rights to any works Gus had ever created. Tourists were tiring of dog-paddling ducks and wind-waggling whooping cranes, so he intended to enforce that. Or, he'd threatened, Gus could go to court, and risk losing the little he had left.

"Son of a bitch." Gus flung the last pieces of wood toward the pile and stomped to the back door. "Greedy blood-sucking bastard. He needed to die."

He ducked into a cramped bathroom and ran a wet wash rag over his face and arms, then rinsed his mouth with baking soda and water and hurried into the bedroom. Yanking off his work boots, he stepped out of his jeans and into the overalls he'd dropped beside the bed yesterday evening. They were a little crusty, but who cared? He'd put on a clean shirt and stick a red bandana in his back pocket. No one looked too hard at an old man, anyway. Especially one who shuffled around town pretending his body was as broken as his spirit. Protective coloration. He hoped it would keep that sergeant from asking him too many questions about what happened the night Grabowski died.

"Just don't fix your gaze a whole lot on the horizon," Mike Donovan cautioned the two men from Nebraska who gripped the rail with their left hands and their rods with their right. "Keep your eyes moving."

The men looked at each other and grimaced. "I'm gonna lose my lunch," the shorter one with the pheasant-hunting-club logo on his jacket whined as he closed his eyes. "Can't you turn the boat sideways or something?"

Mike shrugged. "Only make it worse."

"I didn't get queasy at all when we were moving," his brother-in-law supplied. He wore a faded cap emblazoned with an ear of corn and a crinkly new windbreaker with a price tag attached to the seam under his left arm. "Can't you cruise back and forth?"

"I can, but you won't catch any lingcod or rockfish if I do. No sea bass or grouper, neither. That's what everybody's paying for." Mike gestured toward the other tourists on board, and offered a lips-only smile.

The men exchanged sickly glances, probably wondering why they'd shelled out major bucks for a four-hour fishing trip, why they hadn't settled for the ninety-minute whale-watching excursion. The short one gagged and turned his face into a slight southerly wind. The taller one clamped his teeth and gripped the rail.

"Holler if you get a bite," Mike suggested as he turned away. He'd warned them before they left the harbor, urged them to swallow some of the seasickness pills he kept in the cabin, but they hadn't listened. Just like they hadn't listened when he told them to go easy on the deli sandwiches he and Jeff passed around an hour ago. "Damn candy-ass landlubbers," he cursed under his breath as he walked toward the bow to check on a newlywed couple from California who seemed more interested in playing tonsil hockey than putting lines in the water. Only another two hours of wet-nursing a pack of wobbly-stomached tourists.

Shading his eyes, he looked toward the stern where Jeff threaded bait onto a hook for a heavy-set woman with a slouch hat and a thick German accent. Jeff always smiled at the tourists, and he'd taken to the sea like he'd been birthed by an otter. He already performed his share of the chores aboard the *Helen*, and more. But that presented another problem.

"Goddamn my tired ticker anyway." If Molly agreed Jeff could serve as his mate, she'd go back to Albuquerque. That was no good for him and no good for her, either. She belonged in Devil's Harbor. She just didn't know it. But Mike couldn't tell her that. Or tell her how much he enjoyed having her around. The words just would not come. Short of faking helplessness for the rest of his life, he couldn't think of a way to get her to stay. Unless she met a man.

Mike appraised Jeff again. Strong, quiet, reliable. Of course, Molly went more for big shoulders and a swagger. Like that county mountie. Something about Greg Erdman just didn't sit right with Mike. For one, he didn't have much sense of humor or imagination. He seemed like the kind of guy who'd go to work, come home, drink beer, and watch television. No spontaneity. Every day the same.

Mike sighed. It hurt to think of his free-spirited Molly trying to wedge herself into that life. He was old-fashioned, but he believed that when a man met the right woman, he should close the door on his old ways and open his life up to make room for her, to rebuild himself as Mike had around Helen.

He hated to think of Molly throwing herself away on a man who wasn't willing to risk anything for her. It was a shame she couldn't see that Jeff was a much better match.

"Wow! Look at that!" The California girl pointed to a circle of ripples a hundred yards off the port bow. "Did you see him, honey? A whale!"

She waved to Mike. "There's a whale out there. I've never seen one up close before." She bounced on her toes, ponytail flapping like a pennant. "He has a white spot shaped like a four-leaf clover. Isn't that lucky?"

"Hell!" Mike hustled to the railing. A whale with a spot shaped like a four-leaf clover on his fluke? Double hell. Old Air Biscuit had returned. Just in time for tourist season.

"Which way was he heading?" The California boy shaded his eyes, studying the rolling ocean.

"Right toward us," the girl squealed. "Oooohhh. I hope he comes up next to the boat. That would be awesome."

"You Mother-loving mistake of a sea-mammal." Mike headed for the bridge. "Haul in the lines," he yelled to Jeff. "We're moving."

"Hold it," Jeffrey called back. "We've got a couple of fish on."

"Can't wait! We've got to get underway. Now!" Mike scrambled to the bridge and throttled up the idling engines. One coughed, then quit. He punched the starter button. "Turn over, you worthless piece of congealed crap."

"What's wrong?" Jeffrey's brow furrowed. "Mike, are you okay?"

"That's Old Air Biscuit." Mike punched the starter again and got another asthmatic cough. "Mother-thumping, third-rate, lowest-bidder, oil-burning piece of mechanical crap."

"Who the heck is Old Air Biscuit?" Jeffrey pointed. "Hey. There's a whale. A humpback, I think. Right off the starboard bow. He's spyhopping. Checking us out." He started forward to join the California couple. "I want a closer look."

Mike punched the starter again. "You'll be sorry."

The engine caught as the whale thrust its head from the water, twenty feet away. It twisted slightly, fixed an enormous eyeball on them, and then submerged.

"Wow," the California girl trilled. "Did you see him? This is so cool."

"Look, he's right next to the boat. He's rolling over." Her boyfriend made room for Jeffrey at the rail.

"Frigging blubber-bound flatulating frammerflug!" Mike seized the wheel and edged the boat away, knowing he was too late.

"Isn't that cute? He's blowing bubbles." The girl leaned over the rail.

"Those aren't air bubbles." Jeffrey straightened. "They aren't coming from his blow hole."

"Eeewwww!"

"Oh, Lord!"

"What's he been eating?"

"It's disgusting. Make him stop!"

The California couple stumbled toward the cabin. The Nebraska fishermen turned green, dropped to their knees and hurled ham, cheese, rye, and extra mayo overboard.

"Haul in their lines," Mike bellowed. "We're getting out of here." If I can see, he thought, as the rancid reek from the whale's intestinal system swept over him. The stench enveloped his head like an executioner's hood, burning his eyeballs like a butane torch.

"Captain Donovan! You are experiencing a problem with your engine?" The German woman marched toward the bridge, her sturdy husband close behind. "We are smelling fumes in the rear and—" She halted, peered over the rail, then grabbed a spare rod from the rack beside the cabin door, stepped over the gagging Nebraskans, and began flailing at the water.

"This I do not tolerate!" Whack! "An animal must not do such a thing in public!" Whack! Whack! "We are here for the fresh air!!" Whack! Whack! Whack!

"Hey! She's scaring him away!"

"He's diving."

Through stinging tears, Mike saw Jeffrey give the woman a high five.

"He's gone."

But he'll be back. Mike pounded the wheel. In a twist on a classic, Old Air Biscuit would stalk him like Ahab followed Moby Dick. And the only luck he'd have this season would be bad.

I tapped on the roof of the patrol car parked at the harbor. "Greg? What are you doing here?"

"Hey, Molly." Greg climbed out but kept the open door between us. "How's it going? Come down here to the dock to do some fishing?"

I displayed empty hands. "Without a pole?"

"Ah." He shifted from foot to foot, his eyes darting like minnows. "Well, I'm just down here enjoying the view."

What is he so nervous about? "There's not much view from the dock," I baited him. "You should go up on the bridge."

He shrugged. "It's fine right here."

"Sure. If you say so." Suspicion gnawed at my brain. "What are you really doing here?"

"I told you. Enjoying the view." He focused on my chest, leering and waggling his eyebrows like Groucho Marx.

I rolled my eyes. "And I'm here because I read an article about salt water mud packs and thought I'd scoop up some silt."

He gave up the leer and frowned at me. I frowned back.

He caved. "I came to talk to your father."

A cold feather of fear tickled my spine. *Please don't let him know that Dad argued with Grabowski.* "Why?"

His lips flattened into a thin white line and his gaze darted away again.

"Why?"

"Now, Molly, you know I can't tell you. It's official business."

The feather of fear became a rake He knew. Someone besides Henri had overheard the argument or spotted my father with Grabowski Saturday night. "Is it about Grabowski?"

His eyes narrowed, then opened wide and innocent. *Gotcha!*

"No comment."

"But you're not denying it."

"Damn it, Molly. That's all I'm going to say."

"Give me a hint," I wheedled. "Off the record." Over his shoulder I saw the *Helen* nosing around the spit that stuck into the south side of the bay. The bow slammed into the swells, raising dual fountains of spray. Dad must have her wide open.

"No."

"Come on. I'll buy the drinks next time." Maybe he just wanted to ask Dad a few routine questions, the kind he'd been asking others.

He rubbed his chin. "When *is* next time?"

"Whenever you want. Except for tonight. I have to be up at three to deliver *The Flotsam.*"

He closed the door and stepped closer. "Will it be just you and me?"

"Of course." The *Helen* lined up with the mouth of the channel.

"Not you and me and that geeky poet. I can't believe that crapola he laid on you—that you had an aura like autumn sunlight."

I felt myself blush. I'd kind of liked that. "He's not my type. How about tomorrow night? I'll meet you in Lincoln City."

He grinned. "Okay. Tomorrow night. Promise?"

"I promise." What the heck? I had no other plans and maybe I could gouge more information out of him.

The *Helen* plunged into the channel, six tourists in the bow thrusting their faces into the wind. "Now tell me why you want to talk to my father."

"Off the record?"

"Sure. Off the record."

"You won't get mad? And you'll still have dinner with me tomorrow?"

"Yes. Yes. Just tell me." I saw Dad throttling down the engines, and Jeffrey preparing to leap to the dock.

"Grabowski came to see your dad Saturday night. And as far as I can tell that's the last time anyone saw him alive." He glanced around at the *Helen*. "I want to take your father in and question him."

I felt a fist of fear punch my stomach. "Take him in? Now?"

"Yeah." He pushed past me.

I clutched for his sleeve, and then thrust my hands into my pockets. *Stay calm! Don't make things worse for Dad.* "Can't you question him at the house?"

He shook his head. "It will be better if there are no distractions."

"At least don't put him in the cruiser." My voice sounded strangled. "Let him drive his own truck. You know how people talk."

"Doesn't matter." He turned, and strode along the weathered dock toward the *Helen*. "They'll talk anyway."

To hell with calm! "You're a jerk!"

He turned and put a hand up to smooth back his hair. "I'm guessing this means dinner is off?"

THIRTEEN

Claire Grabowski sneezed so hard her eyes crossed. Vince's cologne hung in the air of the small office, stinging her nostrils with a pungent cocktail of tangerines and testosterone. *Eau de* one-night stand. She could almost feel his malevolent presence in the cluttered modular building beside the Devil's Acres model home. Push-pinned site maps, drawings, and descriptions papered the walls surrounding the broad wooden desk with its executive swivel chair. A half-empty bottle of bourbon sat on top of a tiny refrigerator that squatted beside a card table littered with plastic cups and paper napkins.

Had a detective already searched this mess, or was this the way Vince had left it?

Claire spotted a napkin smeared with bright lipstick that screamed of Vince's infidelities. Her stomach clenched and she braced herself against the wall. Even from beyond the grave he made her feel like a doormat.

"But that's over now."

The words offered comfort and she drew in a long breath and began to hunt for the personal and financial papers she'd need to probate Vince's will. He'd threatened to change it when he'd learned she'd begun the process of annulling their marriage, but as far as she knew, he hadn't.

She'd begun her search by combing the house from basement to attic, emptying every drawer and cabinet, every bookcase and container. In the den, in a tin box under the bar, she'd found a chronicle of Vince's conquests—a notebook he'd kept for thirty years in which he catalogued all the women he'd "nailed," as he so eloquently put it. She'd found his souvenirs, too—silky underwear, hair clips, sunglasses, earrings, lipsticks, stockings, and even a diaphragm. She'd lashed out at the brass wastebasket, kicking it, wishing it was Vince.

Whang.

The pain reminded her that he was dead and she was alive. Alive!

Limping to the executive chair, she sat, pulled out the top drawer, dumped the contents on the blotter, and set the drawer on the floor. She hadn't found much in the house, just a checkbook with a balance of less than six hundred dollars—Vince's personal account. The corporate records and insurance papers must be squirreled away in the office.

A gold fountain pen rolled off the desk, hit the carpet, and clanged against the wastebasket. She'd get it later, she thought, as she pawed through a mass of rubber bands, pencils, candy bar wrappers, matchbooks, message slips, and golf scorecards. She glanced at one of them. Sixty-eight for eighteen holes? What a load of crap! Vince couldn't hit a golf ball two hundred yards with a gale force wind behind him.

"Women weren't enough. You cheated at golf, too."

Flinging the card to the floor, she yanked open a bottom drawer, and spotted a platoon of hanging file folders, one for each lot in the development. The other bottom drawer held files on the golf course and a mass of manila envelopes. Vince had scrawled "bite me" on the front of one from the county planning commission. In the side drawer she found the corporate checkbook and credit card statements. Lots of dinners in

Newport, she noted, and plenty of hundred-dollar withdrawals. The corporate balance was anemic, a mere fifteen thousand dollars, and the statements showed Vince owed three thousand on the corporate plastic.

She leaned back and looked out the window, up at the muddy and sodden slopes of Devil's Acres. Fifteen thousand dollars wouldn't cover more than a day or two of earth moving at the golf course, wouldn't buy enough rock to stabilize the hillside, and certainly wouldn't pay lawyers to defend the avalanche of lawsuits. Adam had claimed Vince teetered on the verge of bankruptcy, but she hadn't believed it. Vince had bought the land for a song, then cheated, chiseled, and cut corners. There should be more money. A lot more.

"Did he gamble it away at the casino?"

No, Vince liked taking risks, but only when those risks involved juggling multiple women.

She reached down and retrieved the pen. "To In-Vince-Able, with Love." No name. She flung it at the wastebasket.

She tried to recall the face value on the insurance policy Vince had bought when they launched the project she believed would help preserve the beauty of the coastline. A million dollars? Two? She shook her head, remembering only that it was much more than the inheritance she'd handed over to help finance his plans.

Well, at least she'd have money to make some kind of restitution—if Vince hadn't quit paying the premiums. "Think, Claire. Think. He borrowed from the bank. Wouldn't they require him to keep up the payments? Or take out another policy naming the bank as beneficiary?"

Wishing she'd paid more attention when they'd started the business, she sorted the litter on the blotter, hoping she'd recognize a vital document when she found one. She read the message slips as she stacked them, noted the restaurant names on match books covers, bound rubber bands together, tossed score-cards in the wastebasket and finally uncovered a tiny scrap of paper with the numbers 12-29-7-22.

"What the heck does that mean?" December twenty-ninth and July twenty-second? Or a phone number for one of his hide-a-honeys.

She tossed it in the wastebasket, retrieved the drawer, wedged it into the track, raked everything into it from the blotter, and shoved.

Grittchh.

The drawer stopped, open half an inch.

Claire shoved again.

Graaawwch.

"Now what?" She crouched, tilting her head, peering beneath the desk.

Adam Quarles hit the remote control and watched the heavy door slide up, revealing one bay of the three-car garage, and more than enough space for his dinged-up Volkswagen. Stopping short of a pristine workbench, he hit the remote again, then trudged up the stairs into the kitchen and checked the clock on the stove. Ten after seven.

"Uggfff."

He slumped onto one of the three sofas in the living room and flexed his shoulders. He'd hoped to finish up at the store earlier so he could crawl into bed, his own bed, and get some shut-eye. He was so exhausted his muscles twitched. Well, most of his muscles. Claire had rendered one of them twitchless—perhaps permanently.

Flopping around, he swung his feet to the cushions. His eyelids fluttered down, screening his view of the ocean, the headland, the trees, the two men in dark suits fiddling with something inside a black suitcase resting on the snout of a white sedan.

"What the hell?"

Snapping upright, he scuttled to the wall of windows, then sidled away. *Stay out of sight.*

Huh? That was paranoid? He hadn't broken in. He wasn't doing anything wrong. And they'd probably seen him pull into the garage.

But who the hell were those guys? Not locals. And definitely not tourists. They looked official. Private investigators? Or specialists sent by the sheriff's department to look into Grabowski's murder?

What was that in the suitcase? A camera with a long barreled telescopic lens? Possibly one of those super-sensitive directional microphones? Henri said they made them so powerful they could pick up conversations hundreds of feet away, right through a wall or window.

Adam backed across the dining area. If they'd seen Claire in that towel in the driveway, like Bart Yamamoto had…He gritted his teeth. In an effort to buy silence, he'd jacked Bart's pay fifty cents an hour, only to have Bart confess sheepishly that he'd already told Jennifer. The shit was definitely headed for the fan. He and Claire would be prime suspects in Vince's death.

"There you are."

Adam jumped like he'd been goosed with a cattle prod. Claire rushed across the kitchen and threw herself into his limp arms. Where had she come from? Why hadn't he heard her? "Oh, Adam, I love you."

"Me, too," he whispered, spinning her around and pushing her toward the garage. "Let's go."

"Go? Where?" She dug in her heels.

"Out. Now!"

117

She gripped the handle on the dishwasher. "Adam! What's wrong? Why are you whispering?"

"Ssshhh." He dropped to floor and flattened himself, the ceramic tile cool against his arms. "Get down."

She knelt beside him and put a hand on his forehead, eyes narrowed with concern. "Are you running a fever?"

"No." He pulled her down beside him and put his mouth against her ear. "There are two men outside. Detectives. They've got high-tech electronic monitoring equipment. They can hear everything we say."

Claire's eyes grew wide. "I want to see them."

She began to crawl toward the dining room. Adam caught her ankle and towed her back. "Don't let them spot you."

"They saw me when I drove up, silly. They know I'm here. Why are we acting like such fools?"

Adam thought about that, scratched his head and sighed. "I don't know," he admitted. He clambered to his feet. "I'm too tired to think straight."

"Well I'm not going to hide." She dusted off her slacks and put her purse on the counter. "Sooner or later everyone in town will know about us."

Sooner, Adam thought. Speculation about Grabowski's widow boffing the town's resident tree-hugger had scorched phone lines all day. He knew that because half the population had popped into Passing Wind claiming they'd decided to give tofu a chance. He'd sold his entire stock—fourteen quivering blocks of the stuff.

"What happens, happens." Claire stood on tiptoe and kissed the tip of his nose. "I know I didn't kill Vince. And I know you didn't, either."

Adam ducked his head, opened the refrigerator, and took out a bottle of organic carrot juice.

"You didn't? Did you?" Her voice climbed the scale.

He poured, the bottle clattering against the rim of the glass, juice sloshing onto the counter top. "Of course not."

"I didn't think so." She leaned over and sipped from the brimming glass. "Hey, I forgot to tell you what I found in Vince's office." She grabbed her purse and emptied it onto the table. "Here. It's a key. And there's this." She plucked the scrap of paper from under a compact. "If there's a safe hidden in this house, I bet this is the combination."

"That witness probably got it wrong," Jeffrey told me for the seventh time. "He must have seen Grabowski with someone else. It was late. It was dark. A lot of men resemble your dad from a distance." He bent to slide a casserole dish into the oven and closed the door gently. "Mike will straighten him out and be back here before the soufflé is done."

"Dad's had a heart attack," I reminded him. "He can't eat anything high in cholesterol. That includes cheese soufflé."

"I know. But he can admire it. And the poached halibut and potatoes and the pear salad are on his diet." He washed the egg whisk and set it in the draining rack. "The soufflé is for you. Comfort food."

I couldn't enjoy food, comfort or otherwise, while my father underwent a grilling at the sheriff's office. I'd argued that I should go along, promising to wait in the lobby, or out on the street. But Greg got all tight-assed and official and Dad had brushed me off, telling me he'd handle it. He'd put a hand on my cheek and kissed the top of my head just like he had when I used to come to him with a skinned knee or a tale of unrequited teenage love. Then he'd told Jeffrey to make sure I ate a good dinner and got to bed early. Following orders, Jeffrey had made a four-course meal with far less effort than I'd ever expended on macaroni and cheese from a box.

"I'm not hungry," I lied as I swallowed the last of my beer and checked my wristwatch again. Ninety minutes since Dad went off with Greg.

Jeffrey turned from the sink, a dripping sponge in his hand, eyes dark with worry. "You need to eat, Molly. If you don't like soufflé, I'll make something else."

"No, soufflé's fine." Exactly what I need right now. Something that will look great for about ten seconds and then collapse to a pile of soggy rubber. Kind of like my hopes that Greg would let Dad go after a few minutes.

Jeffrey put his hands on the scarred wooden table in the center of the kitchen and leaned over me.

I studied the foam sliding down the side of my glass and then, with a sigh, looked up into eyes shadowed with concern. "I'm taking it out on you."

"That's okay."

"No, it's not. And it's not doing Dad any good." I shoved back my chair, retrieved a yellow legal pad from the living room, and plopped it on the table.

"What's that?"

"My list of people who could have killed Vince Grabowski and why they wanted him dead."

"Who's on it?"

I snorted as I dug a pen from the chipped mug at the edge of the counter. "Who isn't?"

"Your father," he answered without hesitation.

"Nice going. You get immunity in the next round." Sitting, I riffled the pages of my list. "You're not on it, either. Should you be?"

"No." He flushed. "I barely knew Grabowski."

"But to know him was to hate him." I tapped the pad with the pen. "Maybe you had some altruistic motive, a sense of poetic justice."

He chuckled. "Poetic justice. That's funny." He knocked on the table and deepened his voice. "Poetry police. You're charged with exceeding the syllable limit on that haiku." He pointed a finger at my nose. "And you. Gross misuse of iambic pentameter. Fifteen days in the library."

The images made me laugh and the ratcheting tightness in my chest began to loosen up. "How about a hundred-dollar fine for onomatopoeia in a public place?"

Jeff's eyes danced. "And a ninety-day suspension of your poetic license." His gaze locked on mine for a moment and we both giggled, but he stared a moment too long. I fidgeted, sending the pen flipping to the floor.

He jumped up, chased it down, and handed it to me. "Well, uh, who are your prime suspects?"

I glanced at my notes. "There's Grabowski's wife and Adam Quarles. They've been having an affair for at least a year."

He pinched the skin between his eyes. "Too obvious. And why now?"

"Hmmm." I hadn't thought of that and couldn't answer. "Prudence Deeds is right up there, and Shelley Perkins. And LaDonna."

"Yeah." He got himself another beer and poured part of it into my glass. "The scored on, the scorned, and the mother protecting her young. Who else?"

"Gus Custer."

He nodded. "The artist forced to whore his craft. What about Maybelline and Chuck?"

I hadn't included them. "Why them?"

"Grabowski threatened to make trouble with their liquor license. I was sitting in the back booth writing and heard him."

"Way to go." It was good to have someone to bounce ideas off of, like in the Albuquerque newsroom. I scribbled their names and the motive, trying to remember what I knew of Chuck's military background. "Too bad you didn't overhear something about Elspeth. A crusader like her might break the commandment about not killing and write it off as divine justice."

He considered for a minute, sipping. "Nope. Nothing on her. But Icky might have a motive."

I sputtered in my beer. "Icky? He's too mellow for murder."

"If someone messed with his supply of dope, that would un-mellow him."

I sputtered again, getting beer up my nose. "Icky does drugs?"

He laughed. "So much for *your* finely honed powers of observation."

"Hey, Sweete Temptations is off-limits since Dad's heart attack."

"Well take my word for it. Icky's a sky-high, full-time major toker and my guess is he's cultivating a plantation in the hills. I hear him going out in the middle of the night two or three times a week."

I sat up straighter, my mind racing. "Did you ever see him with Grabowski?"

He pondered for a moment. "I don't think so."

I gnawed at the pen. "I'll grill him tomorrow. If he smokes as much as you say, he can't be too quick on his mental feet." Flipping to a fresh sheet of paper, I made some rapid notes. "First I'll go see Maybelline—"

"Um, shouldn't we give this evidence to Sergeant Erdman?"

I didn't bother to look up. "No. It's not really evidence. And Greg Erdman wouldn't know what to do with it if it was." I went on making notes, wondering whether Grabowski could have angered Chuck Yamamoto enough to crack his Zen-like demeanor.

Jeffrey peered through the tiny oven window at the soufflé, then returned to the table. "I know reporters are competitive, Molly, but wouldn't it be—?"

"I am not competitive." My knuckles whitened on the pen.

Jeffrey retreated to the refrigerator. "I didn't say that was a bad thing, Molly. In fact, that's one of the qualities I admire about you. But—"

"I am NOT competitive."

He stood his ground, smiling a little. "How can you not know that about yourself? If you weren't competitive, you wouldn't have won those awards your father brags about almost every day."

I stood, my throat thick with peevish anger. Why did this bother me? "I am not competitive. In fact, I'm the least competitive person in the world."

The smile gave way to a burst of laughter. "Okay. So tell me, who exactly was it that came in next-to-last in that non-competitive competition?"

The pen snapped between my fingers. I knew a lot of "competitors" in my business, back-stabbers who'd do anything for a front-page by-line—lie, cheat, burn their sources, and take credit for others' work. I wasn't one of them.

He raised his hands, palms out. "Hey, I was just joking."

I laid the pieces of the pen on the table and my anger receded, leaving me sad and exhausted. I wanted to be alone.

"I thought we were both joking, Molly. I'm sorry. Look, why don't I toss the salad and we'll eat?"

I rubbed my eyes. "I'm too tired to eat. And I have to get up early."

His shoulders slumped and he trudged to the pegs beside the living room door and snagged his jacket. "Okay. I'll go. The soufflé should be done in about ten minutes. The fish is in foil in the refrigerator. It will keep until tomorrow. Cook it for thirty minutes at 375." He slogged to the kitchen door, turned and looked at me one more time. "I'm sorry about your dad." He paused, chewing at his lower lip. "And for whatever it was I said." Raising his hand to his right eyebrow, he closed the door softly behind him.

I watched him melt into the night and wondered if I'd ever be any good at relationships. Not that this qualified as a relationship—it was more like a disaster. And it underlined what I already knew: Jeffrey Wolfe wasn't my type.

"Drinking alone?" Prudence Deeds slid onto the bar stool beside Jeffrey Wolfe and favored him with an encouraging smile. "Need a friendly ear?"

Lucky for her she'd spotted the poet striding away from the Donovan house with a deep frown on his face. A niggle of guilt touched the back of her mind. She shouldn't be here, flirting, thinking about what it would be like to be alone with him. But, Lord, he was fine-looking. And she had needs and desires not fulfilled in the apartment above the fish market.

"Alone is good sometimes," Jeffrey mumbled, the words nearly drowned out by the opening bars of "I Walk The Line" blaring from the juke box. He hoisted the dregs of a brownish drink, drained it, and tapped the glass with his forefinger. Maybelline sauntered along behind the bar and raised her eyebrows. "Again, please."

Maybelline's tinted eyebrows disappeared beneath her orange bangs.

"I'm over twenty-one and I'm not driving. Going nowhere, but I'm making good time," Jeffrey muttered.

Maybelline shrugged, pulled a bottle from under the bar and poured.

"I'll have the same," Prudence told her. "Make it a double."

Maybelline didn't look at her as she tossed ice cubes into a glass and drizzled whiskey over them. "Not your usual drink, Prudence."

"I like variety now and again." Prudence dug a twenty out of her purse and slapped it on the bar.

"That's what everyone says about you. That you like it now. And again." Maybelline made change, winked at Jeffrey and ambled off.

Prudence scowled at Maybelline's back. "That woman has no class. Not one little bit." She gulped her drink, feeling it burn her throat. "How did the fishing go today?"

"Fine."

"Really? Brighton says Old Air Biscuit put in an appearance."

"Yeah. He crashed the party." Jeffrey took a long pull at his drink.

"He's picked Mike Donovan to stalk this season. That's not going to help his business." Prudence drained her drink and tapped the glass on the bar.

"Probably not."

"It would be a shame if Mike had to sell the *Helen* and give up the charter business."

"Yeah."

Maybelline set another drink in front of Prudence, took a few bills, and slid them into the cash register.

"And Molly's such a spark plug." Prudence sucked at the whiskey. "We'll all miss her when she goes back to Albuquerque." She watched his eyes, but saw no flicker of concern or loss.

"Yeah." He drained his liquor in three long swallows and slid off the stool. "Good night, Prudence. Nice talking with you."

She watched him weave toward the door, then gulped the rest of her drink and ran after him, the tapping of her high heels rhythmically punctuating the words to "Third Rate Romance" streaming from the juke box.

"Wait up a minute, Jeffrey. I'll make sure you get home all right."

FOURTEEN

I cocked my left arm and flung the rolled paper at the front porch framed by the headlights.

Whack!

It hit the steps and bounced into a spindly hydrangea. Close enough. Crimping the wheels, I gunned the truck's engine, fishtailed around a clump of lilacs, and rattled down the long driveway, tires spewing gravel into a rhododendron hedge. This was the part of working for *The Flotsam* I hated the most—delivering the rag and filling the boxes outside stores and restaurants. It was the penalty for needing a job so badly I couldn't quibble. It beat ringing up beef jerky and nachos at the Come On 'n' Get It, but not by much. I shivered inside my fleece-lined jacket and cranked the heater up another notch.

Dad had a doctor's appointment scheduled for next week. If he got a thumbs-up, I'd planned to hit the highway for Albuquerque before my leave of absence ran out and somebody "competitive" took my job. But now he was a murder suspect. I couldn't leave until he was cleared.

"Damn!" Jerking the wheel, I spun right onto the deserted highway, and then hung a left down another driveway. As I plucked a paper from the stack on the passenger seat and folded it with one hand, I mentally reran last night's conversation—a conversation from which I'd extracted exactly no information.

Dad had breezed in like he'd been gone for thirty minutes instead of three hours. "Why aren't you in bed?"

Before I could respond, he'd fished the soufflé dish from the sink. "Looks like you baked a studded tire. That dish will never come clean."

I'd felt like a ten-year-old defending a poor report card. Spitting out apologies and scrubbing at the casserole dish, I'd wasted ten minutes before I regained my balance and insisted Dad tell me why Greg Erdman suspected he killed Vince Grabowski. All I got was a soothing "Now Molly. Don't get all worked up over nothing. You know how twisted around gossip gets. A story starts with someone heading north and next thing you know he's southbound. The sergeant will figure it out soon enough."

I'd had so much confidence in that I'd flopped like a beached halibut until the alarm buzzed at three.

Whump!

The paper bounced off the roof of a late-model car and skittered into a rangy rosebush. Slamming the stick into reverse, I wrestled the truck onto a stretch of lawn, turned, and roared away spewing ever-darkening exhaust.

When I got home, Dad and I would have that long talk. This time he'd better tell me the whole story. Then I'd track down Maybelline, interview Icky the ice cream stoner, and see what the widow Grabowski would tell me about her late husband's finances and her inheritance.

Icky squatted, focused his flashlight, and pulled a weed from beside one of the gray-green plants hunched among the young trees on the clear-cut hillside. Around him, birds started to stir, chirping and twittering, gathering a chorus to celebrate the sun still an hour away on the western side of the ridge. He stroked the saw-toothed leaves of the plant between his feet. Starting to dry out. If it didn't rain in the next few days, he'd have to haul water up the ridge. With five hundred thirsty plants to soak, that meant an all-nighter. He couldn't remember the last time Devil's Harbor had gone three weeks without rain in May. The blow-dry weatherman on TV blamed it on ocean currents.

> "Out of the day and night
> A joy has taken flight;
> Fresh Spring, and summer, and winter hoar,
> Move my faint heart with grief, but with delight
> No more—Oh, never more!"

Icky wailed Percy Shelley's words to the waking birds, thinking as he did that lines from "To a Skylark" would have been more appropriate than the final stanza of "A Lament."

"Damn Grabowski!"

He swung the beam across the plants again, reminding himself that Grabowski was dead. If he had to, he could sacrifice most of this harvest, and leave just enough for his own needs. But no. These were living things, stretching up toward the sun. They deserved a chance.

"Damn Grabowski!"

He couldn't rip up plants he'd nurtured from the seeds of last year's crop, set out in tiny pots on his window sills, warmed with lamps through drizzling nights until the days grew long enough, the sun bright enough, the fog thin enough. No, he'd carry water, even if it took all night. Even if he dropped in his tracks on the floor behind the counter while customers waited for him to fill their cones. Or maybe he'd keep the store closed mornings until Jennifer came back. Yesterday she'd informed him she couldn't work at all this week because she feared she'd break a nail. Besides, she'd said, she was busy at Neptune's Grotto. Since Vince Grabowski had floated in, tourism had jumped five-hundred percent. They'd run out of wind-up sea lions.

Standing, he brushed dry soil from the knees of his black jeans and headed into the ravine he'd follow for a quarter of a mile to the edge of Devil's Acres. He clicked off the flashlight, relying on the faint gray light filtering through Douglas firs standing like sentinels. As he walked, he worked through the water hauling problem. Maybe he'd get those canvas and rubber water bags desert travelers used. Adam would know where to find them.

The trees thinned and he spotted mist rising from the dark outline of Vince Grabowski's roof. He checked the black watch on his wrist—not quite five thirty. Cutting it pretty close. Tomorrow he'd start earlier. He didn't want to be seen up here. Stepping from the trees, he picked his way across the washboard surface of a vacant lot scoured by last winter's rains. Behind him, a crow cawed. Icky froze. Off to his left, beyond Grabowski's house, he saw a sweeping flashlight beam, and behind it a dim shape.

Icky hit the dirt. The light swung left, then arced over his head and strafed the trees. Lines of sweat bracketed his spine. This side of the ridge would stay in shadow for an hour or more, but a man sprawled in the center of a vacant lot wouldn't be invisible.

Scrabbling around on his belly, he began to wiggle for cover. Powdery dirt rose in a swirling cloud; the swelling breeze pushed it over his head like a cowl.

"Aaaaah-choo!"

Icky froze again. Sound would carry on the damp dawn air. He squinted over his shoulder. The light had gone off, but he made out two shapes and, behind them, the faint outline of a car. A hundred feet away. He crawled faster, fingers grasping clods of clay and chunks of rock, sweat soaking his shirt, young blackberry vines tearing at his clothing, scratching his face and wrists.

He covered thirty feet in what seemed like thirty minutes, hauled himself behind a thick fir, and realized his lungs were burning—he hadn't breathed since that sneeze.

"Hwuff."

Gasping, he peered around the tree at two men in dark suits and a bulky black suitcase balanced on the hood of the white car. One of the men drew something from inside the case, something that caught the growing light with a metallic gleam. He swung it toward Icky.

He flattened himself against the back of the tree, too frightened to run. Were these hit men from the cartel? Grabowski had claimed the cartel would exact revenge if Icky tried to renege on their "deal," by harming him or destroying the crop. Icky had never believed him. Until now.

But he'd stuck to the deal!

Not that they'd believe him. Cartel hitters killed first and asked questions later. He risked another look. The men swiveled the metal object toward the south. It wasn't a rifle. It seemed to connect to something in the suitcase.

Relief turned to another kind of fear. Was it a locator beacon? Could they home in on a field of marijuana from the ground? The technology changed every day. Maybe some narco-scientist had invented a marijuana meter. If they had, he was screwed. He'd lose everything: the crop, the store, and the mental state of balance he'd worked years to perfect.

Mike Donovan cleared his throat and hawked toothpaste into the sink.

"Rakkk-hooo-ah."

He ran his fingers through his tousled hair, buckled on his watch, and tromped down the stairs. No time for breakfast. He'd grab a piece of high-fiber bread and brew some decaf when he got on board the *Helen*. Ignoring hunger and fatigue, he threw on a worn jacket. No charter today. But he had to get away before Molly returned from her paper route with more questions. He needed time alone to feel the wind in his face and the wheel against his calloused hands. Most of all, he needed time to practice a story so Molly couldn't tell he was lying.

"Not lying," he corrected himself as he closed the door and strode toward the dock, "just evading. Raising a little dust so the truth has a place to hide."

Passing the car wash on the back of the mayor's shop, Mike wrinkled his nose. To old-timers, the smell of fish equaled the smell of money. But the cloying perfume of those scented air fresheners His Stupidness hung around his establishment could make you relish an afternoon with Old Air Biscuit.

"Son of a bitch!" Another problem to wrestle with: that damn whale. Well, he'd get to that. After the Molly problem.

He hadn't lied to the sergeant about arguing with Grabowski on the dock Saturday night. Had even admitted he'd thrown a punch. And why not? Grab-ass had leaned on him to tell Molly to quit snooping around his business dealings, said if Mike couldn't pull her off he'd spread a rumor that Molly had slept with every cop in Albuquerque to get inside information for her stories.

Mike pounded his left fist into his right hand. Amazingly, he'd kept his cool until Grabowski said that Molly's promiscuity wasn't surprising, because she was just like her mother. No one spoke like that about Helen! He'd locked his hands around the developer's neck and squeezed until Grabowski's eyes bulged and his tongue stuck out, thick as a parrot's. Those few minutes had been better for his ticker than all the medicine and tasteless food and efforts to take it easy.

Mike cast off the ropes and jumped to the deck. As for Molly, well, he wasn't the kind of father who pretended his daughter didn't have a sex life. Molly had been married once— even if it had lasted only three months. She'd never told him what went wrong, and he'd vowed never to ask. But she'd never trade sex for information. Never. She had too much pride in herself. Just like her mother.

"Good morning, Captain."

Startled, Mike stared at the bedraggled man wrapped in a tarp on the cushions in the stern. "Jeff? You been here all night?"

"Most of it." Jeffrey Wolfe stood and stretched. "Are you taking her out?"

"Yep."

"Mind if I come along?"

Mike started to say he did, but then changed his mind. Judging from the circles under Jeffrey's eyes, the lad had a few problems of his own to sort out. "Not if you make the coffee."

Elspeth Hunsaker tapped the microphone and cleared her throat as she watched the second hand sweep toward the twelve. Thirty seconds to air. She'd offer the sinners of Devil's Harbor one more chance. They'd better take it. The Grim Reaper awaited.

Now. Pushing a button on the console, she fired up the tape cartridge of her signature music, an organ rendition of "Praise The Lord And Pass The Ammunition." She let the music reach a crescendo, then trailed it out and keyed open her mike.

"Good morning, good morning, good morning. It's another glorious day here and time to remember that the good book is a guidebook."

Elspeth smiled; pleased with the analogy she'd drawn. She'd hadn't planned it. She'd just opened her mouth and the words came. She pulled the microphone closer so not one precious syllable fell by the wayside.

"But before we discuss today's verse, and before I take your many phone calls, I want to share an experience I had last night, and explain what I believe it means for all of us. As many of you know, I have always been steadfast in my love and devotion to Tammy Faye, no matter that—" Elspeth took a deep breath. "Be that as it may." She paused, savoring the words. She loved that expression. "Be that as it may. I draw great strength from the classic programs which I have on videotape, and it is my habit to review them often. And last night, as my weary eyes began to close, last night I saw THE SIGN."

She paused for dramatic effect, imagining listeners leaning toward their radios. She watched the second hand twitch, almost tasting the suspense.

"Tammy Faye, swept up with the spirit, wept copious tears for the world's sinners, and there, in the mascara running down her cheek, I saw it." Elspeth dropped her voice to a whisper. "As clear as day. The letter M." She shivered. "I sat bolt upright and looked at the clock. I'll remember the hour and moment until the end of my days—12:28. I reached for my Bible, which, as you know, is always close to my hand, and I opened it to Matthew and began to read that verse. And there it was, Jesus' answer to the scribes and Pharisees who asked him for a sign. As I'm sure you recall, he said that no sign shall be given except that of Jonah."

Elspeth paused for that to sink in. "Jonah," she repeated, "the man who spent three days and three nights in the belly of a giant fish. And now, friends, a whale circles our bay. But it is not too late to repent! To change the name of our blighted community before we are swallowed by a beast from the deep."

Elspeth panted, flushed with her message. Then she realized she'd forgotten to record it for her archives. Damn. Or rather, darn.

The first button on the phone began to blink and she smiled in eager anticipation. "And now, I'll take your calls. Good morning. You're on the air."

"Ah. Oh, Elspeth. Thank goodness I got through to you." The high-pitched voice thumped the volume needle against the right edge of the meter. Elspeth notched the knob down as the quavery tone filled her earphones. The caller took several sharp breaths. "Oh, excuse me. I'm just giddy, so excited about being on the air with Elspeth Hunsaker. Oh, my goodness. I have to sit down. Can you give me a minute?"

Elspeth glanced at the phone; no other buttons blinked. "Of course." She waited, watching the second hand move across half the clock's face.

"Oh, thank you, and bless you. I just had to breathe into the bag a few times. I'm all right now. Well, not really all right, which of us is ever really all right until we pass the test on judgment day?"

"True. That's so true." Elspeth made a note. Which of us is ever all right? She'd recycle that into a slogan. She'd wait a few weeks, though; it wouldn't do for listeners to think she couldn't come up with things like that on her own.

"So, what I'm saying is that I have a teensy tiny little problem about that sign. If I may?"

Elspeth shot a look of disgust at the phone. "Of course," she sighed.

"Well, it's just this— Now please don't be upset. But you see, when you were telling us about the letter M on

Tammy's cheek and the time on your clock, well, I opened my Bible, just like you did. Only, you see, I opened mine to Mark. M, you see is a *mark*. But it could also stand for Mark."

Elspeth clenched her teeth. Mark? Why hadn't she thought of that? Shit! Or rather, sugar!

"And I read in Mark about the scribes who like to walk around in long robes . . . And, oh, Elspeth, could it be a sign we should wear shorter dresses this year? Or longer ones? Is that the meaning?"

Dress length? Ridiculous! "Well, caller, the—"

"And then I thought," the caller interrupted, "what if that wasn't an M? What if it was maybe an E on its side? So I turned to Exodus and read about the sons of Israel baking the unleavened bread. So maybe the sign means we need to change our diets and give up additives and preservatives. Don't you think that might be what it means, Elspeth? Instead of that Jonah thing? Because, honestly, everyone knows that humpback whales like Old Air Biscuit are baleen whales. They don't swallow people, they just kind of inhale those little shrimpy krill things and—"

Elspeth jabbed the phone button with a stiff forefinger. "Bwaaaaatttt."

She let the dial tone drone for a full ten seconds. "I'm sorry, caller, we seem to be having a problem with our phone lines."

She should hire a producer or a call screener to winnow out the dingbats. But the only calls she got—two or three a day—came from dingbats. "If this is a test," she moaned, "I'd rather wait for the makeup exam."

FIFTEEN

Greg Erdman hunkered in the wooden chair in front of the sheriff's desk, fighting the urge to squirm. The situation reminded him of third grade when Mrs. Blivins had picked him to read out loud and he knew the other kids would laugh at the air whistling through the space where his front teeth used to be. The lesson he'd learned then still held: don't argue. That's how he'd wound up in the corner back in third grade—how he'd wind up pulling an overnight shift now.

"And another thing," the sheriff's initial volcanic roar had subsided to a series of rumbling eruptions, "you swore that all releases to the media would come through this office. From me. You swore no one would leak information those bloodsuckers don't need to know."

Greg nodded warily. He sure as shit wasn't about to remind the sheriff that information could leak from other sources, and he definitely wouldn't mention Barbara Sue's habit of listening at every door. As far as Archie Fletcher was concerned, the dispatcher was perfect.

Smacking the latest copy of *The Flotsam* on the desk, the sheriff built toward another eruption, his face the color of molten lava. "So why does the story in this fish-wrapper say, and I quote, 'Sheriff's investigators'—that would be you, wouldn't it?—'believe evidence points to foul play in

Grabowski's death and are questioning Devil's Harbor residents who may have seen him, or his car, Saturday evening.'"

He slapped the paper against the phone. "If we wanted to withhold information about Grabowski's injuries to trap the killer we'd be shit out of luck, wouldn't we? Because almost everything we know is right here!" He slammed the paper to the floor and glared, his face mottling as his rage subsided.

Greg shifted from one hip to the other, conscious of the gun on his belt and the rising desire to put a hole between Archie Fletcher's eyes. He yearned to inform the sheriff that any reporter worth her salt could have gotten the autopsy information right from the medical examiner or someone on his staff, and anyone with half a brain might figure out that Vince Grabowski hadn't been training to be an Acapulco cliff diver when he landed on the rocks. But Greg said nothing. When someone chews your butt, it's best not to jerk away. It only makes their teeth clamp tighter.

"For two cents I'd take you off this case and assign a man who can keep his mind on his job and off that red-haired reporter."

Greg bit his tongue and didn't remind Fletcher that budget cuts had forced the rest of the department's veterans into retirement last year. Even in his foul mood the sheriff wouldn't turn this case over to a new recruit or part-time deputy hired to pull over speeders.

"What do you have to say for yourself?"

Greg fought temptation and uttered the only words he knew would end the diatribe. "I'm sorry, sir. It won't happen again."

"It damn well better not," the sheriff huffed. He retrieved *The Flotsam*, tossed it into the gray metal wastebasket beside his desk and kicked the container for good measure.

"Now get out and find the asshole responsible for messing up my crime statistics. And don't go near that reporter!"

"Yes, sir." Greg leaped from his chair and strode toward the door.

"Just one minute." The sheriff rocked back in his swivel chair and swung his feet to the corner of his desk. His hand-tooled snakeskin boots gleamed. The soles were barely scuffed. "Who you talking to today?" He pulled a plastic toothpick from his pocket and began worrying his teeth, slinging his jaw forward and curling his lower lip.

"I'll check out Gus Custer's story and stop in at the café. Most everybody comes through there." As he opened the door, Greg heard footsteps scuttling along the hall—Barbara Sue making her appointed rounds. "Then I'll question Prudence Deeds, the mayor's wife. They live by the harbor and she might have heard something." He got one foot into the hall.

"Good. Good." The sheriff slipped the toothpick back into his pocket. "Well, go on then, get going. Let's get this solved before the county tourism board starts riding my rear."

"Yes, sir." Greg closed the door behind him, walked to the front office and nodded to Barbara Sue. "Anything you didn't hear clear enough?"

She shut him down with a scornful glare and he waved with his fingertips as he walked to his cruiser. No point in telling the sheriff that Molly Donovan had called him at home that morning. No point in mentioning his plans to meet her for a late lunch. A tense late lunch. She'd grill him for information, especially about the evidence against her father. But with the sheriff on his ass, he didn't dare reassure her, even off the record, that after interviewing Mike Donovan, he was almost certain he hadn't tossed Grabowski off the cliff. Almost.

Claire Grabowski flipped a hunk of sweat-dampened hair out of her eyes and peeled back a section of wall-to-wall carpeting in the corner of the dressing room off the master bedroom—a section that had been concealed by an antique radio with a half-dozen missing tubes and a compartment in the front containing something that looked suspiciously like fossilized mouse droppings.

"Ah ha."

This was what she'd been searching for: a small door built into the floor and secured with a lock into which the key slid and turned without a squeak. She flipped the door back and peered into a narrow space; a black metal safe with a combination lock rested on its back.

Fingers trembling, she twirled the dial. Left, right, left, right. Nothing. She tried again. Right, left, right, left. Nothing. She started left again, this time passing the first number before hitting the second, and passing the second before going to the third.

"Bingo!"

She tugged the heavy door open and drew out a sheaf of papers. Spreading them on the floor, she spotted Vince's personal life insurance papers and another fat policy payable to Vince's corporation.

She frowned. It was a lot of money, but it probably wouldn't stretch far enough to settle the lawsuits and repay all the investors. Still, she'd throw every bit into the pot to try to repair the financial and environmental devastation Vince had wrought. She wanted to live in Devil's Harbor, with Adam—if that worked out—as a contributing member of the community.

But it didn't take a prize-winning economist to see Vince's rob-Peter-to-pay-Paul tactics had left her between a rock and a hard place. To compensate investors, she'd have to continue to build homes. And that would piss off environmentalists, especially Adam who insisted she cut her losses and return the rest to nature.

"Damn, Vince. You sure were a screw-up."

As she gathered the policies, a small square of paper fell from between them. Several strings of numbers, in Vince's handwriting, filled one side. The first appeared to be a phone number with a 345 area code. Where the heck was that? And what were the others? The second set wasn't a phone number. The rest had dollar signs in front, although they'd all been crossed out. Except for the one at the bottom. $5,879,047.92.

She dropped the paper and ran to the phone.

"Ohmigod, we're hosed Bart. What should we do?" Jennifer waved her copy of *The Flotsam* in Bart's face. "We've got to do *something*."

Bart went on totaling checks. "Why?"

"Why? Because it says that anyone with information about Mr. Grabowski or his car should call the sheriff's department." She stomped one high-heeled sandaled foot. "Anyone. That's us, you spaz. We saw his car Saturday night at the harbor."

"I'll bet a lot of other people did too." Bart wrote a number on a bank deposit slip, zipped up the blue plastic sack of cash and checks, and slid it into the bottom of the cash drawer.

"Not after midnight, doofus." She shoved aside a stack of high-energy, low-fat health bars and laid the paper on the counter. "See, Molly's story says Mr. Grabowski died before midnight."

Bart began re-stacking the bars. "So?"

"Well, duh! So how could a dead man drive his car from the parking lot by the dock up to Perdition Point and jump in the ocean?"

Bart's eyes finally focused on her. She leaned across the counter to kiss his nose. "See what I mean?"

"Yeah. Whoever killed him drove it there." He grinned. "Maybe the body was in the trunk when we walked by."

"And maybe the killer was hiding right there and—"

She scampered around the counter and threw herself into Bart's arms. "What if he saw us? We could be the next victims! Ohmigod, it's just like one of those movies where the guy calls up and says he knows what the girl did and then—"

"Don't be such a drama queen." Bart stroked her hair and kissed her forehead. His voice was calm, but his fingers trembled.

"We've got to tell Molly."

"And have her blab to our folks?"

"Molly's like totally cool. She won't do that."

"She'll just put it in the paper for the whole world to see."

"Ohmigod," Jennifer wailed. "My mother will ground me 'til the next millennium if she finds out I climbed out my window."

"And my dad will lay trust and responsibility lecture number forty-seven on me. The one that starts 'your mother and I are a little disappointed in you, Bartholomew.' I hate it when he calls me that."

She snuffled into his shirt, wondering idly why he never wore the cologne she bought him for Christmas, the stuff that smelled like new leather and lemonade. "What are we gonna do?"

"Nothing."

"But we've got to do something. Ohmigod, Bart, this is a clue." She danced out of his arms, bouncing on her toes, hair flying. "Even if we don't tell the sheriff's department, we've got to tell Molly." Wiggling back into his arms, she planted a long kiss on his eager lips. "Please. She's my idol."

"Okay," Bart sighed. "If they haven't caught the killer by Friday, we'll tell her. By the time the story's in the Sunday paper our folks will be so tired from the Whirligig Festival that they won't have the energy to yell much."

Jennifer shivered. "I hope they catch the killer before then. It really creeps me out that he's still out there." She snuggled up against him. "Guess you'll just have to protect me, Bartholomew."

"Stop calling me that." He lifted her hair to nuzzle her ear.

"Make me," she giggled.

"Now this takes me back to the old days in the locker room." Henri handed a tall pink drink to his guest and offered a tray of hors d'ouevres. "Not the snacks, of course, although how do you like the little caviar puffs shaped like hockey pucks? Adorable, no? I made them myself." He giggled. "Obviously. Where could you buy such a thing? But getting together to study the game films, getting pumped for the play-offs, sharpening our senses."

His guest smiled, took another caviar puff, stuffed it into his mouth, and chewed enthusiastically.

"You approve, *oui*?" Henri settled himself into a recliner he'd had covered in pink brocade. Flipping the footrest up, he sighed and reached for the remote control. "These are purely amateur videos. The videographer was, I suspect, not a little drunk. The camera work is quite sloppy and the composition is hideous, but I think they'll serve our purpose." He flipped the footrest down again. "How's your drink? Need me to refresh it?"

The guest shook his head, leaned back in the recliner covered in deep blue velvet with antique lace antimacassars on the arms, and took a long pull at his straw.

"Some people don't like that combination. Grenadine, gin, and soda over shaved ice. I call it 'the Ice Scraper.' I invented it during the semi-finals against Edmonton." He flopped back and flicked the footrest up again. "Then I guess we're all set. Oh, except for the music." He leaned to the stereo at the left of his chair and punched a few buttons. "I didn't have anything appropriate and the compact disc selection at Passing Wind is limited, so I chose songs of the humpback whale. It seemed to fit with what we're about to see." He remote-controlled a big-screen television to life and hit the "play" button for the VCR.

"Now this first clip was shot two years ago. Billy Bohannon's put on about thirty pounds since then. All in his gut. If I had a figure like his, I'd buy a girdle or padlock my lips." Henri patted his flat stomach and took a pull on his drink. "I may be big, but every ounce is muscle. My buns, too." He peeked at his guest from the corner of his eyes. "Too much information? You're blushing, *mon ami*."

Henri fingered his tinted hair and snagged a crab croquette from the tray balanced on the back of a carved wooden elephant. He pointed at the action on the screen. "Now some of these human hippopotami," he raised an eyebrow, "sort of circle around, get up on their toes and trot forward, thrusting out their stomachs. As you can see, that posture tends to throw them off balance and, since the rules call for their hands to be clasped behind them, most are propelled out of the ring and into the crowd upon impact and so are disqualified."

Henri paused the tape and studied his guest. "Keep your weight on the balls of your feet and your knees flexed so you can take a quick step in any direction. You'll outlast most of these buffoons, wear them down, catch them off balance. Big Billy, though, is another matter."

Henri started the tape again. "His technique relies on brute strength, with not a single dollop of nuance. But, of course, he doesn't need any. He overpowers his opponents." They watched an unfortunate contestant bucked into the juke box. "Three bucks against him is the record, and that belongs to a tourist from Wisconsin who broke four ribs and took the experience as a sign he should quit drinking."

Henri slurped the last of the Ice Scraper through his straw and munched down the three maraschino cherries in the bottom of the glass. "You must stay balanced and absorb the impact a few times. Raise his frustration level; perhaps taunt him so he takes a hard run at you. Then you pivot and . . ."

He set his glass down on the end table. "You may be called the champion. Or perhaps the deceased. We will see."

Flipping down the footrest, Henri went to a spindly legged table in the corner and dug shaved ice out of a bucket, filling his glass. "I just love these. I could drink them all night." He poured the ingredients, stirred with a small plastic hockey stick, tossed four cherries on top, and popped three more into his mouth. Chewing, he returned to his chair and started the tape.

"Don't even say it. I can hear your mind working. 'How do I make Big Billy Bohannon lose control?' Well never fear, Henri has been shaking the Bohannon family tree for information. And I have a cunning plan."

I dragged my eyelids up and squinted at the glowing red numbers on the digital clock. Fifteen minutes before five. Groaning, I clamped the lids closed again. I'd conked out less than an hour ago. But Dad would be home any minute. This time I'd force him to tell me the truth about his interview with

Greg Erdman—the truth I couldn't pry out of the tight-lipped sergeant at lunch even though I'd ponied up for the captain's platter out at the fish place on 101 and handed over what I'd learned about Grabowski threatening Maybelline's liquor license.

When I'd talked to her, she'd made no bones about hating him. But she'd also made it clear that Chuck had told him he'd see him in court. "Lawyers don't need to strangle people," she'd said. "They just litigate and bleed them dry."

Greg hadn't traded a single syllable I could use. "Nuh-uh," he'd muttered, his mouth full of fried oysters and coleslaw, "I'm not saying another word, especially not about your father."

"Oh come on, Greg. I know you can't seriously think my father killed Grabowski." I'd signaled the waiter to bring Greg a refill on his soda. "So tell me what made you take him to the sheriff's office."

"Nice try, Molly." Greg had rammed his fork into a pile of home fries, dragged his captives through a puddle of tartar sauce, and stuffed them in his mouth. He chewed, swallowed, and leaned into my face. "But you're not getting anything else out of me. Not about the Grabowski case. Or any other cases, for that matter." He straightened his shoulders against the dark wood of the booth and stabbed at more fries.

I'd debated spilling my suspicions about Icky, the only thing I had left besides the information I'd gleaned about Grabowski's investors—a list that included my father. "Okay, so you're testy because the sheriff chewed you out. But off the record you can still—"

"No!" He slammed his fork on the table and a home fry catapulted against the wood beside me, spattering tartar sauce on my T-shirt. "No more information. Not on the record. Not off the record." He'd shoved his plate aside. "Look, I can't work this case with both you and the sheriff attached to my butt.

I need to shake one of you loose." He'd slid out of the booth, brushing at his slacks, avoiding my eyes. "Dating you is a conflict of interest. The sheriff wasn't happy before, but now that your father's a suspect—"

"But not a real suspect!" I wiped at the sauce splatter.

Greg sighed, eyes slewing toward the door. "They fought, Molly."

"That doesn't prove a thing. Dad had no reason to kill Grabowski." Not counting the money he'd lost when those homes slid down the hillside last winter. I dug my nails into my palms, half wishing I had never checked my e-mail when I got back from pounding in vain on Icky's locked door.

"Not that I can see," he'd admitted. "But I have to investigate him just like anyone else. I can't show favoritism."

"Of course not." I'd tried to disguise the bitterness in my voice. Part of me acknowledged what a difficult spot Greg was in; another part wanted to punch him out. "Well, that doesn't leave you much choice."

He'd shrugged, not meeting my eyes. "Maybe we should cool it for now."

Or forever. Except I needed the information I was sure he'd spill when he forgot about being careful. "Maybe so."

I paid the bill and he held the door for me as we walked out. Like a civilized adult, I waved as he drove away. I only kicked the pickup's tires three times before heading home. Molly Donovan, calloused queen of uncommitted relationships. That's why you pick the men you do, I reminded myself. There's no danger you'll ever have a conversation about love or trust. And because you won't miss them much when they're gone.

An unexpected twinge of regret stung my brain as I remembered the piece of gossip Maybelline had shared about Jeffrey Wolfe stumbling out of the bar with Prudence Deeds hot on his poetic heels. I couldn't visualize Jeffrey tumbling for her aggressive brand of sexuality. I thought he was a cut above the kind of man who'd do that, but what did I really know about him? Not much. And I'd been wrong about men before. My eyes burned and I blinked back tears, remembering the day I'd swung by the house for lunch and found the man I'd married three months earlier in bed with my maid of honor.

No point in dwelling on that. I rubbed my eyes and blew my nose. Rolling over, I swung my feet to the floor, then scratched my head. What was wrong with this picture? Well, for one thing, I couldn't see the floor. My room, which should have been bright with western sun, was dark as octopus ink. Had I slept for thirteen hours, instead of one?

Sagging back on the bed, I snapped on the light and noticed someone had pulled the shades, unplugged the phone on the night table and flung a quilt over me. Not Dad. Well, he might have gotten the quilt, but he wouldn't have thought about the phone. This smelled of Jeffrey Wolfe.

"Damn him!" I threw the quilt on the floor and kicked it into the corner, then crossed to the windows and yanked the shade up on a dim pre-dawn world. What right did he have coming into my bedroom after letting Prudence Deeds into his? I opened the window on a cool salt wind, breathed deep, and let my anger go. As soon as I figured out who killed Vince Grabowski, I'd be out of this stupid town.

SIXTEEN

"Ummmm." Prudence Deeds blinked at the clock and snuggled deeper into her satin sheets. 6:00 a.m. She knew she should get up and start her morning routine, but cocooning felt better. Besides, she wasn't sure she could face her image in the mirror after the debacle at Jeffrey Wolfe's apartment.

Until she followed him from the bar, she hadn't realized how desperately she needed male companionship. As guilty as cheating on Brighton made her feel, doing without a man admiring the body she worked so hard to maintain caused an ache she couldn't ignore.

If she pulled herself together now, she had time to give her hair a hot oil treatment, exfoliate her skin, use the pumice stone on her feet, smooth that new lotion all over her body, and make it to the Realtors' breakfast.

She moaned and curled into a fetal position. Or maybe she'd spend another day in bed like an overweight teenage outcast as she replayed that humiliating scene in the tiny apartment over the ice cream shop. She'd followed him like a homeless puppy, struggling to keep up with his long strides, her attempts at suggestive conversation met with only an occasional grunt or a disbelieving stare. She should have quit then. But no, she'd wheedled her way inside by inventing a headache. While he'd hunted for the aspirin, she'd raced to his bedroom, shed her clothes, and slid between the sheets.

"Prudence?" She'd heard his footsteps cross the living room and sat up, allowing the covers to slip from one breast. "Here's your aspirin and wa—"

With great satisfaction, she'd seen his jaw drop and his mouth form an involuntary O as she bared the other breast. Then he blinked, set the pills and the glass on the nightstand, spun on his heel, and walked out.

She'd given him fifteen minutes to realize what he was missing and come back. He hadn't.

Woozy from the drinks, she'd drifted into an uneasy sleep. She'd awakened, shivering, to an empty apartment and a shrieking headache. Sheepishly she'd swallowed the aspirin, pulled on her clothing, and slunk out.

Nothing had happened. But Maybelline would tell everyone they'd left together. And Adam Quarles would testify that he saw her sneaking down the stairs the next morning.

She groaned and pried herself from the bed. Hiding would only make things worse. Better to get on with her life. Besides, she couldn't afford to ignore her calls and messages another day. Festival week always drew a bumper crop of real estate prospects. Sure, most of them were only tourists passing through. They fell in love with the "quaint" houses hunkering around the harbor, exclaimed over weather vanes and whirligigs, and cooed about wooden whales and gulls. Coastal kitsch. Most of them just ate up her time poking through other people's closets. Most couldn't scrape together a down payment on a doublewide beside a salt marsh, let alone a lot with a view. But you never knew when someone might open a checkbook and plop down real earnest money.

She turned on the shower and steam filled the bathroom. Setting the shower head to "pulse," she stood beneath the throbbing fists of water and lathered her body, taking her time, enjoying the sensuous pain of the spray.

Then her brain dredged up a thought that gave her a chill. That sergeant might return to ask more questions about Vince. She'd better think about what she'd say, make sure her workout-tightened rear was covered. The sergeant had no need to know about the knock-down-drag-out fight she and Vince had gotten into last Wednesday when he informed her that he needed a kickback from commissions on Devil's Acres sales to solve all of his cash-flow problems. "In your dreams," she'd answered.

With a smirk, Vince had asked her to reconsider. He'd pointed out that Brighton's political prospects would be damaged if explicit details of their sexual encounters leaked out.

She'd been expecting Vince to take the low road, and countered by hinting that his standing in the business community could also be damaged if investors found out about his account in the Cayman Islands. When she told him she'd spotted a letter on his computer screen, his eyes widened and his lips clamped. Smugly, she'd reminded him that if investors knew he'd siphoned off their money, they might be inclined to, well, throw him off a cliff. Talk about prophecy.

Shifting into a practiced and obsequious, repentant-little-boy persona, Vince had apologized for any "misunderstanding." Still, he said, it might be better if they "cooled it" for a few months. No fool, she knew that meant he planned to turn up the heat with someone else—like Shelley Perkins—and she'd stormed out after throwing a stapler and calling him a few choice names.

With a sigh, she turned off the shower and toweled her hair, mapping out her day. A door slammed in the fish shop beneath her. Brighton. One thing you had to give the little runt, he was punctual. Hearing a couple of thuds and a creak, she imagined him moving things around in the walk-in freezer. Then she heard the front door open again and the sound of a squeegee on the windows. Brighton was constantly fixing or cleaning. Even in the middle of the night she'd hear him puttering around in the market or out back at the coin-operated car wash.

She selected a teal blouse and skirt that showed off her figure. If Brighton would work out and give up greasy foods he could lose fifty pounds easily. Then maybe . . .

She tugged her belt tighter.

She finished her makeup, checked herself in the mirror and started down the stairs. Maybe she'd make a big sale today. Or maybe that Sergeant Erdman would come by to interrogate her. A little danger could be thrilling.

Gus Custer flipped the eggs sizzling in a quarter inch of bacon grease and turned off the burner under the cast-iron frying pan. Over easy. The way he liked them. He pulled the one remaining clean plate from the knotty pine cabinet, fished two slices of browned bread from the toaster, laid a cube of butter on each, and piled six slices of bacon beside them. Cutting the eggs apart with the spatula, he fitted them into the remaining space on the plate. Only sissies counted fat grams and cholesterol. He didn't buy into food-police hysteria. He was more likely to choke to death on a spear of broccoli or have a seizure trying to digest organic seaweed and millet.

Bacon and eggs. Plenty of butter slathered on the toast. Black coffee with sugar. A real by-God breakfast. He'd started his days like this since he was a kid. Hadn't hurt him a bit, neither.

He set the plate and double-sized mug of coffee on a battered table by the picture window in the living room and followed a trail of crumbs and splotches back to the kitchen for a knife and fork. The drawer stuck, and then opened with a clatter, as the utensils inside abruptly shifted to another tangled configuration. He pawed through the jumble and found a fork with two bent tines. Glaring at the mountain of dishes in the sink, he admitted he'd have to wash them this evening or eat at the Devil's Food Cafe tomorrow.

"Not a bad idea." LaDonna cooked up a good plate of chow, and he liked to watch her work. She never wasted motion. Or words. Gus liked strong quiet women. The kind of women he didn't like much were the pushy, nosy ones, like that reporter who'd come around yesterday asking about his finances and what happened the night Grabowski died. He told her exactly nothing. If you didn't open your trap, then your words couldn't come back around and bite you in the ass.

Settling himself in his chair, he ate the first strip of bacon in two bites, forked a load of egg in behind it and stared out the window. From this side of his house, he couldn't see Devil's Acres. A meadow dappled with wildflowers dropped away toward a thin stand of Douglas fir. Twenty acres. That's all he'd saved from Grabowski's big land grab.

A deer raised its head at the edge of the meadow, tested the breeze as it chewed, froze, and then leaped into the trees, flipping its tail. A fawn Gus hadn't noticed followed close behind. He picked up a dented pair of binoculars and scanned the area, trying to see what had startled them.

"What the hell?"

Gus stood to get a better look at the two men in dark suits walking across the field. Tax collectors? No, they sent threats through the mail first. Census takers? Not the right year, was it? Government biologists? In suits? Not likely. Guys from the liquor commission? Maybe. He thought about the jug of white lightning under the sink. Two decades old and strong enough to eat through the plastic paddles on those damn whirligigs.

Gus put the binoculars down, forked in a load of dripping egg and chomped toast. If they started his way, he'd dump the stuff down the sink. No evidence, no crime.

The men turned and pointed off toward Devil's Harbor, then down the coast. One put his finger to his ear and held it there. Gus grabbed the binoculars again and spotted an ear-plug and a wire like something those Secret Service guys used in the movies. He set the binoculars down and rubbed his chin. Secret Service? Was the President coming to Devil's Harbor?

Gus grunted out a laugh and demolished another strip of bacon. For what, a chance to compete in the belly-bucking competition?

"Hell, that would be worth a year's salary!"

The two men started down the hillside, one still holding the earplug in place. Gus mopped up egg yolk with toast and grinned as he made a mental note to tell His Gullibleness that the President was coming for the festival. Brighton Deeds would wet his pants. And no telling what kind of lame-ass plans he'd make. Maybe he'd paint the streets again.

Gus guffawed. This year's festival might be worth attending after all.

"Okay, Dad," I plunked into the seat across from him at the table. He'd left me no choice but to play my ace. "Remember when I was twelve? Just after Mom died. The day we looked through the photo album?"

My father nodded and blinked with the wariness of a cornered lemming as he forked off a strip of low-fat waffle smothered with fresh strawberries and non-fat dessert whip. I'd put in an hour of hard labor and, by the time Dad got up, I'd had a world-class breakfast waiting, right down to the hazelnut-flavored decaf coffee and an egg-white, onion, and mushroom omelet. Food hadn't loosened his tongue so it was time to bring out the big gun—guilt.

"I remember."

"And do you remember what you said then?"

He set the fork down and gazed at me, his faded blue eyes damp. "I said a lot of things, Molly. I was trying to make us both feel better."

"I know, Dad. But one thing stayed with me. You promised we'd always be honest with each other, no matter what."

His shoulders slumped. "I remember. But when I said that, I couldn't foresee . . ." He frowned at his waffle.

I felt like the black scum that grows down inside the drain in the sink—the stuff you know is there, but can't get at to clean. Dad wanted to absorb the pain and protect his little girl. I wanted him to acknowledge that I didn't need protecting anymore; I was an adult who could not only take care of herself, but also help him. I turned the knife in his emotional wound. "So you're saying it was a conditional promise?"

He chewed his lip wiped one eye with his napkin. "No, I'm not saying that. I'm—"

"Mike! Molly! I brought breakfast! And I have a great idea about how to get rid of Old Air Biscuit." Jeffrey Wolfe plunged into the kitchen, holding a white bakery sack and a bag of coffee. "Hey, those waffles look great."

"Jeff! Pull up a chair. Grab a waffle. Did you sleep well?" Dad clutched the distraction like a condemned man grasps a stay of execution.

I shot a glare at each of them, but neither seemed to notice. With a bright grin, Dad watched Jeffrey load muffins onto a plate. "Better than the night before," Jeffrey answered.

"Jeff slept on board the *Helen* Tuesday night," my father supplied.

"Really?" I took a casual sip of coffee, and kept my voice light and innocent. "Why was that?"

Jeffrey half turned, licking a smear of blueberry from his thumb and peering at me from the corners of his eyes. "I had, um, unanticipated company at my place."

"Oh? Relatives from out of town?" I baited him.

"No." He frowned and muttered something I thought sounded like "small town gossip," then squared his shoulders and pulled a chair up to the table. "I'm sure you know. Prudence Deeds followed me home from the Belly Up."

Dad uttered a grunt of surprise. I merely raised an eyebrow.

"She forced her way into my apartment."

I gave him ten points for honesty, and subtracted two for the word "forced."

"Well, not exactly forced," he amended before I could utter something sarcastic. "She claimed she had a headache and needed some aspirin. When I went to the kitchen to get a glass of water, she . . . well, she got into my bed and . . ." He stammered to a halt and flushed fuchsia. "She was naked."

"So he got out of there fast. Like any man with good sense would have." My father grinned and took a bite of waffle.

Jeffrey chewed his lower lip and studied my face. I kept my eyes on the syrup bottle. In twenty years of dating and three sorry months of marriage, I'd listened to so many lies from so many men that I wasn't sure I could identify the truth. My father looked from one of us to the other like he was following a tennis match.

Finally Jeffrey rose and brought the coffee pot from the counter. "Can I pour you a refill, Molly?"

"No thanks." I shoved my chair back, stood slowly, lifted my camera bag from the counter, and walked toward the door. I needed time alone. "I'll pass. I've got a lot of work to do. Good luck with the charter today. And Dad?"

He ducked his head, avoiding my eyes. "Yes?"

"We'll finish our talk this evening."

SEVENTEEN

Greg Erdman riffled the sheaf of pink "while you were out" message slips.

"Twenty-seven," Barbara Sue supplied. "Not counting the six calls the sheriff took before he told me he didn't want to be bothered anymore and I should write down the messages and give them to you."

Greg grunted and pulled one of the slips from the pack. "I can't read this one. 'Unflob.' What's an unflob?"

"Unidentified flying object," Barbara Sue huffed. "Any fool can see that."

Greg suppressed an eye roll. "So this says someone saw Vince Grabowski beamed aboard an unidentified flying object filled with," he squinted at the paper, "little green men who proceeded to skin, no, scan his brain and prod, no, probe his innards and then show, no shove, him—"

"Well, I beg your pardon." Barbara Sue put her hands on her hips. "I'm a dispatcher, not a stenographer. I'm sorry my secretarial skills don't meet your exacting standards." She marched toward the door. "You can bet I'll never take a message for you again! Unless I get a direct order from the sheriff!"

She slammed the door twice. No easy trick, Greg acknowledged, given the hydraulic device designed to prevent that.

"What the hell is going on in here?"

The beleaguered door opened again and Sheriff Archie Fletcher glowered at the pile of messages in Greg's hand. "How'd you piss her off now?"

"I asked her to translate these messages about the Grabowski case."

The sheriff leveled a forefinger at Greg's chest. "This is your fault."

Greg blinked. "My fault?"

"Damn straight. If you hadn't run off at the mouth to that media jackal girlfriend of yours, and if she hadn't encouraged those wackos to call, Barbara Sue wouldn't have wasted a whole day writing down a bunch of claptrap."

Greg shuffled the message slips once more. Twenty-seven scribbles didn't look like a day's work. Deciphering those scribbles might be.

"One woman told me she spotted Grabowski with Elvis," the sheriff said, "and another accused that retired hockey guy of selling black market abalone shell ashtrays. Then there's the guy who said he's forming an exclusive club of men who haven't been involved with Mayor Deeds' wife and wanted to know if anybody in this office was eligible." The sheriff's flushed face darkened. "And I hope to hell you *are*, mister. Because if I find out you've been in bed with a suspect in a murder case . . ."

He let that hang, turned toward his office, and then rounded on Greg again. "How many times do I have to tell you? You solicit calls, you're asking for every crackpot, malcontent, and smartass in the county to rat out anyone they've got a grudge against."

Greg gripped the edge of his desk. "But—"

"No buts. Barbara Sue isn't your secretary. Anybody else calls, she'll take a number, that's all. You can call back on your own time and listen to their malarkey." Without waiting for an answer, Fletcher smoothly rotated on one polished heel, disappeared into his office, and slammed the door. Greg heard an echoing slam from the ladies room door. Barbara Sue celebrating her victory.

"Crud." He ran a hand over his face, wiping away a sheen of sweat. He hated to admit it, but the sheriff was right. Waste of time wading through this crap. He leaned back in the aged vinyl swivel chair he'd claimed at a yard sale in Netarts and then started flipping the messages into the circular file. Narrowing his eyes, he tried to decipher the scrawl across the bottom of one. Maybe, no that was Maybelline, kissed who? Wait, it must read Maybelline killed Grabowski because . . . He scratched his head. Licorice incense? Liquid assets? Liquor license! Yeah, Molly had mentioned something about that.

He pulled out his notebook and wrote a reminder to call the state commission, then squinted at another message slip with something about a major, no make that the mayor, and first base, or maybe fish paste. Greg let that flutter to the waste basket and looked at the next one. Something about a card in the deck, or possibly a carp on the—

"Oh, to hell with it!" He wadded the pile and slam-dunked it. "Crackpots."

He squinted at the wad in the wastebasket. Or maybe just one crackpot, like the one he'd heard deviling Elspeth Hunsaker on her call-in program. Barbara Sue wouldn't notice if all the voices sounded similar. Not if more important things occupied her mind.

He checked his pager battery and flipped through the paperwork in his "in" basket. Nothing that couldn't wait. "See you later," he called to the ladies room door as he passed. Then he strolled out to his cruiser and headed north. Mike Donovan had been evasive about his reasons for throwing a punch at Grabowski, but Greg didn't believe Molly's father had killed the developer. He needed to get on the stick and interrogate the others on his list, like Grabowski's less-than-grieving widow.

First thing, though, he'd look up Prudence Deeds and see if she was ready to stop waltzing around and admit the affair with Grabowski. Had she gotten angry enough to kill him when he dumped her for the sweet young thing at the cafe?

Jennifer Daley waved as Molly Donovan roared by, then leaned over and poked the two-foot long metal rod attached to the roadrunner-and-coyote whirligig into a metal bracket on the outside of the bridge railing.

"A hundred down, four hundred to go," Bart Yamamoto called from the opposite side of the road.

"Thank you, Mr. Future Bean Counter," she wailed. "Cheer down, okay."

They'd been working all morning, first lugging boxes from the storage room at the factory, then setting up the giant whirligigs at the city limits—devils with whirling pitchforks riding whales, same as the pictures on the coffee mugs.

The slipstream from a passing car sent plastic paddles into motion. Cartoonish flamingos, ducks, sharks, hillbillies, pirates, and Las Vegas showgirls twirled their wings, arms, feet, and tassels in the breeze, frantically getting nowhere as they whirled in single file at five-foot intervals down either side of the highway toward the center of town.

She retrieved a whirligig golfer from the wheelbarrow beside her and wedged it into the next bracket. "Eewww! My hands are all covered with rust and oily stuff. Ohmigod, Bart, this job is disgusto-mundo!"

"Queen candidates have to do community service," Bart reminded her. "At least it isn't raining. You can work on your tan."

"True." She watched him secure a whirligig beagle, and held up her arm for comparison with his bronze skin. Hers was as pale as that no-fat tofu stuff she'd forced herself to try last week. Maybe she should use the quick tanning gunk Shelley had loaned her or the body makeup she'd bought last month.

Honestly, she thought as she firmly stuffed a whirligig hippopotamus into its slot, being beautiful took so much effort. After they crowned her with the whirligig salmon, she'd let it all go. Eat peanut butter and not worry about zits and get one of those haircuts she could just blow and comb with her fingers. And as far as makeup, well, look at Molly. She wore like next to none at all and she had a guy who really dug her—the cute dude who worked on her dad's boat and wrote poetry that didn't rhyme.

"Come on, I'm getting ahead of you," Bart called from the end of the bridge. "Last one done buys ice cream."

"I'm not racing! I might break a fingernail." She made pout-lips. "If I do, you'll be on my invisible person list as long as you live."

Bart laughed and raised his hands in surrender. "Okay. If I get done first I'll come back and help you."

Jennifer flashed a smile and turned to stick a whirligig nun into its bracket. The black-robed figure flashed a ruler at a student's knuckles as the wind rotated its arm. What was the rush anyway? As soon as they finished, an adult on some stupid festival committee would find another job for them. And later they'd have to decorate the gym with Mrs. Deeds. Torture-rama.

And what if she didn't win? She'd have done all this work for nothing. She wouldn't get the scholarship. And she might never get out of Devil's Harbor. She might turn into Shelley. Or Mrs. Deeds. She clutched her stomach. "Ohh!"

"What's wrong now?" Bart called.

"Nothing. Never mind." Of course she'd win. Practicing the wave she'd almost definitely decided on, she snagged an octopus whirligig from the wheelbarrow with her left hand and slid it into place.

"Good morning, good morning, good morning! Welcome to KYMR, You Must Repent. Elspeth Hunsaker here to lead you to salvation. It's another fine morning. The sky is clear, it's seventy-three degrees, and although there's a chance of rain this weekend, we know the sun always shines on true believers."

Elspeth paused and tucked a loose strand of hair into her bun. "I want to speak with all of you this morning about sin and redemption. Yes, I know confession can be painful, but we must acknowledge our transgressions if we are to make meaningful progress on that shining road."

She shuddered as she thought about the blasphemous curse on this lovely town. She hoped the foul-mouthed sailor who'd pasted the name "Devil's Harbor" on it was roasting to a fare-thee-well.

"Now, it's time for a new feature, confession on the air. Just call the hotline." She punched a button, playing the recorded jingle for her toll-free number.

She frowned. Lately she'd considered giving up that line. After all, her signal barely reached the border of the local calling zone. But an 800-number sounded important. "To start things off, I'll offer my confession."

She cleared her throat and flashed a confident smile at the microphone. This would definitely trigger an avalanche of calls.

"Ahem. Well, a few weeks ago, as I was singing in the choir, I noticed that the woman next to me was wearing a beautiful ring. I imagined how it would feel to slide that gold band, plump diamond, and glittering rubies along my finger, how it would glint in the light through the stained-glass window."

She paused to let her listeners see the image in their own minds. "And while I coveted that ring, I stopped singing and began humming a show tune. Yes, right there in church. 'Diamonds Are A Girl's Best Friend.' There, I've admitted it."

Elspeth clasped her hands and bowed her head, sneaking a peek at the buttons on the phone. Not a single light winked. The panel was as dark as her high-necked dress. She sighed.

"Well perhaps, given the examples some of our political leaders set, you believe this sin doesn't amount to much." She took a deep breath. "I've done worse. Much worse." She lowered her voice and leaned into the microphone. "Once, when I lived in Salt Lake City, I had a neighbor who could . . . well, frankly he could try the patience of a saint. His lawn was smoother and greener than any golf course." She paused, remembering that emerald patch of grass. "This man would mow exactly to the property line, would rake the leaves that fell on his side but would not touch a single twig on mine. And he demanded that I water, weed, and mow to meet his standards."

Even after ten years, Elspeth felt her throat constrict with anger. She grasped her water glass, gulped, and sputtered. "I got down on my knees and asked for love in my heart, but I felt hatred creep into it instead. And one night, one dark night, after reading another of his notes insinuating that my yard resembled a pigsty . . . well, I could not put Satan behind me. Satan urged me to spread a twenty-pound bag of rock salt across my lawn and tell everyone that this man who placed so much false pride in his grass had poisoned mine. He protested, but the neighbors shunned him, and finally he sold his house and moved to Duluth."

She realized she sounded a bit too gleeful and fought back the memory of how good it felt when she saw the sign on that cretin's lawn. Firmly, she concluded. "I begged for forgiveness, crawling through my house until I picked bloody splinters from my knees."

The unblinking buttons on the phone panel mocked her. "Now, let's enjoy this message from Divine Investments." Jabbing a button, she heard a rich baritone voice exhorting listeners to call a 900 number where they could learn how to find stock tips in scripture.

"Drat!" She'd have to raise the stakes. But what had she done that could titillate listeners in a town where enormously fat men drank gallons of beer and then charged each other in sport, where an actual homosexual was one of the leaders of the community? What kind of horrible crime did she have to confess to in order to get their attention? Murder?

She slammed her fist on the console. If that's what it took, that's what she'd do.

The commercial ended, she shot another look at the phone, and opened her microphone. "I'm Elspeth Hunsaker and I guess you can tell I've been holding something back. That's why you're not calling. So here it is. Last week I poured poison into a cup of tea. I killed a man." She paused to let her listeners visualize that. "There! It's off my chest and— ah, we have a caller."

She punched the blinking button. "You're on the air."

"Uh, yeah. You the broad who just confessed to killing someone?" The voice was hoarse and low, barely audible above a humming rumble.

Elspeth's heart leaped. "Yes. Yes, I am. I've confessed and I am free."

"Great. Where can I meet you?"

"Meet me?" Elspeth tucked another strand of hair into her bun. Was this man what they called a radio groupie?

"Yeah. I'm a long haul trucker. I'm out on 101 parked next to some ham and clam joint. I got this problem with my mother-in-law. I thought you could come along to Sacramento and brew up a pot of that tea for her."

Elspeth punched at the phone button.

"Bwaaaatttt." The dial tone pegged the meters into the red. This time she let it go on for a good long time while she slumped over the console. What would she have to do to reach the people of this town?

I squinted through the viewfinder, wondering how a wide shot of the main street with an inset of a specific whirligig would look on the front page of *The Flotsam*. Or perhaps an artsy shot of the three-piece bucket brigade whirligig with the street out of focus behind it? Or maybe a high-angle shot of whirligigs marching along the dock and around the harbor?

I decided to play it safe and let Ben Galloway pick his favorite. The important thing was to get done and get over to Claire Grabowski's house. I'd heard Elspeth's confession on the air, but until the toxicology report came back, I was going with my gut feeling and leaving her at the bottom of my list. Maybe it was Vince's tea she'd poisoned, but that didn't explain his other injuries, and I couldn't see her hauling him to the headland and dumping him without leaving a trail of clues like breadcrumbs leading to her door.

"Looks like we're getting all decked out for the festival. Good, good." Brighton Deeds bustled toward me, making his way to the Devil's Food Cafe for his usual lunch—a triple-decker sandwich with extra mayonnaise, a double order of fries, a chocolate milk shake, and a slab of the pie of the day piled with whipped cream. He tugged his shirt over his prodigious gut and waddled around my tripod. "Molly, I've been meaning to talk to you."

"Have you?" I mumbled, distracted by an impossible choice: bow-legged cowgirl whirligig or whistling woodpecker?

"I saw your father drive off with Sergeant Erdman the other night."

I clicked off a shot of the woodpecker and zeroed in on the buckarooette. Heck, they were all adorable. Why not photograph every one of them?

I sighed. Sarcasm wasn't as satisfying when you didn't share it.

"Well. Um, I hope everything is okay."

"It's fine." I aimed at a gaggle of whirligig geese and clicked.

"Um. What I mean is I hope that, you know, your dad isn't called down to the sheriff's office for questioning again."

My resolution to stay calm and controlled dissolved. "Don't you mean that you hope he doesn't get arrested during the festival?" I straightened and looked down into his beady little eyes. "Or if he does, that it happens after the parade of ships, and that tourists won't notice. That's what you mean, isn't it?" I left the words "you sanctimonious little weasel" implied but not spoken.

"Now, Molly."

I snapped the tripod legs together and stomped twenty feet down the sidewalk to get a shot of a paddling platypus painted a bright fuchsia. Deeds sidled up beside me.

"Your father and I go way back. Why, he and my dad used to play poker on Saturday nights. I'm sure Mike didn't have anything to do with Vince's death and I hope the sergeant doesn't make any more trouble for him."

He was so oily he practically left a slick on the sidewalk. I nudged up the shutter speed to compensate for the wind that set the paddles whirling.

"I hope he doesn't make trouble for you either, Mayor."

His eyes widened. "Trouble? Over what?"

"Over that investment in Devil's Acres you might have lost if Grabowski went to bankruptcy court where the rumor mill says he was headed."

His eyes narrowed and he pointed a finger at my chest. "I had perfect faith in Vince," he insisted. "My money was safe with him."

"As safe as your wife?" I kept my tone matter-of-fact.

His rubbery lips snapped down at the corners and his face turned the color of a heart attack waiting to happen. His gaze shifted left and right, but then he resurrected his chamber-of-commerce smile.

"Molly. Surely you don't suspect me of murder?" He chuckled, his belly shaking. "No, of course you don't. No more than anyone honestly believes your father killed Vince. But this is a small town and you've been gone a lot of years. Maybe you've forgotten how important it is that we all work together and stay on good terms. So I'm sorry if I upset you when I asked about your dad."

I nodded, noting he hadn't answered my question. Pretending to adjust the focus, I watched him shuffle his pudgy little feet. His shoes were smaller than mine. And the heels were higher. Too bad that couldn't raise his IQ.

"So, we're still friends? I wouldn't want to get on the wrong side of the media, especially when it appears I'm headed for Washington."

Talk about delusions of adequacy. I ordered my eyeballs not to roll.

"Well, I've got a scoop for you. Guess who's coming to the Whirligig Festival."

I hated games like this. "Elvis."

"No. Guess again."

I sighed. "I give up."

"Come on, guess again."

"I'm out of guesses."

"You won't believe it." He leaned so close his cologne seared through my nostrils. Essence of three-day-old bacon cheeseburger? "The President!"

"The president of what?"

"The United States." He hummed an off-key rendition of "Hail To The Chief."

"Right." I turned back to the camera. "He's in Africa this week."

"I have it on good authority that he's making a special trip out here for the festival. Devil's Harbor is practically on his way home."

His Cluelessness had obviously ditched his high school geography classes along with civics and physical education. "So you've been notified by the White House, right?"

He scratched his head. "Well, not exactly."

I clicked off another shot. "Then what makes you think the big guy will show up? Meaning no disrespect, Mayor, but I've covered presidential visits, and believe me, if he had Devil's Harbor on his itinerary, this town would be crawling with Secret Service agents."

"It is," Deeds assured me as he waddled off. "Guys in dark suits with special ear pieces, right? Two of them were in the cafe yesterday. And Gus Custer spotted more this morning."

I snapped a final shot, considering the information. The sketchy description sounded like Secret Service, but the idea of the President dropping in on the festival was too ludicrous to consider. So who were those men? Did they have something to do with Grabowski's shady business dealings? Or his death? Or both? I folded the tripod, stuck the camera in my bag, and headed for my truck wondering where the mystery men might be.

EIGHTEEN

Greg Erdman checked his shirt and fly as he pulled up in front of the Grabowski house. All buttoned and zipped. Still, just a few minutes with Prudence Deeds had left him feeling exposed, violated. She hadn't touched him, but her eyes had roamed every inch of his body. The experience had been erotic, but disturbing. It had required every ounce of concentration he could muster to maintain his "just the facts ma'am" manner and, reviewing it in his mind, he wasn't certain he'd managed.

"So," he'd said, "let's go over this again. You and Vince Grabowski had a business relationship?"

"Yes." She'd licked her bottom lip and prickly heat had tingled in his loins. "And we were . . . friends."

"Friends?"

"Good friends. Close friends." With a whisper of nylon stockings she'd rearranged herself on the chair in her living room office. Her skirt slid another inch up long, smooth thighs.

"Were you and Vince Grabowski sleeping together?"

She'd fluttered long eyelashes. "Neither of us got much sleep, Captain."

"Sergeant, ma'am."

"Whatever. If you must know, we were . . . intimate."

She drew out the syllables and Greg felt himself flush, imagining the ramifications of intimacy. Prudence Deeds smiled and tugged at her skirt. His tongue thick and dry, he'd forced himself to go on. "Did your, um, intimate relationship affect your business dealings?"

"No. Why would it?" A hint of defensiveness tinged her confident tone.

"There weren't any disagreements? For example, did the landslide and the fallout from it create any tension between you?"

Prudence took a deep breath, something that didn't help his concentration. "Sex is sex. Business is business. We kept them separate."

Greg had never managed that. "Were you still involved when he died?"

A pink tide washed up her neck. Had he struck a nerve?

"No. But we were still friends. I gave him a gold and diamond medallion for his birthday."

"Did you see him Saturday?"

"No. I was . . . out of town."

"Is there someone who can corroborate that?"

"Maybe." She shrugged. "I played blackjack at the casino until after midnight. The dealer's name is George. He'll remember me."

"Because you won?"

She smirked. "Because I turned him down when he asked me out."

Greg had made a note to look for George and ask him if he'd noticed when Prudence left. He decided to drop one of the rumors he'd picked up. "One of my sources tells me that Grabowski cooked his books. Skimmed some of the investors' money."

"I wouldn't know anything about that." Her syllables dropped like icicles.

Direct hit. "Are you sure? There will be an extensive audit of everyone involved with all phases of the development."

She'd sagged and, for the first time, he noticed crows' feet at the corners of her eyes. "All right. He had a bank account in the Cayman Islands. But that's all I know."

Damn, he was good. "Did you confront him? Or tell anyone else?"

"No. No, I just found out a couple of days ago." She lowered her eyes and Greg knew she was lying. But his instincts told him he'd gotten all he could. For now. He'd peeled himself from the turquoise lounge chair and started for the door.

"Leaving so soon, Captain?" A playful lilt returned to her voice and he felt her eyes probing his back.

"Sergeant, ma'am. And, yes. I've got an investigation to conduct."

"You're finished with me?" The double meaning in her question hung between them.

"I . . . uh . . . er . . ." His primal, testosterone-driven, whoever's-around-at-closing-time male libido screamed at him to turn around, pick her up, and carry her to the fluffy four-poster bed he could see through the open bedroom door. A cubic inch of cerebral sanity insisted that it would be sleazy, sweaty, over in a few minutes, and probably get him fired.

"Thank you for your time, ma'am," he'd mumbled as he escaped through the door into midday sunlight, gulping air like a man who'd been trapped by an undertow.

"Damn!" Greg slapped his hands against the steering wheel. If Grabowski had ripped off investors, the list of suspects could be longer. And if Mike Donovan had sunk his savings into the development and lost a bundle, it gave him a stronger motive. But right now Greg couldn't worry about that; he had to concentrate on the widow Grabowski.

He opened the cruiser's door, crossed her asphalt driveway, climbed the steps to the deck, and confronted the carved front door looming beside a wall of windows. If what he'd heard about her affair with Adam Quarles was true, she had the strongest motive of all. Except she'd been in Chicago. He tugged at his ear. Chicago. A good place to find someone who specialized in murder for hire.

Greg punched the doorbell and heard a muffled chime in the distance. The final five notes sounded like the payoff line in that Frank Sinatra song. What was it? Oh yeah. "I Did It My Way."

Feet scuffled and a tentative voice called, "Who is it?"

"Sergeant Greg Erdman. Sheriff's Department."

"Oh."

Greg waited, but the knob didn't move.

"I'd like to talk to you, ma'am."

"Oh. Just a moment. I'm not dressed." The footsteps retreated and Greg looked at the runneled, weed-encrusted yard. Grabowski must have channeled the landscaping budget into that offshore account, too. Greg set his face in an expressionless mask. If she was like her husband, she'd try to run roughshod over the yokels. It wouldn't surprise him if she planned to keep that offshore account for herself and continue the family tradition of milking Devil's Harbor. He squared his shoulders. Well, she wouldn't get away with it.

The footsteps returned and the door opened on an attractive middle-aged woman wrapped in an apricot-colored robe. She smiled, displaying freckles scattered across her nose and cheeks. "I'm sorry to keep you waiting. Come in."

"Thanks." Greg stepped through the door into a small alcove and looked around at a living room the size of his entire apartment and a view that tacked at least a hundred thousand onto the price of the house. The sofa lay on its back, the bookshelves had been emptied, and liquor bottles lined the carpet beneath the bar cabinet. Was she getting ready to move to the islands and live off the interest from that slush fund?

"Shall we go into the kitchen?" Then Claire Grabowski walked ahead of him, without waiting for an answer. "It's cozier, and to tell you the truth, I was just making breakfast."

Greg checked his watch. At 2:30? He followed her to a kitchen cluttered with boxes, cans, and bottles.

"Sorry about the mess." Claire pulled the toaster from behind a stack of dish towels. "I tore the place up looking for Vince's safe." She turned, damp curls bobbing. "That's why you're here, isn't it?"

"Yes," Greg answered automatically. What was she up to? He moved a drawer full of silverware from a chair and sat, watching Claire feed bread into the toaster and measure coffee into the filter basket of the drip machine she'd unearthed from behind a stack of bowls.

"I found it set in the space under the floor in the loft. His insurance papers were in it—the personal policy that I knew about, and a corporate policy, too. And I found the number for his offshore account. It looks like he transferred a lot of money out of the development." She turned, leaning against the counter, the robe belted tight around her narrow waist. "Naturally I called my attorney right away. He said he'd notify the authorities, so I was expecting you." She ruffled her hair.

Knowing he was two steps behind and losing ground fast, Greg decided to say as little as possible. "You were?"

"Well of course." Her hazel eyes widened, then narrowed. "I may be naive, but I'm not stupid, Sergeant Erdman. I know Vince stole that money from his investors. I also know that when a man is killed, the wife is usually a prime suspect. Especially when she wanted to annul the marriage." She removed the toast, excavated a plate from beneath a heap of pot holders, then extracted a knife from the drawer Greg had moved and began to slather butter on the browned bread.

"Actually, I hadn't heard about your lawyer's call. I've been on the road all morning."

"Well, I'm sure there's a message on your desk."

"Yeah." He didn't mention that the odds of ever getting another telephone message slip amounted to exactly zilch. Except for those from his ex-wife. Barbara Sue would pass them along, word for bitter word.

"Frankly, I'm surprised you didn't talk with me sooner." Claire took a big bite of toast. "Before that reporter got here."

Greg's head snapped up. "What reporter?"

"Molly Donovan. She left just a few minutes ago."

Greg clenched his fists. "What did she want to know?"

Claire poured coffee and smiled. "Why, everything, of course."

Greg cursed under his breath. While he'd been staring at Prudence Deeds' cleavage, Molly had gotten ahead of him. Again.

"No one from your office had questioned me, so I assumed I wasn't a suspect."

Greg coughed, his mind struggling to catch up. "We haven't ruled anyone out yet, ma'am. However, since we can place you in Chicago when your husband died, we—"

"But I wasn't." Claire set her cup on the table. "Would you like some?"

"Yes. Uh. No. Okay. Half a cup. Black." What the hell was she talking about? The Chicago cops told she'd answered the door when the chaplain went to notify her Sunday night. He stalled again, waiting until she handed him the cup. "You weren't in Chicago?"

"No." She sat across from him, located a jar of jam in the debris and slathered some on the toast. "I was up in the

Columbia Gorge near Portland. With Adam Quarles." She blushed and pushed a pile of curls off her forehead.

"Adam Quarles." Greg feigned ignorance of the affair. "He's the guy who owns Passing Wind, right? The one with the dreadlocks?"

"Yes." She smiled faintly.

"The one your husband had arrested for trespassing when he picketed this development a few years back?"

"That's him." Her smile widened.

"Kind of the exact opposite of your husband, isn't he?"

"Exactly." She grinned.

Greg sipped his coffee, buying time. It was good. Some kind of chocolate flavor, with maybe a drop of vanilla. Not like the sludge Barbara Sue brewed from recycled tires. "So you spent the weekend in the Gorge?"

"Right. Camping near Beacon Rock."

He watched her smear jam on the second slice of toast. Two people conveniently on a wilderness expedition just a three-hour drive from Devil's Harbor. Or two killers providing mutual alibis. They both gained from Grabowski's death.

"Listen." She set the toast down and stared into his eyes. "Why don't I tell you the whole story? Then you can ask me anything you want. Believe me, I'll tell you the truth."

And sell me some swamp land in Florida. "Why?"

"Why what?"

"Why are you volunteering so much information?"

She studied him, not in the bluntly sexual manner of Prudence Deeds, but more like someone trying to decide what to wear so her outfit wouldn't clash with his. "First of all, I'm an honest person."

An honest person who sneaks around having an affair. He wondered whether she intended to use a little bit of truth to disguise a big lie, and whether she'd told Molly the same

177

version of the story that he was about to hear. He grunted in annoyance.

Claire studied him for another moment. "Sergeant, I was married to Vince Grabowski for almost half my life. In that time I heard more lies, unsupported half-truths, cons, limp excuses, amazing coincidences, alibis, and just plain bogus horse manure than anyone else on the face of this planet. The sad thing is that for most of our marriage, I bought into that because I didn't think I was entitled to more."

Greg nodded, fighting to keep his stern cop face in place.

"Then I met Adam." She flushed and brushed crumbs from the lapels of her robe. "The builders had nearly completed work in this house and Vince and I drove over from Portland to look at it. Adam stood in front of the main gate with a protest sign and shook his fist at us. Vince called him a disgruntled tree-hugger and told me to ignore him. Anyway, Adam barged through the gate and quickly ran up to us. He called Vince an 'environmental rapist' and threw something."

She laughed and ran her fingers through her hair. "Vince, as usual, thought only of himself. He ducked and ketchup spattered all over my coat. My ranch mink. Vince bought it with some of the money I inherited from my grandmother. He was generous that way."

She laughed again. "Well, Vince called somebody from your office and tried to file charges, but I was the one who'd been assaulted, and I refused." She paused to stare out the kitchen window at the ocean. "You see, that incident finally made me see Vince in a clear light. He cared more about himself than anything or anyone. I told him I wanted a divorce just as soon as we could manage it. I'm Catholic, you see, so these things can be difficult. Vince said if I tried to dump him he'd declare bankruptcy and I'd lose everything. We compromised on a separation and I moved back to Chicago."

She sipped coffee. "A few weeks later I got a letter from Adam. He said he felt bad about hitting me, but he wanted me to know about animal cruelty, so he sent me some literature. When I was done reading, I took that coat out of the closet and gave it to charity. Then I took a long look in the mirror. I saw a greedy woman who'd stayed married to a horrible man simply to protect her investment. I started annulment proceedings, and then I wrote to Adam and apologized for Vince's lousy existence and my insensitivity. He wrote back to me and I wrote back to him and . . . we became friends."

Friends. Right.

"We met every other month. Sometimes in Chicago, sometimes in Portland. Or in between. Last fall we spent a week backpacking in Yellowstone." She shrugged and looked around the kitchen. "Gradually we realized we'd fallen in love."

Enough of this fairy tale. "Did your husband know about this?"

"Oh, no. We were very careful. No one in Devil's Harbor knew."

Right. In a town of busybodies, no one knew a thing. "Did he know you were going ahead with trying to annul your marriage?"

"Yes, he did." She unconsciously chewed at her lip. "He was notified." She looked directly into Greg's eyes. "But I didn't kill him. And neither did Adam. Like I told Molly, we were prepared to go on as we had been."

"It's convenient that you didn't have to."

"Yes," she said without registering his sarcasm. "It is. But we didn't kill him. You believe me, don't you?"

How many times had he heard that question from a suspect? "I believe only what I can verify, ma'am." Greg took a final swallow of his coffee. He stood and started toward the door. If he could place her or Adam Quarles in Devil's Harbor on Saturday night, he'd turn up the heat. "I'll be in touch. Don't leave the area."

He clattered down the steps to his cruiser, intending to find Molly Donovan and tell her to butt out of his investigation.

I knotted a length of string and cut the free ends as my father looped another section of garland along the rail—strands of mock evergreen with silver-blue tinsel and white lights wound among them. "This is getting pretty ratty. I thought you planned to buy new decorations this year."

"I did. Until Grabowski came down here acting like a four-star general and ordered me to."

I tied another knot and clipped the string, tucking the ends into my pocket and ignoring the chance to ask again about the Saturday-night argument with Grabowski. Why continue to beat my head on that door if it wouldn't open?

"And this afternoon His Porkiness started riding my ass about it: 'We have to put our best foot forward this year,' he tells me, 'we're getting special attention. It's important we show the world our community spirit.' As if the damn festival's beamed on some worldwide satellite link. The runty little son-of-a-bitch can kiss my ass. He's lucky I'm taking the *Helen* out at all."

"But Dad, you love the parade of ships." I tried to settle him down before his blood pressure shot up. "It was your idea. And you'll have the lead position this year."

"Big frigging deal. Year after year. The same stupid people doing the same stupid things and the mayor strutting around like a pot-bellied rooster with hemorrhoids."

I tied the last knot and sent up a trial balloon to see just how serious he was. "Then why don't you put the *Helen* and the house up for sale? With the inflated prices for coast property, you'd come out with a pretty good chunk of change. Take the interest from that, and your Social Security check, and you could afford to live almost anywhere. How about the South? Florida, maybe? Or you could move to Albuquerque. Be my roommate."

I didn't know I'd thought it until I said it. But I liked the idea. I could resume my career and keep an eye on Dad's health at the same time.

He stopped unpacking the box of whirligigs destined for the roof of the cabin and a smile softened his lips. "Why the hell would I leave, Molly? There's no place better on earth. We've got sun and sand and all that ocean, birds and fish and storms."

"Yep. Sixty-five inches of rain a year. Four months when the sky's so gray and the fog's so dense the town looks like an old black and white photograph. Mold spores so thick in the air we can barely breathe. It's a little piece of paradise, all right." I moved to the bench in the stern and began turning the cushions, putting the sun-faded sides down.

"Your mother loved this town." His voice was slow and sad. "I don't understand why you don't. Or why you're mad at Jeff. He's a nice boy."

"He's a man, Dad. Not a boy." I turned another cushion. "And I'm not mad at him." That was true, I realized. I wasn't.

"Well, it just seems to me that you two—"

"Listen, Dad. I know you'd like me to settle down and give you some grandkids." I gave him a quick hug. "But I'm not ready yet." I returned to the stern, grabbed the last cushion and flipped it. Something beneath it flashed in the sunlight. Pulling the cushion off, I retrieved a gold chain.

Dad pointed at it. "What's that?"

"I don't know. Something one of your charter folks left, I guess."

The medallion on the chain spun in the breeze—a stylized "G" set with tiny diamonds. G for Grabowski. "Oh, no."

"What is it?" My father stood and took a step toward me.

"It's evidence," a voice said. "That's what it is."

I spun as Greg Erdman vaulted the rail and held up his hand like a traffic cop. "Sorry, Molly, but I've got to take that to the lab." He fished a plastic bag from his pocket. "Put it in here."

Gritting my teeth, I let the chain and medallion drop into the bag with a sound like death rattle. "This doesn't mean a thing. My father didn't—"

"That's what I'll have to ask him." He folded the envelope and slipped it into his shirt pocket. "Looks like you'll be taking another ride, Mr. Donovan. You told me Grabowski never came aboard the *Helen*." He shook the bag. "You lied."

I stepped between them. "Anyone could have put that chain there."

"It's okay, Molly." My father laid an arm across my shoulders. "I'll be back in no time." He kissed my cheek and headed for the ladder.

I glared at Greg. "I'm going to call a lawyer."

"That's your legal right, Molly. By the way, you have to get off the boat. It could be a crime scene." He started across the dock toward the parking lot, steering my father by his elbow. "I'll send a deputy down to keep an eye on it. And we'll impound your father's truck, too. I'll be back with a warrant."

I watched Greg help my father into the back seat of the cruiser, and then I dug for my cell phone to call Chuck Yamamoto.

NINETEEN

Margaret scooted past with a defiant "meorrw" as Henri Trevelle opened the door to his shop. Hefting a bucket of marked-up whirligigs out to the sidewalk for the tourist trade, he called after her, "If you're not home by seven, you'll be out all night in the cold, you little trollop. Daddy's dance card is full. I don't have time to chase you around town."

He flipped around the open sign in the window, got a bottle of glass cleaner and a wad of newspaper, and wiped grubby fingerprints from the display cases. Some of the smudges looked suspiciously like that new flavor of ice cream Icky had stocked for the festival: Whirligig Whirlwind Ripple. It stuck like glue and Henri wondered if that might be one of the ingredients. Adam claimed it tasted like a mouthful of jellyfish, but tiny tourists loved it.

Squatting, Henri sprayed a stubborn smear. Was it too early to call Molly? According to Jeffrey, the tight-assed sergeant with the yummy shoulders had hauled Mike off again yesterday afternoon, and this time actually booked him on suspicion of murder. Maybelline, who got her information from her husband, said Molly had vowed to sue the socks off of Sergeant Greg Erdman and bring the real killer to justice.

The bell over the door jingled and he watched two pairs of black shoes and two pairs of dusty black trousers approach.

183

"Excuse me; do you carry nine-volt batteries?"

Henri hauled himself up and studied the men he'd heard rumors about. Were those the tackiest off-the-rack suits, or what? And the eyebrows on the tall one! If these guys were Secret Service, he was a perfect size twelve. They might work for the government, but he'd bet his bunny slippers that they'd never been any closer to the President than he had.

"Batteries? Certainly. If you can wait a moment. They're in the back." Where the little tourist children can't pilfer them, he thought as he bustled off. "Back in a tick," he chirped over his shoulder. "Browse to your heart's content."

He chuckled at the image of them soberly pawing through tourist trinkets, but much to his surprise, that's what they were doing when he returned. The shorter one clutched a T-shirt emblazoned with the words "I'm with stupid," and the tall one seemed to be torn between a clamshell nightlight and a seagull tape dispenser.

"Those are very popular this year," Henri offered. "*C'est vrai.* I've sold more than I ever imagined." And that's not a lie, he thought, remembering his one sale to Elspeth Hunsaker who'd been convinced the bird was a dove.

"Hmmm." The tall man raised a questioning eyebrow at his companion who shrugged and dug through the rack of T-shirts.

Take your time," Henri urged. "I'm open until six." He straightened the miniature whirligig lapel pins stuck in a coffee cup beside the cash register. "Are you staying for the festival?"

"When's that?" The shorter one held his T-shirt against his chest.

Definitely government types, Henri thought. They've been in town for two days and haven't noticed the posters and banners and the platoon of whirligigs marching down the highway. Or else they're playing dumb. "It starts tonight with a cocktail party." He leaned over the counter conspiratorially. "That's for locals and invited guests, but perhaps the mayor could arrange tickets for you." And wet his pants in the process.

The men exchanged glances, and the tall one elevated a bushy eyebrow again. "Cocktail party?"

Henri remembered one of the first rumors, that the men were checking liquor licenses. "Oh, it's all legal. We get a permit, or something." He giggled. "Although it would be amusing if someone forgot that little detail and we found ourselves arrested and handcuffed." He suppressed a shiver of excitement at the thought.

Neither man laughed. The tall one shifted back and forth as if his shoes didn't fit. The shorter one twitched lips the width of the rubber bands on the wilting broccoli at the Come On 'n' Get It.

"After everyone's loosened up, we send out the parade of ships." Henri heard himself prattle on. "Quite spectacular, really. Those twinkling lights on that inky black water. And after that, the evening's main event, the belly-bucking competition at the local watering hole." He ran a hand over his moussed hair. "I'll be the ringmaster and emcee for that. And then Saturday morning, of course, there's the whirligig parade—floats, marching bands, the mounted posse with their horses pooping everywhere. And in the evening we crown the festival queen and trip the light fantastic in the school gym, then sober up at the pancake breakfast on Sunday. It's not at all cosmopolitan, but it's quite the highlight of life in Devil's Harbor, so we make the best of it."

The men traded sidelong glances again and the short one laid the T-shirt on the counter and pulled a small spiral notebook and pen from an inside pocket. "You lived here long?"

Henri narrowed his eyes. "Is this an official inquiry?"

The men eyeballed each other; then the shorter one spoke. "Let's call it a fact-finding mission."

Henri considered pressing them, but decided to bide his time. "Five years and two weeks tomorrow. I came here shortly after I hung up my skates." He nodded toward the poster behind him. "That's me in all my glory."

The two men looked up at the poster, then back at Henri, then did a tandem double-take. "Five years." The shorter man's tongue followed the pen as he wrote.

The tall one inspected the poster again, and then studied Henri. "You must know a lot of the townspeople."

"*Certainement*. I know them all." He watched the short man hurriedly write that down. These guys weren't with a law enforcement agency. They hadn't shown any interest in his guns or in that sweet little potted plant he'd gotten from Icky and set in the front window—the one he intended to swear was an hybrid tomato if anyone ever asked.

"How would you say people in town obtain news and information about local and regional events?"

What a strange question. "They gossip. All day, every day. *Tout le monde*. They set the phone wires on fire."

The men looked at each other and the tall one cleared his throat. "Any other sources? Like newspapers? Television? Radio?"

Henri laughed. "The only area newspaper is *The Flotsam*. It comes out on Wednesday and Sunday. The motto should be 'two days a week and two days behind.' If you don't have cable or a satellite dish, you get only snow on your television set, and if it weren't for Vince Grabowski's murder and last winter's mud slide, no television reporter could find Devil's Harbor on a map of Oregon. And as far as radio is concerned, well, the headlands block most of the signals, so about all you can pick up is KYMR and up-to-the-minute news for Elspeth Hunsaker is a list of who got off the ark with Noah. The last sports score I heard on her station was David one, Goliath nothing."

The tall man didn't crack a smile. "So, you'd say Devil's Harbor needs better media communication?"

Henri shook his head. "No. Not at all."

"No?" Slack-jawed, the men stared at Henri. "Why not?"

"Because people here enjoy being out of touch with the world. This is a backwater. And with a few exceptions, one of them now deceased, we prefer it that way." Henri unlocked the cabinet behind him, took down a rifle, and began running a rag over the stock. "Who are you and what you're doing here?"

"Um," the short one swallowed and clicked his pen.

"We're both sociologists," the tall one supplied. "We're gathering information on small town communications for a local university."

Henri sighted through the scope and flicked dust from the barrel. "Which university?"

The men winced and exchanged glances.

Henri laid the rifle across the counter and pulled out a box of ammunition. "Such nonsense. Tell me who you really are."

The short one swallowed twice, sucked the end of his pen and lowered his eyes to the rifle. The tall one measured the distance to the door, then dragged his eyes back to Henri. He shrugged. "All right. But it's privileged information. You're sworn to secrecy."

Henri danced onto his toes and ran an index finger across his mouth. "My lips are zipped."

Shelley Perkins pushed open the door of the Sweete Temptations Ice Creame Shoppe and looked around. Where the heck was Icky Ferris? He'd promised to deliver three gallons of ice cream to the Devil's Food Cafe at 9:00, but hadn't shown up. Now it was 11:15. What a pain! The lunch rush would begin any second and they were down to a pint of Venomous Vanilla Bean and a few scrapings of Brimstone Brickle. Shelley never ate ice cream because of the calories, but the lunch special printed on the blackboard promised strawberry pie a la mode, so here she was.

Slamming the door with a satisfying jangle, she marched to the counter and hammered the button on top of a silver bell. She intended to give Icky a piece of her mind. Maybe goad him into actually saying something. She didn't know how Jennifer, who was like the ultimate chatterbox, could work for a man who doled out syllables like diamonds. She waited, examining her fingernails, wondering if she should apply a fresh coat of polish after lunch or wait until just before the cocktail party. And what about her hair? Should she put it up, or curl it and let it fly loose? She decided she'd ask Henri what he thought once the lunch rush was over.

She slapped the bell again. "Icky! Icky Ferris! I need ice cream! Now!"

Something on the floor behind the counter shifted and moaned. She stood on tiptoe and spied Icky, wrapped in a blanket and curled up on a thick rubber mat.

"Icky? Are you okay?"

He moaned again. His eyelids fluttered.

"Icky?" She darted around the counter and knelt beside him, putting two fingers against his neck to check his pulse. It was strong and regular. Maybe he'd smoked himself into a coma. "Icky!" She patted his cheeks and he moaned again. "Icky, wake up!"

She stood, slid open the case and grabbed an ice cream scoop. Gouging out a heavy and very gooey scoop full of Beelzebub Bubblegum, she dropped it on Icky's forehead.

"Whaaaa?" Flailing at his face, he swiped the pink glob from his eyes, then sat up, blinking.

"'He lives, he wakes—'tis Death is dead, not he; Mourn not for Adonais.'"

Icky stared at her for a moment, blinked again, then struggled to his feet. "That's Shelley."

"I know." She pulled a couple of sheets of paper towel off a roll by the sink and handed them to him, then yanked off more and cleaned the mat.

"That's from 'Adonais,' his Elegy to John Keats."

"The very one." Shelley tossed the dirty towels into a small wastebasket at the end of the counter. "What were you doing down there?"

"Uh, meditating. I didn't think anyone in town except me and Jeffrey read poetry. Especially not—"

"Especially not me?" Shelley glared at him. "Because I have blond hair? Because everyone says I—"

"No." Icky put two fingers against her lips. "Because I'm stupid and insensitive. Please forgive me."

His fingers seemed to burn against her mouth. "Um . . . okay."

"Shelley's my favorite poet of all time." He removed his hand and wiped his face.

"Mine too." She dipped another towel into the tub of water that held the scoops and used it to blot ice cream from his faded black T-shirt. "No one speaks to me like he does."

"Really? That's how I feel, too. 'Make me a lyre, even as the forest is: What if my leaves are falling like its own!'"

Shelley felt a tingle at the base of her spine. She smiled and wiped a small smear of ice cream from the corner of his mouth. "'Drive my dead thoughts over the universe, like withered leaves to quicken a new birth!'"

Icky took her hand, bowed a little, and then kissed each knuckle. "'Teach me half the gladness that thy brain must know.'"

Her skin felt fiery, her legs wobbled. "'Our sweetest songs are those that tell of saddest thought,'" she gasped.

He sighed, drew her into his arms and slowly laid a trail of soft kisses down her forehead, across her cheeks and onto her lips.

Shelley's breath caught in her throat. Was this how it was supposed to feel? Like a warm whirlpool? She closed her eyes as they kissed, something she'd never done before, and sucked the taste of ice cream from his mouth.

"Why didn't you tell me Grabowski had been on the boat? Why didn't you tell Sergeant Erdman that the first time he questioned you? What were you thinking, Dad?"

Chuck Yamamoto laid a hand on my arm and Dad inched his chair away from the rickety wooden table in the jail visitors' room. "Now, Molly."

"Don't 'now, Molly,' me." I brushed off Chuck's hand. "I'm trying to help you."

Dad put on the indulgent smile he'd perfected when I was six, the one that made my blood boil. "And don't give me that smile. This situation is scary, Dad. All this circumstantial evidence piling up. There may be others with stronger motives, but right now all Greg Erdman sees is that medallion, and the fact that you seem to have been the last person with Vince Grabowski, and that you lied about him being on the boat."

"It will get straightened out, and meanwhile I'm just fine. I've got the books you brought, special meals so I can stick to my diet, and they gave me a room at the back so it's quiet and—"

"This isn't a motel, Dad!" I pounded that table painted the color of despair, then got control of myself. "It's not a room, it's a cell, and you can't check out until they set bail or clear you!"

"Now, Molly!"

I stood, thought about kicking my chair into the wall, then took a deep breath. "You're not taking this seriously, Dad. You've got to trust me, and Chuck. You've got to tell them what Grabowski said to provoke you. Tell them exactly what happened. Everything!"

My father glanced at Chuck Yamamoto who nodded in agreement. "I'm going outside," I told Chuck. "See if you can talk some sense into him."

I bolted into the hall and nearly collided with Greg. "Having fun, Sergeant Erdman?"

He raised his hands. "Molly, you know I'm just doing my job."

And does your job description maybe read 'jump to stupid conclusions'? I kept my lips zipped and settled for a glare. Dad was in enough trouble.

"It's all about facts. You know that, too." He bit off each word. "Vince Grabowski struggled with your father on board the *Helen* and your father lied about it. No one seems to have seen Grabowski after that."

"Except the real killer," I interrupted.

Greg brushed that aside and forged ahead. "Next fact—your father won't tell us what Grabowski said, but he admits he choked him."

"But he didn't kill him. And he didn't pitch him into the ocean from the headland. He'd have had another heart attack if he tried."

Greg sighed and squeezed the bridge of his nose. "Prisons are full of people who didn't do it. Unless I get a lot more information, your father will have to stay here until he's arraigned Monday morning. If the district attorney agrees to bail, that's fine. If you can raise it, your father can go home."

I studied the gritty floor, remembering my checking account balance. Would a bail bondsman take a house in New Mexico as collateral? A house mortgaged to the hilt?

"You can talk to him on the phone whenever you want. Because of his age and condition, we're bending all the rules to make him comfortable." He stretched a hand toward my shoulder, but didn't touch me. "I'm sorry it worked out this way, Molly. Let Barbara Sue know when you're ready and she'll call a deputy to escort your father back to his cell." He hesitated, then raised the hand in a half-salute and walked away.

Facts, I fumed. You want facts. I'll get you facts. I'll do your job for you. I'll get you the killer if I have to turn Devil's Harbor inside out. I'll—

The door opened and Chuck stuck his head out. "Your father wishes to speak with you urgently. He requires your help. I will wait in the lobby."

I hurtled into the room. "What is it?"

He gripped my hands. "Molly, I need you to promise me something. Promise you'll do what I ask."

The daughter in me started to say "yes," but the reporter held back. "What am I promising?"

"Don't ask. Just promise." His voice had the tired but resigned tone people get when they talk about death and I felt my stomach clench and my pulse begin to race. I felt the warm roughness of his skin, the smooth ridge of the wedding ring he'd put on more than forty years ago.

"Tell me what it is."

"Please, Molly, just say you'll do what I ask." Tears welled up in his eyes.

I couldn't hold out against that. "Okay. What is it?"

He snuffled into his shirt and his voice emerged as a hoarse and halting whisper. "Sergeant Erdman says they've finished searching the *Helen* and we can use her again." He clutched my hands. "Jeff will take her out for the parade of ships. Please go with him. It will be dark when he brings her in."

He didn't say any more, but I knew what he was thinking—Jeffrey had only run the channel in daylight. If Dad lost the *Helen* on top of everything else it would kill him. I cursed the corner he'd painted me into and answered through gritted teeth. "Okay."

TWENTY

Jeffrey Wolfe tipped the delivery service driver, and then hauled two bulky boxes up to his apartment, set them on the sofa, and unfolded his pocket knife.

"I hope this works," he muttered as he sliced the tape. If it didn't, he'd be a huge laughingstock, emotionally tarred and feathered, and without even enough cash to leave town. He'd invested the last of his meager savings in the contents of these boxes and, with Mike Donovan in jail; he wouldn't get a paycheck any time soon. Icky sometimes held his rent checks for two or three months before cashing them; he probably wouldn't notice if Jeffrey fell behind. But food would be a problem. Up until two days ago, he might have been able to run tabs at the Devil's Food Cafe and the Belly Up Bar. But now that the whole town knew Prudence Deeds had followed him home . . .

He shoveled foam crinkles from one of the boxes, pulled out an oblong glass container, and set it on the coffee table. It looked large enough and the gasket appeared strong enough to take the weather. He decided he would add windshield sealant for insurance.

He yanked open the second box, flinging aside a wad of tissue paper. The hue of the device inside reminded him of the "flesh-colored" crayons he'd had as a child—they always kept their points long after the reds, blues, and greens had been worn to nubs and ground into the carpet. He pulled the object out, walked to the bedroom, and held it up in front of the mirror. "Bizarre," he muttered, turning it upside down, then backwards.

"I'll pull this off, or I'll make a complete ass out of myself. Maybe both."

He flung the object on the bed and walked to the cramped kitchen to scrape something out of the refrigerator for lunch. It wasn't like love hadn't driven him to action in the past, but those actions had been the kind of soul-baring, ego-humbling, walking-through-fire deeds that inspired poetry worthy of Whitman. If verse sprang from this, he thought, it would be along the lines of limericks etched above toilet paper dispensers in public restrooms. Something beginning, "A poet who'd run out of luck . . ."

"Good morning, good morning, good morning. And a wonderful morning it is," Elspeth trilled into the microphone. Today's show would be special. She'd warn them of impending doom. They'd *have* to listen.

"I'm Elspeth Hunsaker, inviting you to join me here on KYMR. She played the recorded jingle and waited for her faithful listeners to write down the number knowing that her spiritual bombshell would send them racing to their phones. "Yes, it's a glorious morning beside the rolling Pacific Ocean. But although the sun shines, I am here to tell you, brothers and sisters, that all is not well!" She thumped the console for emphasis.

Just like the big time soothsayers on television she, Elspeth Hunsaker, was about to say some sooth that would swivel heads. "Our time is running out, friends and neighbors. Stalking our streets, are two men clad in black. Two men who make notes of everything they see and hear. And what *do* they see? Sniveling sinners teetering on the rim of the burning pit, sinners with one chance at redemption who refuse to seize it! And what do they hear? They hear the glorification of Lucifer!"

She thumped the console again, and then rubbed the edge of her hand. Perhaps she should invest in a set of those sound effect recordings. Maybe use a thunderclap for punctuation. Yes! A stroke of genius. She scribbled a note on a blank white pad beside the console. When she talked about damnation, she'd use that sizzling sound lightning makes. To remind them what would happen to their souls if they continued to ignore her.

"We must change the name of this community, and we must do it today. This very minute. We must petition Mayor Deeds and demand that he cast the symbols of Satan, the pennants and cups and banners and T-shirts, yes, even the whirligigs bearing that blasphemous name, into the sea. Demand that he ban the swilling of demon rum and the grotesque spectacle of pagan competition scheduled for this eve—"

"Ah, I see we have a phone call." Elspeth punched the button with a trembling finger. "You're on the air, caller."

"Elspeth! Elspeth, this is Mayor Deeds! Are we on the air?"

"Yes. Everyone can hear you, Mayor. I was just talking about you."

"I know you were. That's why I called."

Elspeth ran a hand over her hair and sat up straighter. The mayor listened! She felt a tingle of elation. She'd arrived!

"Elspeth, I've tolerated your petition to change the name of Devil's Harbor. I've put up with you making the same monotonous, simple-minded comments at every single city council meeting, and your ridiculous efforts to have the school ban practically every book including the dictionary. But this harebrained theory about those men is the limit!"

Elspeth clenched her fists. Now who was *he* to be talking about harebrained ideas?

"Those men are with the Secret Service, you nitwit!" Deeds' voice rose to an eardrum-shattering howl. "They're here to secure the town so the President can attend the Whirligig Festival!"

Audio needles pegged into the red. Elspeth clutched at the volume knob.

"And another thing. If you, or anyone else, comes down to my market and harangues me about changing the name of the town one more time, I'll call the sheriff and have you arrested for creating a public nuisance. And while I'm at it, I'll have—"

Bwaaaaaat!

Elspeth let the dial tone hum for a few seconds, then disconnected the line. "I apologize for that, Mayor Deeds; we're experiencing some technical difficulties here at KYMR. I hope you'll call back so we can continue our conversation." Like I hope a bolt of lightning will come through the ceiling and strike my chair. "And now, let's listen to this message from the D River Excursion Company."

She killed the mike, punched the commercial cart and leaned back in her chair, listening to the first few words of the spot: "Why should a river-rafting trip be exhausting? Why should it take all day? The world's shortest River, the D River, measures only one hundred twenty feet and . . ."

Elspeth lowered the volume. She refused to believe the mayor. Those men must be emissaries of the devil. How else could you explain those suits?

As the commercial ended, the phone button twinkled; she reached for it, but then hesitated. She wouldn't give Mayor

Deeds any more airtime. But what if some desperate sinner had dialed her? She punched the button and took the call off-air.

"Elspeth? Elspeth is that you, dear?" The voice quavered and dissolved into a delicate cat-like sneeze.

Not the mayor! The commercial ended and Elspeth opened her mike and put the caller on the air. "Go ahead, caller."

"Oh, thank goodness. For a moment I was certain I'd dialed the wrong number. It's these new trifocals, you see. I don't know how that doctor expects me to see when I have to keep flopping my head up and down trying to get the lines in the right place. Why yesterday I discovered I'd been cleaning all my windows with hair spray. And the day before, the paramedics came because of that unfortunate incident with the tub and tile caulk and my dentures. The tube looks very much like the toothpaste, you see, and so I—"

Bwaaatttt.

"Thank you for calling." Elspeth didn't want to hear how *that* turned out. Had these cranks been sent to test her? She slapped in a public service announcement for the beach clean-up to fill time while she regained her composure. In a moment she saw another telephone line light up. This one would be genuine. She just knew it.

She opened her microphone as the announcement ended. "And we're back talking with another of our faithful listeners. You're on the air, caller."

"Why, thank you Elspeth. You are such a dear. Such a beacon of truth for this community." The voice was female, and firm, with a touch of a British accent.

Elspeth relaxed. Finally, someone with some sense. And some culture.

"Elspeth, I don't believe for a minute that those men are from the Secret Service."

Elspeth beamed. Finally, someone to back her up.

"They don't look at all like Clint Eastwood did in that movie. You know the one I mean?" The British accent dropped away. The voice began to quaver. "The one where he has the ice cream cone at the end. Or was it one of those frozen juice things? Oh, well, that doesn't really matter, does it? Because the point is that . . . The point is . . . Well, never mind. Have I told you about the tub and tile caulk and my trifocals?"

Bwaaaaatttt.

Once again I stared at that damn blinking cursor, willing words onto the screen. I'd finished the piece about preparations for the Whirligig Festival, including thumbnail sketches of the five contestants vying for the title of Festival Queen and the interview with Big Billy Bohannon on what it takes to be a belly-bucking champion and his training diet. My stomach rumbled in rebellion as I scanned the list of what he ate. No matter what Ben Galloway said about details being crucial, even readers of *The Flotsam* didn't deserve to suffer through the entire menu. I edited copiously with the "delete" key. Let the beer, pork rinds, raw onions, and jalapeno dip speak for the rest.

I glanced at my watch. Forty-five minutes until Ben Galloway called and started chewing on my butt if my copy wasn't in. Five and a half hours until the stupid dockside party that preceded the parade of ships. What a joke. Canapes, cocktails, and the scent of low tide. I glanced at my watch again. Forty-four minutes. Kicking back the chair, I paced into the kitchen and back again.

"Unbiased," I told myself. "I'm supposed to be unbiased. So even though my father's behind bars, I have to present a complete and fair look at the murder investigation and his arrest."

"Hah!" I slumped into the chair again. Greg Erdman couldn't tell circumstantial evidence from clam chowder. And that's all he had against Dad, circumstantial evidence: the fight, the mark on Grabowski's neck, and the medallion I'd found under the cushions.

I sat up straight, nerves tingling. "If Dad used it to strangle Grabowski, why didn't he get rid of it? All he had to do was drop it over the side. And why hadn't that thin chain snapped?"

I closed my eyes, trying to recall every detail. The clasp had been fastened, no question about that. And when I'd handed it to Greg, all the links were intact. And the chain was short—too short to fit over a man's head.

I was certain Dad was innocent, so if that chain had been around Grabowski's neck Saturday night, there were three possibilities: Someone had strangled Grabowski without damaging the chain and then removed it before dumping him off the cliff; the chain had broken in the struggle and someone had repaired it; or the chain had broken and someone had substituted another. Part two of each scenario was that someone had planted the chain and medallion on the *Helen* to frame my father.

I reached for the phone. It might not be enough to convince Greg Erdman, but I'd feel better if I told my theory to Chuck Yamamoto.

TWENTY ONE

Mayor Brighton Deeds sucked in as much of his gut as he could, tugged his vest down, hoisted his double chin high, and marched between rows of sluggishly twirling whirligigs to the dock. Wisps of mist slipped across the bay and a solid bank of clouds loomed on the horizon. He hoped the President arrived before that damn foghorn started blatting, obliterating what passed for ambiance down here.

He tugged at his vest again, ran a finger under his collar, and glanced at the sky. Weather forecasters on the Portland television stations called for rain, but the storm could slip by to the north.

He crossed his stubby fingers. Please let the President see Devil's Harbor in the best possible light. And quickly, too, before the residents slugged down so much liquor they forgot their best-behavior pledges. Not that he'd ever witnessed *any* of them displaying what he'd call good manners. Loaded or not, they generally sniped at each other almost as much as they sniped at him. He palmed back greasy hair. No one appreciated the difficulty of holding a position of leadership and power without aides or assistants. It would be easier once he got to Washington and had people on his payroll to read up on issues and tell him how to vote.

He reached the dock and nodded to Chuck Yamamoto who offered a tray of drinks. The liquid looked venomous. Frothing greenish blue. And what was with those ice cubes? Were they yellow or was that his imagination?

"We call it a high tide hummer," Chuck informed him. "Maybelline's creation. It symbolizes the ocean and the sun from which we draw all life."

Deeds nodded, put the glass to his lips and took enough of a sip to make Chuck move on to Gus Custer who ambled up in a pair of coveralls that smelled like mothballed canvas. Deeds stalked away, swallowing his drink in two gulps. How the hell did Gus get on the list? Did he just invite himself? Why the hell was he, Brighton Deeds the Third, the only person worried about the important stuff, the only one who cared what the rest of the world thought?

And what was this? Deeds squinted in dismay at a custom-made whirligig featuring a porky man riding what appeared to be an ice-scraper and holding a twirling fish in each hand. He plucked it from its bracket and flung it over the railing. Damn Gus Custer. This was his dirty work.

Deeds patted his wallet and looked around for Big Billy Bohannon. For a hundred bucks, he might be persuaded to take Gus for a walk. A one-way walk.

Chuck hurried by with the tray and Deeds snagged another drink. If he held his breath and swallowed fast they weren't bad. And they certainly weren't weak. After last year's debacle, when Harlan Winkle got stinko and announced that State Senator Coogan's wife had a great set of hooters, he'd told Maybelline to ease back on the alcohol content. But no one in this town seemed to give a rip about his opinion. What the hell, with the fog growing thicker by the minute, a few tots of rum could take the chill off.

"Good evening, Mayor." Bart Yamamoto and Jennifer Daley pranced up, offering trays of appetizers.

Deeds studied the violet, orange, and cerise spreads piled on crackers and topped with olives, cocktail onions, pickled lima beans, salami, and something that resembled raw fish. He regretted using the expression "be creative" when LaDonna had asked what she should make. Why hadn't he insisted on those smoked cocktail weenies he liked so much? Or some of that cheese in a can spritzed onto potato chips? My God, if the President saw this kaleidoscope of slop he'd probably climb right back into his helicopter. Deeds peered at the thickening sky wondering if a helicopter could even land in this soup.

"Aren't these cool?" Jennifer grinned and pointed to an orange pile topped with a pickled beet slice. "LaDonna says the colors represent the stones polished by the tide and tossed on the sand like a necklace for a sea goddess. Isn't that just awesome? I hope the President likes them." She plucked off a purple one topped with a radish and gulped it down.

Deeds did the same with his drink and looked around for Chuck. He'd need another before he got to the dessert cart and risked a peek at what Shelley Perkins had prepared and learned what it signified. He peered around and spotted his wife, standing at the edge of a small cluster of people, laughing at something that Jeffrey What's-his-name, the poet was saying. What did she see in him, anyway? He didn't have any money. He wasn't a mover and shaker like Grabowski. He crewed for Mike Donovan and camped out over Icky's place and the whole town knew she'd spent the night there.

Deeds felt his face redden. Well, they'd be in Washington soon enough. She'd see her husband dealing and wheeling and get so turned on her underwear would scorch. What did they say about power being the ultimate something?

Afro-freezy-ack? Effru-Hackensack? What was that word, anyway? Whatever, it meant Brighton Deeds the Third would be getting lucky. Soon.

"Refill!" Deeds bellowed to Chuck.

He took two drinks from the tray. Weird, but tasty. He drained half of one. He'd have to compliment Mayllabine. No. Maynelleebe. Damn. Maybelline. There.

LaDonna Perkins spooned a dollop of orange glop onto a cracker and topped it with a Brazil nut.

"Those are so unique," Maybelline told her as she shook up another batch of drinks. "And yummy. What did you use, anyway? I've had three, but I can't decide whether you ground up shrimp or scallops or both."

"Neither," LaDonna grinned. "Not on the budget His Stinginess set: a dollar a person for hors d'oeuvres and desserts. You couldn't cater an anorexia convention for that!" She topped off another cracker with a chocolate-covered raisin. "And his wife's a social-climbing shrew! Told me I should buy lobster and cover the extra cost out of my own pocket!"

"Yeah, she mentioned French champagne to me," Maybelline laughed. "I'd tell you what I told her, but it might burn your ears."

LaDonna giggled. Topping off another cracker with a carrot twist, she offered it to Maybelline. "It's just tofu salad and that phony crab," she whispered. "Crab with a K."

"Get out of here!" Maybelline bit into the cracker and chewed. "Really?"

"Really. Toss in enough green onion and hot sauce and mustard, lay a bunch of artistic leftovers on top, and you can fool anyone."

"Well, you sure faked me out." Maybelline poured her mixture into an array of plastic cocktail glasses. "Next it will be filet mignon with a PH."

"Exactly," LaDonna chuckled. "But I couldn't have done it without those." She pointed at the brimming glasses. "Momma always said the secret of a good dinner party was cocktails. By the time the guests sit down, you can dish up cat food on toast."

She nodded across the dock at the dessert cart where Shelley presided. "Same with the desserts. That mousse is just instant pudding and whipped topping and that cake is from a mix I got at a warehouse store over in Portland. The cookies are the real thing, though, white chocolate and macadamia nuts. Shelley blew the budget, but I couldn't say no because she was so happy: dancing around the kitchen, even singing while she washed up."

"Hmmm." Maybelline loaded the glasses on a tray and handed it off to Chuck, then looked across the dock. "Hey, isn't that Icky Ferris?"

"Where?"

"Over there with Shelley. The one she's feeding that pudding to."

"It can't be." LaDonna studied the man in the flowing yellow embroidered shirt who grinned at Shelley between bites. "Icky always wears black. And he never smiles."

"He never talks, either, but he's chattering up a storm. And it appears he's washed his hair."

They stood on tiptoe for a better look. "It could be Icky," LaDonna admitted.

Maybelline watched as the man stroked Shelley's cheek, fed her a bite of cake and followed it with a kiss. "I bet you'll be seeing more of him." She patted her friend's arm. "And I'll bet you get a discount on ice cream."

"And this is Gus Custer, our resident whirligig wizard," Adam said.

Claire Grabowski reached for Gus' gnarled hand and shook it with both of hers. "Adam has told me so much about you."

Gus grunted and tried to pull his hand away. Claire held on. "I know what you must be thinking." She glanced at Adam for support. "That because I married Vincent Grabowski I'm the same kind of person. Well, I'm not!" She tightened her grip. "This morning I tore up that contract Vince made you sign. And I have a proposition if you'd care to listen."

Gus narrowed his eyes and pulled his hand free. "No."

"Aw, give her a minute, man." Adam laid a hand on Gus' shoulder. "What could it hurt? I'll get you another drink."

Gus grunted and Adam trotted off to find Chuck Yamamoto. Claire shifted from foot to foot, trying to decide how to convince this old curmudgeon she meant well. She knew that more went on behind his clouded blue eyes than most people suspected.

"Mr. Custer. I'm painfully aware of the shoddy way my husband treated you. Between lying about his intentions for your property and shackling you to that sham of a factory, well…" She lowered her voice to a whisper. "All I can say is that if you pushed Vince off the cliff, I wouldn't blame you."

Gus grunted, finished his drink, and set the plastic glass on the railing.

"I don't know what the situation will be like when the police finish their investigation, but I want you to know I intend to use any resources I can salvage to try to right the wrongs he inflicted on this community. And on you."

Gus spat into the water. With a nod he accepted a drink from Adam who slung his arm around Claire's shoulders.

Claire plunged on. "Adam told me you're a genius with wood and stone. I believe that art, genuine art, expresses and defines our culture. I'd like to enable you to express yourself in a way that would benefit all of us."

Gus snorted, shook his head and started to turn away, but Adam clutched his shoulder again. "Just one more minute. Okay?"

Gus blinked but said nothing.

Claire took a deep breath. She must sound like such a goody-two-shoes. She wished for once she possessed just an ounce of Vince's salesmanship, a drop of his force of character. But she could offer only the germ of an idea and the desire to do penance for his sins. "When the lawyers finish sorting through Vince's unholy mess, I hope to be able to repay all the investors. I can't promise a profit, but at least I won't declare bankruptcy like Vince intended to do. I'm also going to halt home sales and turn the undeveloped land back to nature."

Gus' lips twitched into a small fraction of a smile.

"In the meantime, I know you need an income. I hope you'll stay on at the factory and—"

"No way in hell!" Gus hurled his plastic glass onto the dock.

"—create your own designs!" Claire yelped. "Oh, I got it all backwards," She turned to Adam and knotted her hands in her hair. "I'm no good at this. He thinks I'm just like Vince and—"

"My own designs?" Gus blinked. His eyes grew clear and sharp.

"Yeah," Adam told him. "We thought you could create limited-edition whirligigs. Like they do with prints and lithographs. Quality, not quantity. We'll sell off that schlock from overseas as fast as possible, and then produce only your designs."

"And the rest of the time you'd work on your sculptures." Claire blotted her eyes with a cocktail napkin. "We'll turn part of the factory into a gallery."

"Maybe we could attract other artists, too. Make it a co-op. A place they could work and show their art, and talk to people who come to watch."

Gus rubbed his chin. "I know a couple might be interested, might even teach classes."

"Yes!" Claire crowed, flinging her arms around both of them. "Oh, that would be fantastic. An artists' colony."

"Yeah," Adam said. "Vince will spin in his grave like a whirligig."

"Won't he just," she giggled.

"Uh, Mrs. Grabowski . . . ?"

Hearing the name she now hated shriveled her enjoyment. "Claire," she insisted.

"Uh, Claire, you know this won't make a big profit."

"No," she admitted. "But profit doesn't matter to me anymore."

"The important thing is that we take back the town. Bring people together," Adam said. "We'll set up a board, get everyone involved. Do it right."

Gus grabbed Claire's hand and shook until her fingers cramped, then marched off across the parking lot.

"The old man's stronger than he looks," she mused as she watched him go. She remembered that he'd never really answered the question she'd never really asked—the one about whether he killed Vince.

I wrapped another cocktail napkin around my plastic glass and wished I'd put on my turtleneck sweater. A light jacket wouldn't cut it when we got underway. Neither would the running shoes I'd slipped into without benefit of socks. After we shoved off, I'd go through the cabinets and see if I could find an old jacket of Dad's and maybe a pair of wool socks that weren't too mildewed. Possibly a knit cap to shut out both the wind and the bleating foghorn.

In the meantime, I'd stand here beside the *Helen* like the invisible woman. Having your father in jail was a conversation stifler. I'd endured dozens of sympathetic looks, and a score of comments about the weather, but no one lingered by my side. Except Prudence Deeds. She'd been pleased as punch to inform me that she, as the mayor's wife, always rode in the lead boat, and she intended to ask Jeffrey if she could "drive."

I'd been tempted to toss my drink in her face, stomping on her toes as I stalked off. Had Dad known about this when he made me promise to go along, or had Prudence cooked it up?

I'd kept my cool, a toothy smile on my face, while I'd fantasized an unfortunate accident: the *Helen* floundering in the bay, passengers leaping into the swells, slapped under by curling waves. My smile had broadened as I imagined a shortage of life preservers. And Prudence with all the buoyancy of the average refrigerator.

But as she'd prattled on about the unfortunate situation with my father, I hadn't been able to keep my mouth shut. In the most pleasant tone of voice I could summon, I'd informed her: "Touch the wheel, Prudence, and I'll use you as an anchor." Still smiling, I'd shoved past her, snagged another drink, and smacked into a tall man in a navy blue suit.

"You must be Molly Donovan."

"Only because somebody has to be," I muttered at the red, white, and blue tie and the "Benton for Congress" button on his lapel.

His forehead wrinkled, but he forged on. "I'm Joe Benton, county commissioner." He mangled my hand like he was wringing out a rag mop. "I haven't seen you at any of our meetings, but I recognized you from your picture in *The Flotsam*. Never miss your stories. Ben Galloway is lucky to have you."

"Really? He doesn't seem convinced of that."

Benton rolled on, seemingly oblivious to my sarcasm. "You must be very excited about the festival."

"Words can't express my feelings." Not the kind of words that wouldn't get me thrown out of public places.

"Ha ha. That's funny. A person who makes her living with words can't find the right ones. Ha ha."

I sucked at my drink. Pretty darned hilarious, all right.

"Well, nice talking to you, Molly. I've got to mingle. Got to press the flesh. Let people see who the best man is."

"Sure thing."

"Say, uh, can you aim me toward Claire Grabowski? I want to offer my profound sympathies."

"She's right over there." I pointed toward the far side of the dock. "Next to the man with the dreadlocks."

He licked his lips. "Ah. She's a very attractive woman. And younger than I thought she'd be."

"Yes." Having an unfaithful two-hundred-pound lump of slime removed from your life could take years off a woman.

"I know this isn't a good time but . . ." Benton leaned down and spoke into my ear. Ordinarily I hate that, but since his breath was warmer than the air, I didn't move away. "Vincent Grabowski promised a contribution to my campaign, and I need to know if she'll honor his commitment."

Even my cold ear perked up. "A contribution?"

"Yes. You see, since I, well, helped expedite a matter for him in the past, and since I have a firm commitment from the party to run for Nathan Sedgewick's seat, he offered to help me out with a sizeable chunk of cash."

"That's interesting." I patted my pockets and remembered I didn't have my tape recorder with me. No note pad, either. "I thought Grabowski planned to back Mayor Deeds for Congress."

"Deeds?" Benton's smile became a puzzled frown. "No, he's always been in my corner, since the day of poor Nathan's funeral." He brushed mist from his lapels and straightened his campaign button. "Now, if you'll excuse me, I do need to speak with Mrs. Grabowski before you all shove off."

He loped away just as Deeds hauled himself up on a crab pot. Had he just assumed he'd had Grabowski's support, or had Vince lied to him? And what about the party commitment? Was Deeds clueless about that, too?

"Ladiesh and gennlemen, frens and neighbors. It is sho wunnerful to see all your schmiling faishes looking up at me." The mayor wobbled; several hands reached out to prop him up. "And wunnerful to be here in Devilsh Harbor for another Whirligug Feshtival."

Jeffrey Wolfe pushed through the crowd to my side. "Boy is he flying."

I ignored him, focused on Deeds.

"Ash your mayor, it givesh me great pride to be here tonight. And I promish that when I am electorated, I will return eesh year to be with you on this schpecial night." His face turned the color of Maybelline's drinks.

"And now, let the parade of schleps, Watergigs on Whirly Water things get, hic, underway." With a final wobble that no one intercepted, he belly flopped to the dock.

With cries of "All right!" and "Let's go!" the crowd surged toward the boats. No one paused to help the mayor who twitched amid a litter of discarded napkins and plastic glasses. Kind of a metaphor for his political career.

"I'll cast off the lines if you want," Jeffrey offered.

"No. You're the captain tonight. I'll get them." I stepped aside and watched him help the guests on board, rolling my eyes when Prudence Deeds pretended to stumble and clutched his arm. Didn't the woman have any shame? When they were settled on the bench in the stern and Jeffrey had the engines humming, I cast off, grabbed the rail, and swung aboard.

Studiously ignoring Prudence, I glanced back to see the mayor flailing to his feet. Dad had stocked wine in a cooler in the cabin, but my hands were too cold to grip the bottle and one look at our guests told me they'd already had enough alcohol. Put wine on top of what Maybelline had mixed up and everyone would spend the evening hanging over the rails up-chucking hors d'oeuvres. Given the color of those things, that wouldn't be pretty. I handed out pinwheels instead.

Decorative lights twinkling, the *Helen* churned toward the channel, whirligigs spinning atop the cabin, tinsel fluttering, and a string of boats chugging in our wake. Even in the fog, and even with my stomach tied in knots of concern for my father, it felt a little magical. Against my will, my lips lifted in a small smile. In a minute we entered the channel and I admitted to myself that Jeffrey knew his stuff. His knuckles shone white against the wheel, but he took us through without a single scrape and we swung out into the bay with the others forming up behind us for a serpentine dance up and down the coast.

"Wheee!" Prudence Deeds had made her way to the prow and leaned against the rail, a pinwheel in each hand, hair flapping in sprayed clumps, sweater dress molded to her body. "It's just like that wonderful movie, isn't it?" She threw her arms out, tilted her head back and screamed into the twilight. "I'm the queen of the world."

Snorting in disgust, I made my way to the cabin. As I dug an aging slicker out of a cabinet, I heard Jeffrey cry out, "Molly! Molly, come up here! Quick."

Shrugging into the slicker I clambered up beside him. "What?"

He pointed to a dark shape lurking in the water about a hundred yards ahead. A shape with flippers and flukes.

"We've got a problem."

TWENTY TWO

Pirouetting in front of the full-length mirror in his bedroom, Henri Trevelle studied the effect of his outfit.

"What do you think, Margaret? Is the cape just a little too-too? I thought that with the basic black turtleneck and slacks I could carry it off. And what about the shoes? The silver platforms?"

The tabby yawned, sat on the gold jumpsuit Henri had removed when he returned from the cocktail party, spread the toes on her right front paw, and groomed them slowly.

"Point well taken." Henri dropped beside her on the puffy satin comforter. "They *do* pinch my toes. And I *will* be on my feet all evening. The jeweled sneakers it is. And maybe just a touch of glitter in the coiffure." He stood, shook the scarlet velvet cape out behind him, and searched the drawers of the antique gold and white dressing table. "Ah, here it is. Now, a touch of hair spray, the glitter, and *voila*! What do you think?"

The tabby purred and kneaded the spread.

"*Merci beaucoup.* I thought so myself. Perfect." Henri saluted his image in the mirror, let himself out the back door of the Gilded Puffin, and headed for the Belly Up and the opening round of the annual belly-bucking competition.

"He's closing fast," I yelled, pointing to the whale that had resurfaced on the starboard side. "Looks like this will be the shortest parade of ships in festival history. Especially with the wind dropping and the fog getting thicker."

Jeffrey snatched the two-way radio microphone from its hook. "*Helen* to parade of ships. *Helen* to parade of ships."

"Oh look. A whale!" Prudence's squeal sliced the fog. "And so close." She waved her pinwheels. "Isn't this exciting?"

A response crackled through the speaker. "Go ahead."

"We have contact with Old Air Biscuit," Jeffrey informed the other captains. "Suggest you hang back and give us some room."

A static-filled string of expletives crackled back.

"Ohhhh. He's disappeared." Prudence leaned over the railing.

"No argument," a voice cackled from the radio. "Take all the room you need."

"Take the whole bay," another voice chimed in.

"Look, he's coming up again." Prudence pointed with a pinwheel. "Right there. Out in front of us."

"Damn!" Jeffrey throttled back as Old Air Biscuit's head rose from the swells. The whale scanned us with one huge eye, winked, then settled back into the water.

"Ohhh. He's gone." Prudence turned toward the cabin, pouting. "Find him, Jeffrey. I want to see him up close again."

Suddenly my miserable little day looked a whole lot brighter. Under the influence of Maybelline's drinks, Prudence seemed to have forgotten that Old Air Biscuit was stalking the *Helen*. "You'll see him, Prudence," I called. "Lean over the rail again."

"Molly, get her out of there before he rises," Jeffrey ordered. "Put her back in the stern with the others. You don't know how bad this is going to be."

I hesitated, childishly considering how much I'd enjoy seeing Prudence hurl her appetizers.

"Oh, look. He's blowing bubbles."

"Damn! Prudence! Get away from the rail!" Jeffrey yelled.

"But the whale—"

"Get away from there now!"

"Owwww." Prudence doubled over.

Jeffrey jumped from the platform. "Take the wheel."

As I did, the noxious odor overwhelmed me. Gagging, I knuckled tears from my eyes. Did marine biologists have special equipment to measure stuff like that?

"Hold your breath, everyone," I called to the guests in the stern. "We're downwind from a forty-mega-whiff whale floofer."

Ignoring a chorus of retching and moaning, I concentrated on the depth finder and the swells ahead of us, breathed through my mouth, and watched Jeffrey grapple with Prudence. What some women won't do to get a man to put his arms around them, I thought, as her knees buckled and she sagged to the deck.

Oddly enough, I found myself feeling jealous of the attention he was giving her—until he slung her over his shoulder. Clambering to the stern, he dumped her on the bench beside an unctuous little man who owned a used car lot out on Highway 101 and whose eyes darted furiously while he clamped both hands over his mouth.

"Take her out, Molly!" Jeffrey headed toward the bridge.

"Out where?"

"Just out!" He pointed to the western horizon. "Now!"

I hit the throttles and felt the *Helen* shudder, then respond. Jeffrey hauled himself up beside me and keyed the microphone.

"*Helen* to *Neptune's Bride*."

"Go ahead, Jeff. Looks like you caught a dose of him."

"A big dose. Listen; lead the boats up the coast. We're going to try to get him away from here."

"Understood. Better you than me."

I gulped down a double lungful of fresh air and looked back to see the other boats dropping away and Old Air Biscuit spyhopping in our wake.

"Slow down," Jeffrey told me as he replaced the microphone. "We don't want to lose him."

I stared in disbelief. "We don't?"

His lips curled. The first time I'd seen him smile at me since soufflé night. I'd forgotten what a nice smile he had.

"Not yet. Keep heading out. I have a plan."

"Does it involve coating Prudence with fish oil and trolling her as bait?"

He rolled his eyes, but smiled again. "No." Then he jumped to the deck, ducked, and disappeared into the cabin.

"Too bad," I muttered to the depth finder.

The *Helen* plowed into a dense fog bank and I peered around nervously, expecting hulking shapes to materialize out of the mist, trawlers or freighters that would mow the *Helen* down. I tried to remember the last time I took the helm. High school, probably. And Dad had never left my side. Fresh tears formed and the wind blew them to the corners of my eyes. He should be here now. Instead of in that miserable jail cell.

"Take a slow turn to port now, Molly. Then head due south. I'll relieve you as soon as I get this set up."

"No need," I lied as I turned the wheel. A rocky cape jutted somewhere to the south. Would I be able to see the lighthouse through the fog? "I'm fine."

"Okay."

Looking down, I saw Jeffrey fitting a cassette into a small boom box which he balanced on the edge of what appeared to be an aquarium.

"What the heck is that?"

He held up the cassette. "Whale songs. Humpback whales. Like Old Air Biscuit."

I glanced back and saw the whale break the surface two swells behind us. "Whale music? What's the album called? *Live from Big Stink?*"

"No scoffing." Jeffrey pointed a warning finger at me. "Just wait." He slid the tape into the boom box and hit the "play" button. Even above the engine noise I heard an eerie sound: part wail, part whine, part hollow hum.

"Ladies and gentlemen," he addressed the guests in the stern, all of whom were squirming on the benches, anticipating Old Air Biscuit's next pungent appearance. "You've probably noticed we've departed from the usual route. Our plan is to lead this digestively-challenged creature out to sea."

Two passengers stood and applauded. Prudence, her face the color of wet cardboard, covered her mouth with both hands. For a fleeting moment I felt sorry for her. Her triumphant role as queen of the world wasn't playing out the way she'd planned.

"Unfortunately, we have to let him approach the boat one more time."

The guests booed. Prudence's eyes widened with alarm.

"In the meantime," Jeffrey made a soothing motion with his hands, "I'm going to pass around the wine and the brandy we keep for emergencies. I think this qualifies."

Henri studied the tiny platinum and diamond watch on his left wrist and considered the twisted path he'd traveled in the pursuit of fashion. First it took forever to find exactly what he wanted. And when he'd spotted it, hiding in the women's section of that chic little jewelry store in Newport, he'd been forced to pay extra to have the band extended. Now he had somehow become ever so gently myopic and couldn't read the microscopic dial. And he'd be damned if he'd squint in front of all these people crammed into the Belly Up.

And he had to face another truth. He'd actually begun to enjoy this barbaric interlude. Granted, most of the belly-buckers were little more than slope-shouldered Neanderthals with no sense of style or technique. But one, the young stud wearing the leather thong over the purple tights, had demonstrated a certain swashbuckling flair, that instinct to seize the day and capture the imagination of the crowd. And if Henri hadn't misread his repeated glances, or his rooster strut, Margaret's companions wouldn't be the only ones yowling at the moon tonight.

No time to think about that now, though. He must focus on the job at hand. He strode to the center of the ring and bellowed to be heard above the drunken bedlam. "And now, ladies and gentlemen, it's time for the seventh match of our tournament. On my left, sponsored by Grover's Clam and Ham and proudly displaying their insignia, a thick smear of ketchup over a glob of tartar sauce, we have Larry Murphy, the Human Jellyfish." He raised Murphy's hand and waited for the drunken crowd to eke out a miniscule roar of support.

"And on my right, sponsored by the Come On 'n' Get It convenience store, and clad in a pair of coveralls last washed in early March, an impressive cluster of fat cells calling himself Bernard 'Jiggles' Jackson."

Henri waved Jackson's limp hand in the air and waited for a meager rumble of approval to die away.

"All right, gentlemen—and I use the term with severe misgivings—you know the rules, such as they are. Prepare to buck bellies."

Henri backed out of the ring, peered again at his watch, and then checked the clock over the bar. The matches were moving more quickly than he'd imagined. And the Mango Marauder had yet to make his appearance.

"That was pretty clever, Jeffrey," I admitted as I wiped something best left unidentified off the rail. After the second dose of the by-product of Old Air Biscuit's bottom-of-the-tide-table diet, our guests had proceeded to drain every bottle on board and the second we docked they'd bolted like rats. "Rigging a cassette player in that watertight box and setting it adrift in the current. I can't wait to tell Dad. Hey, why don't you drive down to the jail with me?"

"You're going now?" Jeffrey tossed two empty brandy bottles into a plastic sack. "I thought you'd be covering the bucking competition."

"I changed my mind. Henri will give me play-by-play later. Besides, I promised Dad I'd tell him how the parade of ships went."

"I'd like to see him." He retrieved a dirty napkin and shredded it into the bag. "But I can't make it tonight. I, uh, have a project to finish."

"Okay." Trying to keep my voice light and show rejection didn't bother me, I scrubbed at a crusty blotch on a cushion.

"Maybe tomorrow," Jeffrey offered. "After the parade. If you can take a break from doing your former-queen stuff."

I scoured the now-invisible blotch, cleared my throat, and went for casual. "Yeah. Tomorrow. I'll save the best parts for you to tell."

"Don't worry about that." He flushed. "I just hope we found a current and that Old Air Biscuit stays with it. The tape reverses when one side finishes. It'll play as long as the batteries hold out. Maybe he'll latch onto some poor tuna fisherman, or a freighter."

"And if he comes back, you can get another tape and take him farther away."

He climbed to the bridge and flicked off the lights, leaving us in the purple-white glow from the two vapor lamps up in the parking lot. "How about to Baja California? Would the *Helen* make it that far?"

"Sure." I peeled off my slicker and spread it out in the cabin to dry. "The *Helen's* in great shape. Why, when he gets out of jail, I'll bet you and Dad could probably take her all the way to Tierra del Fuego." I bent to close the cabinet from which he'd liberated the brandy.

He jumped from the ladder and stood in the doorway. "I was thinking maybe you and I could take her somewhere."

His shadow seemed to fill the room, and I realized his chest was broader than I'd thought, his arms more muscled, his thighs thicker. My cheeks grew hot and my breath caught in my throat. "Uh . . ."

"It doesn't have to be far. Maybe just to Newport." He took a step forward and laid a hand on my arm. "We could have dinner. Or I could pack a picnic. No soufflé."

Why not? It was only dinner. And it wasn't like he was really my type. Not that I didn't enjoy intelligent men. And he did have a nice smile. Since I'd left college, I'd only dated the kind of people I'd been around all the time—cops, lawyers, and reporters—not "civilians." "Well, I—"

"Just think about it, okay?" His voice was both eager and wistful.

I smiled at him. "Okay."

"Good."

"Are you sure you can't come with me to see Dad?"

"I'd like to, Molly, really I would, but I . . ." He chewed on his lower lip. "No. I can't. I have a commitment I have to honor." He checked his watch. "In fact, I'm late now. But I'll see him, and you, tomorrow."

"Okay. Tomorrow," I muttered.

He swung to the dock and strode away. As I made a final check of the *Helen*, I wondered if that commitment had anything to do with what Prudence Deeds had whispered in his ear as he'd helped her off the boat.

"And now the final match of the evening," Henri bellowed over drunken rumbling hoots from the crowd. "The match that will determine whether this year's champion is Larry 'The Human Jellyfish' Murphy from Grover's Clam and Ham, or the seven-time defending champion from Bucky's Body Shop, Big Billy Bohannon."

Big Billy and the Human Jellyfish wobbled unsteadily beside Henri, exchanging slack-jawed, glazed-eye expressions of mock hatred. Henri latched onto meaty hands grubby from an evening of holding perspiring beer bottles and adjusting jock straps and raised them for the crowd's approval. Slewing his eyes to the left, he cast a surreptitious glance at the man in the leather thong who'd been eliminated in the semi-final round. Then he glanced at the clock and made a quick appraisal of the packed bar. No Molly yet. And no sign of the Mango Marauder. The best-laid plans had gone astray. And he couldn't stall any longer.

"Gentlemen, take your places."

Both men hitched at the jeans defying gravity and the pressure of watermelon-sized guts created by years of beer, burgers, fries, and hours logged on couches while clutching remote controls. They paced to the edge of the ring, pawed at the litter of sawdust, peanut shells, and popcorn on the floor, and grunted like rutting rhinos.

"And ready! Set! Buck!" Henri backpedaled quickly from the ring as the two men thudded together like under-inflated tires.

Big Billy stumbled back, off balance. "Oooohhh!" The crowd moaned in astonishment as one of his boots nearly touched the circle and ended the match, but he recovered and moved crab-like around the ring.

Henri checked out Thong Man again. Did he detect a wink, or just a reaction to the noxious cloud of cigarette smoke? Touching his hair, Henri wondered how much glitter remained and whether his deodorant would live up to its twelve-hour promise.

"Ooowwww!"

Henri checked the action in the ring again. The Human Jellyfish hunkered on hands and knees, gasping for air. Big Billy strutted the perimeter, hands clasped above his head.

Should he stop the match? Declare Billy the winner? Start CPR on Murphy? Henri couldn't remember anything in the rules that covered this.

Then The Human Jellyfish stumbled to his feet, tucked his head, and ran at Big Billy. Clearly an illegal move.

Henri grabbed for his silver whistle, but before he could get it to his lips, Big Billy shuffled to his left and kicked Murphy in the rear as he charged past. The Human Jellyfish hurtled out of the ring and sprawled across a ringside table occupied by Mayor Deeds and political supporters from Lincoln City to whom Chuck had just delivered a fresh pitcher of beer. The table collapsed in a spray of brew, broken glass, and sputtering politicos.

Henri brushed beer from his sleeves. Another delightful end to another unforgettable evening in Devil's Harbor. He must remember to plead for this assignment next year.

"Gimme the trophy," Big Billy grunted, raising his fists and preparing for the traditional parade around the bar which would be followed, Mike had warned Henri, by a testosterone-fueled offer to belly-buck the referee.

"Halt!" A voice boomed out over the crowd. "I demand the right to challenge the winner!"

Everyone, except the unconscious Jellyfish, turned to look at the man with the billowing orange satin shirt and the matching mask covering the upper half of his face. A green velvet cape rippled from his shoulders.

Big Billy sucked in a half-bushel of gut and puffed out his chest. "Who the hell are you?"

The man strode toward the ring, the crowd parting before him. He cleared his throat and proclaimed in a high-pitched British accent: "*I* am the Mango Marauder."

"Well, *you* are too damn late." Big Billy seized the trophy from the end of bar. "I won this fair and square."

"You are mistaken." The challenger untied the cape, twirled it, and then flipped it to Henri. "The rules specify that before the winner is declared, anyone, even those who did not compete, may challenge." He stood, hands on hips, the beginning of a sneer on his lips. "Is that not correct?"

"Yes," Henri agreed. Who the hell knew? If it wasn't a rule, it should be.

"Bullshit! I'm the winner. Nobody can stay in the ring with me. Nobody. So take your little prissy-boy outfit and run home to your mommy."

The Marauder peeled black leather gloves from his hands, one finger at a time. A nice touch. Henri felt miffed he hadn't thought of that himself. "Not until I have propelled you from yonder ring."

"You and whose army?" Big Billy set the trophy on the bar and looked around at the crowd for support. No one made a sound or returned his glare. All eyes focused on the man in orange who drew his shoulders back and thrust out a bulging gut.

"Just me."

"I ain't gonna fight no sissy boy."

The Marauder surveyed the crowd, "Would that be because you are a sissy boy yourself?" He stepped into the ring.

"Fight. Fight. Fight. Fight!" The chant built from the crowd. Henri stepped to the edge of the ring, angling toward the end of the bar and the hallway to the back door. He'd open an escape route for the Mango Marauder. It would be just like his last game in the league.

"Who are you calling a sissy boy?" Big Billy shuffled into the ring and faced the challenger. His nostrils flared and his pupils shrank to pinpoints.

"You," the Marauder thundered. "I say you watch *Masterpiece Theater.*"

Big Billy scowled. "What's that?"

"I say you like those drinks with little umbrellas."

"What the hell are you talking about?"

"I hear you collect dolls."

"Shut up. I ain't no sissy boy."

"Fight! Fight! Fight! Fight!" The spectators stomped their feet and slapped their palms on tabletops. Even The Human Jellyfish lifted his head, pounded one fist, then slumped back into oblivion.

"I say you are."

"Am not." Big Billy roared, his fingers balling into fists.

"Prove it, big-bellied sissy boy." The challenger grinned and danced around the edge of the ring on his toes. "Come on, Billy. Prove it to them," he gestured toward the crowd then moved in so close that only Henri heard what he said next.

"Prove it to that inflatable doll in your bedroom."

TWENTY THREE

Maybelline Yamamoto flipped through the papers clamped onto her clipboard and grinned at LaDonna Perkins. "You should have been there. I tell you, I don't know what that fellow decked out like a navel orange said to Big Billy. But it looked like someone lit a firecracker under him. Big Billy reared back and charged, but the Mango Marauder didn't give an inch."

She found the right page of the pre-parade check-off list and put a mark beside the Synchronized Cheese-Cutting Squad from Tillamook. The twenty-two member team, rehearsing a difficult maneuver, circled a fifty-pound wheel of cheddar shaking boxes of crackers like castanets. "Big Billy just snapped. You could have heard his teeth gnashing all the way to Netarts. He made a noise like a constipated hippo and charged again. I almost couldn't watch, but damned if that orange fellow didn't do a little twinkle-foot fox trot and catch Big Billy a glancing blow. All with less of a stomach than I had when I was carrying Bart. But that's all he needed. Big Billy flew right out of the ring and barreled smack into the mayor. Second time His Tubbiness bit the dust inside ten minutes. Laugh? Why I thought I'd bust a gut. And then—"

LaDonna held up one hand, checked her own clipboard, and squinted across the school parking lot. "Hold on a minute,

Maybelline. Do you have that cross-dressing drill team before or after the mechanical clam sandwich?

Maybelline riffled through her papers, pausing to shoot a glare at the white-booted drill team members and the moth-eaten spray-painted papier-mache mini-float. "Before. No, after. No, put them before. And I'm gonna talk to Grover about that clamwich. This is absolutely the last year for that thing. Why, it's getting so tatty you can see the chicken wire right through the paper stuff on the bun. Anyway, like I was saying, Henri called Big Billy out and declared the orange guy the winner and then all hell broke loose." She shook her head and grinned again. "We lost the big mirror over the bar, six chairs, two tables, and I can't tell you how many glasses and pitchers. But it was almost worth it."

LaDonna doubted she'd be so cheerful if her cafe looked like it had been downsized by a tornado. But Maybelline's insurance probably would cover it, and once word got around, last night's free-for-all would generate more business than five years of paid advertising. "I wonder if Big Billy will think it's worth it after he coughs up bail money."

"If the judge gives him bail. Folks lined up three deep to file assault charges against him."

"I heard it took four deputies to get him in the squad car."

"Only two. But that's because Lou ran home and got one of those tranquilizer guns he uses to bring down elk so they can put on those radio collars. Dropped Big Billy just as he threw some fellow in purple tights through the front window. Poor little guy. He'd intended to drive back to Portland last night, but he got so shook up Henri took him home. Said he'd let him sleep on his sofa."

LaDonna snorted and pretended to be interested in the antics of the members of the clown club who were trying unsuccessfully to stuff sixteen unlucky people into a Corvair. Maybelline knew Henri was gay, but refused to acknowledge the full extent of what that meant. "And nobody knows what happened to the man in orange?"

"No. Henri tossed him the trophy and the prize money and he bolted out the back door like he'd put both feet down in a hornet's nest."

"And nobody knows who he was?"

"No one."

Except Henri, LaDonna guessed. From Shelley's accounts of the contents of Henri's closets, she could guess where the Marauder's outfit originated. But LaDonna could keep a secret. She put her megaphone to her lips. "Okay. Everybody get with your group. The parade starts down that hill at eleven sharp. We've got twenty minutes to get it together."

"Don't you think we should wait until dark?" Shelley asked.

Icky Ferris stopped uprooting marijuana plants and gazed across the mist-shrouded field. "No. Everyone's involved with the parade this morning. And last night's heavy rain will discourage hikers."

But not, he thought glumly, those two enforcer-types in black suits. He'd seen them on the hill just that one time, so maybe they weren't from the cartel after all. Shrugging, he decided not to worry about who they were and what they might do to him, especially now that he'd decided to destroy the crop. To sacrifice one love for another. What would be, would be. "'Naught may endure but mutability,'" he muttered.

Bundling up an armload of plants, he carried them to a pile in the center of the field. "I want to get this part of my life behind me. I intend to devote the rest of my days to loving you, my Aphrodite, my Diana, my Athena. I can't blur my senses with a drug that will alter my experience of you."

"Oh, Icky. That's so sweet. So noble. But are you sure I'm worth giving up all this?" Shelley spread her arms.

"'Best and brightest, come away! Fairer far than this fair Day,'" Icky quoted.

"'Where the earth and ocean meet, and all things seem only one in the universal sun.'" Shelley quoted back as she placed a small load of plants on top of the pyre and twined fingers, green and sticky, with his.

Icky sighed contentedly and lifted their hands to shoulder level. "This is all I've ever dreamed of. Someone who knows my inner soul. Someone I can talk to. Really talk to."

Shelley leaned against his chest. "Me, too. All my life."

Icky pulled her tight against him and kissed the top of her head. "Why didn't I hear your soul calling to mine? Why did I waste so much time?"

Shelley tilted her head back, tugged down his T-shirt and kissed the hollow between his collar bones. "I'm here now. That's all that matters."

"So true." Icky pushed her away gently. "But I will not be worthy until I have cleansed my misguided ways with fire."

Shelley nodded. "Purified by flame, true love will burn brighter."

"Shelley?"

"Yes, dearest."

"I mean, I didn't recognize that. Was it Shelley?"

"No. I just tossed it off."

"Wow. That's profound." He kissed her deeply.

"Icky," she finally breathed, "if you start the fire, I'll pull up the rest of the plants."

"Thank you, my love. I do long to see bright flames engulf these symbols of my pursuit of money, the filthy bills and coins that divide man from nature." He opened a can of lighter fluid and spritzed the pile. Maybe, if those guys were from the cartel, he could blame this destruction on the feds, paint himself as a little grower caught in a squeeze play.

"I hope you brought plenty of that," Shelley called. "These plants are awfully wet." She shook water droplets from one.

"They'll burn, once the fire gets going." Icky licked a forefinger and held it aloft. "There's almost no wind, just a slight breeze downhill. The fire won't get out of control and jump to the trees."

"I thought we planned to stay and watch it until it's out."

"Oh yeah, that's right." Icky wondered how many short-term memory brain cells he'd killed by smoking so much pot. He struck a kitchen match, tossed it onto the pile and watched it fizzle out. Striking another, he held it to a spot he'd saturated with starter. The flame caught, spread to a six-inch circle, and then sputtered to a halt.

"Damn!" Icky leaned close and inhaled the aroma as he held a third match to the heap. This could take all day. He glanced at the bulging paper bag filled with brownies, cream cheese, black cherry soda, tortilla chips, salsa, cashews, custard-filled doughnuts, and a big slab of peanut butter pie. He anticipated a major case of the munchies. Even someone who'd sworn to give up pot couldn't be expected to resist the kind of high this pile would deliver. Surely both Shelleys would forgive him one last indulgence.

Tweet. Tweet. Tweeeetttttt!

The red-faced drum major blew his whistle and a marching band called the Musty Melody Makers began bleating out something that might have been "Stars Fell On Alabama," as they stumbled down the road behind two red-clad youngsters with crimson plastic horns on their heads and the Whirligig Festival banner strung between their pitchforks.

"They should call themselves the old Geezers with Glockenspiels. I hope they make it the whole two miles," Maybelline observed. "That trombone player looks like he's about to launch a coronary. And the woman in the support hose with the saxophone appears to have a nasty case of hemorrhoids. She's walking like a duck on ice."

"That's why we put them up front," LaDonna reminded her friend. "More people to notice and yell for the medical response unit if someone keels over."

"Check out the clarinet player. He's wheezing like a broken accordion. If he's got a solo, he's toast. And if the sun comes out, his bald head's gonna fry like an egg."

"I don't think that'll happen." LaDonna peered up at the sky. "The fog's getting thicker. And there isn't enough wind to twirl the whirligigs, or blow away this god-awful smell." She fanned a hand in front of her face. "Reminds me of something. Creosote, maybe? It's getting stronger, too."

Maybelline waved her clipboard as a giant seagull on stilts followed the band out onto the road. "Kind of sicky sweet, whatever it is. Maybe Gus Custer's doing some woodworking. Or burning reject whirligigs."

"Could be."

"Let's hope a breeze clears it out when they get down to the main road. Otherwise we'll get a lecture from His Stupidness. Like it's our fault."

"Where is the little runt, anyway?"

"You know, I haven't seen him. The cars for the princesses are up by the school. He should be driving that classic Impala there, next to the Sidesaddle Mounted Posse." Maybelline pointed to a fiery red convertible with a banner proclaiming "Whirligig Royalty, Past and Present" across the hood and a fleet of whirligigs shaped like bathing beauties mounted on the rear fenders.

"Molly's not there yet, either. Do you think she decided not to come?"

"Could you blame her, what with the trouble with her father and all?"

"No," LaDonna admitted.

"Me neither. But she promised. And Mike claims Molly never breaks a promise."

"Ohmigod, where is she?" Jennifer Daley whined to Bart Yamamoto as she paced beside the parade car. "She's ruining the most important day of my life. How does my hair look? Do you think the stinky smoke is taking the body out of it? I don't have a run in my stockings, do I? Is my dress all crushed? Is there mud on my heels? Do my goose bumps show? Did I put on too much eye makeup? You'd tell me if I did, wouldn't you?"

Bart alternately nodded and shook his head, avoiding words that could land him in deep doo-doo. Silence, he'd learned from his father, while not always the right answer, was generally the safest.

"I'm sure Molly will show up before we start," Traci Walker consoled Jennifer from her seat on the car's folded top. "Mellow out, Jen."

"That's easy for you to say. You already put your fat butt down in the good seat. The one on the side with the most spectators."

"I got here first." Traci squared her shoulders and brushed imaginary lint from the banner that crossed the front of her puffy pink chiffon dress. "Besides, I'll be the next queen. And my butt is not fat."

"Then why do you buy jeans with the 'wide load' label?"

"I do not!"

"Do so!"

Bart sighed loudly, then grabbed Jennifer by the shoulders, and turned her around. "Look, there's Molly."

"Where?"

"Down there." He pointed to a milling mass at the far side of the football field. "She's trying to get through the Garden Tool Drill Team. See her?"

"Ooohhh! And she's wearing the dress she wore when they crowned her. I hope I'm that buff when I'm really ancient."

Bart seized Jennifer's arm. "Let's go meet her, okay? Then we can tell her about Mr. Grabowski's car. We have time. The mayor's not here yet, and the way those fogies at the head of the parade are going, it will be twenty minutes before we move out."

Normally I hate being late. Normally I try to get places on time, early even. But as I stepped on a clown's oversized rubber shoe and elbowed a baton twirler out of the way, I decided I'd make this silly parade the exception to my rule. And as soon as it was over, I'd burn this polyester disco dress from hell.

I turned an ankle on a clump of grass, cursed, and glowered at the mini-majorette who shook a finger at me. I couldn't believe I'd once worn four-inch heels. Really couldn't believe I'd saved this dress. And definitely couldn't believe my father had used emotional blackmail once again.

Thirty minutes ago I'd decided to bag the parade, stripped off the dress, slid on my jeans and a sweatshirt, and started for the back door. I'd planned to drive south to the headland where Vince Grabowski took his final dive, to review everything I knew about him and everyone on my list of suspects. Dad had put up a brave front last night, but he'd been pale and his hands had quivered. I had to get him out of that cell before his heart went gunnysack.

Then, as I was about to leave, the phone had rung. Dad, calling from the jail, told me he wished he could see me in the parade.

"I'm not going."

"But Molly," he'd gasped, "you promised the parade committee."

"I'm breaking my promise."

He'd said nothing for a moment, then sighed. "It's your decision, honey. But I was hoping to see the pictures of you, waving like you did twenty years ago. You made me so proud. Queen of the Whirligig Festival. The smartest girl in town, and the prettiest, too. I felt your mother looking down on us."

I'd steeled myself for the guilt finale. "I love you, Molly. And I'm proud of you. Whatever you do." He hung up before I could respond.

I'd stomped around the house and jammed four no-fat cookies into my mouth before I'd admitted defeat, repaired my makeup, and rammed myself back into the mutant dress and medieval shoes.

Goosebumps clustered on my arms. I could freeze to death in this smoky fog. It smelled like someone had torched a marijuana plantation. My news nerves tingled and I recalled what Jeffrey had said about Icky's nocturnal excursions.

"Molly. Molly! Ohmigod, you look so cool." Jennifer Daley bounced up with Bart Yamamoto trailing in her wake. "I just love that dress. Look at the hem. That's so neat the way it goes up and down like that. And those shoes are awesome."

"And painful. Where's our car?"

"Up there," Bart pointed past a half-dozen people dressed in yellow and brown slug costumes to the top of the parking lot. "By the side of the school."

"Good. I can't walk much farther." My toes had curled under, my arches ached, and my calves screamed with every step.

"Molly, we've got to tell you something. About Mr. Grabowski."

"About his car," Jennifer corrected Bart. She took my right arm and Bart latched onto my left. "It might be a clue."

I managed a grim smile. "A clue?"

"Well, maybe," Bart hedged as they tugged me through a cluster of tambourine-thumping women in black and white cow costumes with swinging udders. "And maybe not."

"No, you loser nerd. It's definitely a clue. That car was totally dirty."

"Not totally," Bart amended, "just around the tires, and up the doors. Like you get when you drive down a dirt road."

Like the road up to Gus Custer's place. Had Grabowski driven up there looking for revenge after Gus had whacked him with the whirligig?

"And it was real late when we saw it," Jennifer supplied.

I snapped to attention. "How late?"

They exchanged guilty looks and flushed.

"After your curfew?" I grilled them.

Jennifer flushed. "Ohmigod, Molly, don't tell my Mom I snuck out. She'll ground me for a year."

"It was after one," Bart conceded. "And I'd rather you didn't tell my parents, either."

According to the medical examiner, Grabowski had stopped breathing some time before midnight. I paused in front of a blackened float commemorating the 1936 gorse fire that had burned down much of the city of Bandon. What had Greg

Erdman told me about the car? That it was clean, inside and out. No, not just clean, he'd used the word "sparkled." So someone had polished it after Jennifer and Bart had seen it. I gripped Jennifer's hand. "Where did you see it?"

"Down by the dock." Jennifer pointed toward the Impala. "We've got to hurry. It's almost time for us to start."

"But the mayor's not there yet." Bart swiveled his head.

"Then you drive," Jennifer informed him. "I'm a princess and Molly's the queen. And we're more important than any old fish-stinky mayor."

I processed information as we fought through a knot of bagpipers grappling with "Louie Louie." Why would someone clean the entire car before he took it to Perdition Point? Why not just wipe off the fingerprints? Who would go to so much trouble? And why?

TWENTY FOUR

"Coming through. Official business." Sergeant Greg Erdman hitched at his belt, elbowed a couple of hefty tourists aside, and then leaned against the mailbox in front of Passing Wind. When the parade approached down Sin Street, he'd be ready. Pissed off, but ready. The job of stopping traffic on the Coast Road usually fell to a deputy; a sergeant shouldn't be assigned to this crap. But thanks to Barbara Sue, the sheriff had found out that Greg had arranged for Molly to visit her father long after lockdown. Naturally, Archie Fletcher went ballistic.

So here Greg stood on his day off, ears still blistering from the sheriff's tirade. But at least he hadn't been suspended. He'd log overtime pay for today, and get to keep most of it thanks to Patsy's surly message on his machine instructing him to take the kids for two weeks in June while she went on her honeymoon. Honeymoon. He smiled. No more alimony.

"Sure is a peculiar smell in the air," the woman beside him observed.

"Yeah," another agreed. "Like something burning."

"It's the engines on those parade cars," a pompous man in Bermuda shorts informed them. "They drive so slow that they overheat."

Greg realized that his eyes had been watering since he got out of his cruiser. And now his nose was stopped up.

Definitely something burning. But the thickening smoke didn't sear his sinuses like the stench of a hot engine would. Definitely organic—half sweet and half acid.

He drew in a deep breath and held it for a moment. Whoa! The air exploded from his lungs. Feeling light-headed now.

He checked his watch, and then shoved his way through the crowd and into Passing Wind. Maybe he needed some food—a sandwich without those damn alfalfa sprouts. Chocolate milk would be good, too. And something crunchy. Maybe nuts. With lots of salt.

Elspeth Hunsaker stepped out on the porch of her home on Temptation Way, peered up the street, and cupped a hand to her ear. She thought she heard an off-key version of "Let Me Call You Sweetheart." Stiffening her spine, she checked her reflection in the grimy front window. Despite three hours in front of the mirror upstairs, she still hadn't settled on the proper expression to present as the parade passed. Anger? Scorn? Divine condescension? Or perhaps benevolent forgiveness for this heathen demonstration? Or should she simply turn her back on such depravity?

"I have prayed for guidance. Please show me the way that I may lead others." She closed her eyes, turned her face to the sky, and drew in a long breath of hazy air.

"Uh-huff." Coughing, she peered up the road through wisps of strange-smelling smoke. Almost like the pagan incense Adam Quarles burned in his degenerate little shop. But this wasn't incense. It was stronger. Something like the sweet scent of heaven. Perhaps she *had* seen a sign. Perhaps Devil's Harbor was right now teetering on the brink of consumption by celestial conflagration.

She took another deep breath and struggled to contain the heavenly smoke signal in her lungs. She, being pure of heart, must allow it to sanctify her soul. Inhaling again, she unleashed an unholy wracking cough followed by an involuntary giggle.

"This is grim business, Elspeth," she cautioned her reflection before she sucked in another breath. "Grim business."

Vowing to lose thirty pounds and get more exercise, Mayor Brighton Deeds huffed across the football field, scattering members of the Tiny Tots Talent Team and leaving a tangle of batons and spangled leotards in his wake. Not that he'd start that health program today. Not with a cut on his cheek, a black eye, a split lip, and a lump on his head the size of a lemon. He'd spent half the night picking splinters of glass out of places he couldn't mention in mixed company.

If he didn't know better, he'd swear that Henri and the others who punched him hadn't really been aiming for Big Billy Bohannon like they claimed. But, no sense in pointing fingers and alienating voters. He'd show them Brighton Deeds could take his lumps. Still, if he ever found that idiot in the orange outfit, he'd file charges for inciting a riot and whatever else he could think of.

"Good morning," he called to Maybelline and LaDonna as he puffed past, tugging his sash. "Where the hell is this smoke coming from?"

The women shrugged, then looked at each other and snickered.

"It's no laughing matter," Deeds snapped. "It could drive away tourists and ruin the festival. If Gus Custer's burning a brush pile I'll have him arrested. I'll have the fire marshal slap him with every fine in the book."

"Yes, sir!" LaDonna and Maybelline snapped to attention and saluted, then collapsed against each other, howling with laughter.

"Why am I the only person in this godforsaken town who takes anything seriously?" He gestured for Bart Yamamoto to get out of the convertible. "I'm here!" he bellowed. "I'll drive, damn it!"

Jeffrey Wolfe dumped cold coffee into a patch of weeds, crumpled the cardboard cup and tossed it into a rusty trash container beside the Come On 'n' Get It convenience store. Squinting through the misty haze, he peered up the Coast Road.

"You'll get a better view if you walk up into town." A young deputy with a three-millimeter buzz cut leaned from the window of his cruiser. "The parade goes up and down every street in Devil's Harbor. Even the alleys."

"Thanks." Jeffrey didn't move.

"Suit yourself." The radio on the dashboard crackled and spat garbled words; the deputy keyed the microphone. "Yes, sir, Sergeant Erdman. I'll set up the roadblock now." Slapping the car into gear, he reversed out of the lot and onto the highway, roared south a hundred yards and, with a squeal of tires, turned the car broadside in the road.

"If I had any sense at all, I'd just walk home," Jeffrey told himself. "Forget about Molly Donovan." He kicked the trash can. "She probably thinks I went home with Prudence Deeds last night."

He rubbed at his ear and kicked the can again. He wasn't sure Molly believed that he'd left his apartment and slept on the *Helen* after his previous encounter with Prudence. And if she didn't, it would be impossible to convince her Prudence had apologized when she'd left the *Helen* last night, "I'm sorry if I caused you trouble with Molly. I was drunk. Please forgive me."

He peered up the road again. "Maybe there's a poem in this: 'Blank Verse For Empty Hearts.'"

"You ladies look lovely, just lovely. Are you ready?" Deeds asked.

Jennifer and Traci giggled, squirmed on our perch, and nudged me. "Yeah," I told His Sweatiness. "Let's get this dog and pony show over with. I've got better things to do." *Like locate the source of this cloud of pot smoke before I get so stoned I can't walk.*

Maybe the feds in the bad suits had set fire to the cannabis crop Jeff suspected Icky had. If so, it was the news story of the year—a story even Ben Galloway couldn't bury. The minute this stupid parade disbanded, I'd bolt home, put on some real clothing, and hike into the hills. With this much smoke, the source shouldn't be hard to find.

"Now, Molly," the mayor gave me a cheesy grin. "I know you don't mean that. These young women have worked hard for the opportunity to win the coveted whirligig crown." His eyes narrowed. "By the way, where's yours?"

"Oh, did I forget my crown?" I patted my head in mock panic. "Gosh, it's like a raincoat, the one day you don't wear it is the day you need it."

We traded glares. I held mine longer.

"You were supposed to wear it," he mumbled as the turquoise convertible carrying last year's chortling queen and three other cackling princesses swept past. Someone must have told a great joke because all four hooted and laughed hysterically, the queen flutter-kicking the back seat. Cranked to the max, the tape deck blared out "Lucille" and the driver stood and steered with his knees while pounding the top of the windshield like Little Richard thumping piano keys.

"Well, we don't have time to argue." Deeds opened the door, running his hand along the side of it as he did. "Nice wax job," he commented. "And the whitewalls shine like new money. Couldn't have cleaned this baby up better myself."

Something niggled at the back of my marijuana-impaired mind, flashed like a leaping fish, then vanished. Jennifer and Traci inhaled, leaned forward to look at each other, puffed out their cheeks, and guffawed. Deeds shot an inquiring look at me.

"It's that new car smell," I offered. "Gets them every time."

He sniffed the upholstery. "Smells like mildew. This thing could use one of my air fresheners. Banana, or pine, or maybe—"

"Mayor, if we don't get rolling, we'll lose our place to Dolly's Llama Club." I nodded at a phalanx of prancing beasts carrying sacks filled with the traditional seaweed-flavored saltwater taffy their handlers would toss to the crowd. Dolly herself smacked the nose of one particularly contrary beast, warning him to, "Knock it off, Fernando."

Deeds scowled, but slid into the driver's seat, slammed the door, and stretched his arms toward the wheel. "Damn." He groped under the seat. "Who drove this last, a giant?" With a grunt and a lurch, he moved the seat as far forward as it would go, tugged his banner into place, settled his feet on the pedals, turned the key, released the emergency brake, and pushed the automatic shift lever into "drive."

And just like that I knew who'd killed Vince Grabowski.

"Get out of the car," I whispered to Jennifer. "Take Traci and slide down over the trunk."

"Are you crazy," she hissed back. "I haven't had a chance to wave yet. And I've been practicing for a month." She demonstrated a limp hand flip.

I tried Traci. "Get out of the car."

She looked at me through vacant eyes, and then flopped back across the trunk, arms flailing and feet kicking in time with raucous laughter.

"Watch her," I told Jennifer as Deeds swung the car in line. "If she falls out she could be trampled by llamas."

"Her butt is too big to trample," Jennifer chortled as he grabbed a handful of Traci's puffy dress. I stepped onto the back seat, hiked up my skirt and swung a leg over to the front.

Deeds turned his head and scowled. "What the heck are you doing, Molly? Get back with the princesses."

"Oh, I will, Mayor." Grabbing the top of the windshield, I swung the other leg over and plopped onto the seat. Flipping open my miniscule purse, I pulled out the tiny tape recorder I'd brought along to record my impressions of the parade. This interview would top even the source of the marijuana smoke, which grew more pungent by the minute. This interview would bypass *The Flotsam* and go straight to the Associated Press. "I'll get back right after you answer a few questions."

He flashed another chamber-of-commerce smile. "Why certainly, certainly. I'd be happy to talk about the parade and the Whirligig Festival as we drive along." He spun the wheel, sending the car down Styx Street toward the ocean. A cluster of spectators waved at Jennifer who had both arms going like the blades of a windmill. "But leave out this smoke. Don't write anything negative about our big day."

"This piece won't be about the festival, Mayor. It will be about you."

He puffed out his lard-laden chest. "Well, I guess that's only fitting. I *am* the driving force behind the event."

"Yes, you are. You're the big frog in this little puddle."

He fanned smoke away from his eyes, lips curling into a simpering smile. "I think of myself as a born leader. A man with vision and courage. A man who sees no obstacles, only opportunities." He waved at an elderly couple squatting in lawn chairs in a yard filled with garden gnomes.

"That's good. Obstacles and opportunities." I paused, glancing at Jennifer who'd taken off her green satin sling-back shoes and put them on her hands like puppets. Traci, snoring, curled up on the folded down roof.

"So tell me, when you took care of Vince Grabowski, were you removing an obstacle, or creating an opportunity?"

He stomped on the brake, tossing me against the dashboard, hurling Jennifer and Traci into the back seat with a cascade of screams, wails, and ripping fabric.

"What the hell are you talking about?"

I scrabbled for the ends of the seat belt. "I'm talking about murder."

"Well you're talking to the wrong person." He moved his foot to the gas and the car reeled down the road. Whimpering, Jennifer and Traci crawled back to their perch. "I don't know anything about what happened to poor Vince," he told me from between clenched teeth. "The last time I saw him, he was walking toward the dock to talk to *your* father."

We turned onto Evil Way and he waved at a man with a home video camera. "But right now isn't the time to discuss this."

"I think it's exactly the time to discuss a— what should I call it? How about a falling-out between thieves?"

"Molly," he hissed from the corner of his mouth, "we are engaged in an important civic endeavor. We must fulfill our duty to the citizens of Devil's Harbor." He acknowledged a wave from a woman in tight shorts holding a whirligig dachshund. "And I know absolutely nothing about how Vince died."

"I think you know plenty. And I think this is the perfect time to tell me, while we're surrounded by all these potential voters."

I fluttered my fingers at a trio of white-haired women in neon walking shoes. "You can tell me how you put up with Grabowski boinking your wife, but when you found out he planned to support Joe Benton you couldn't take it anymore. You can tell me how you killed him and how you're so anal-retentive you didn't just wipe off a few fingerprints, you scrubbed his entire car. 'Clean as his wallet before payday,' that's how Sergeant Erdman described it. Then you can explain how you used that medallion to frame my father."

I nodded and smiled at two boys with skateboards under their arms and held the tape recorder up to his face. "Come on, Mayor. The citizens of Devil's Harbor should know what kind of scheming scum they elected when they checked the box next to your name."

"You can't talk to me like that." He trod on the brake, chucking Jennifer and Traci onto the back seat again. "I'll call Ben Galloway. I'll have your job."

"A: I don't think so. And B: you'll have to make that call from jail."

"I'm getting carsick," Traci wailed.

"And my dress is ripped. This is zero fun." Jennifer struggled upright. "Stop the car."

"We're not stopping!" Deeds hit the gas. "This is a parade, damn it!"

We roared up behind the queen's convertible which had slowed to turn onto Brimstone Boulevard.

"Urrrrpppp." Traci unloaded her breakfast on the floor.

"Ohmigod, Traci. Gross-a-rama. Are those jelly beans? No wonder you have more zits than brains."

"Get out!" Deeds punched the brake again and pulled a gun from his jacket pocket. That gun was not, I deduced, a pot-smoke-induced illusion. "Get out before I shoot you both."

Jennifer and Traci gaped, then slithered over the trunk and ran for Bucky Mallory's house, screaming. Three llamas bolted in the other direction. I fumbled at my seat belt clasp with frozen fingers.

"Not you, Molly." Deeds pointed the gun at my head. "You come with me."

I swallowed bile. Even if I'd known I'd end up confronting the mayor, I wouldn't have imagined he'd be armed. Deeds never struck me as the type. But until five minutes ago I wouldn't have figured he had guts enough to kill Vince Grabowski, either.

"The gun was my father's." He jerked the wheel and goosed the car over the curb and through Olive Mabry's flower garden. "I've never fired it, but it wouldn't be smart to bet that I couldn't hit you."

I nodded. His glazed eyes and clenched fingers convinced me an escape attempt was lunacy. That left only the reckless pursuit of my story and the faint hope that he could be distracted. "You didn't use that gun on Grabowski. So how did you kill him?"

Tires sucked mud and Olive hollered from her back door. Right-handed, he muscled the car across Jim Parsons' lawn, leaving deep gouges. He kept his left hand, and the gun, tight against his belly, out of sight of spectators. "I bashed his head with a frozen halibut and strangled him with the chain on that medallion Prudence gave him. Broke the damn thing. Stowed old Vince in the cooler until I could haul him to Perdition Point."

"And then you bought a new chain and framed my father."

"I only meant to confuse things. I can't go to jail. This town needs me."

Snatching his hand from the wheel, he laid on the horn as we jounced across the sidewalk and spun onto Styx Street aiming straight at the Netarts Precision Knitting Team. Balls of yarn and needles flew as the women dashed for the sidewalk. I braced my right hand against the dashboard and clutched the tape recorder with the other, fighting the whirlpool of his insanity.

"He deserved to die." He jerked the wheel right again and we jumped the curb and roared through the slatted sides of the rose garden gazebo Myrtle Perry had built in a bid to win the Garden Club's blue ribbon. Leaves, petals, and shards of wood swirled around us and I saw Myrtle's mouth stretched into a silent scream as she peered out an upstairs window.

"He took my money, he took my wife, and he tried to take my political future." With a series of twangs and pops, the car lurched through the maze of poles and wires Del Sadler had strung for his grapevines. "Then he said that I was a blubbery blimp, a pungent pile of pork, and that Prudence would never love me again."

He turned to me, eyes flickering like a feral cat's. "I had to kill him! I had no choice! You understand, don't you?"

Without waiting for an answer, he slewed the car across another sidewalk into Damnation Alley then plunged downhill toward Temptation Way, leaning on the horn. We scattered The Young Women's Anti-Profanity Unicycle Team. Several of them flipped us the bird as they dove for cover and their single-wheelers crunched beneath our tires. Elspeth Hunsaker, skirt hiked up to her thighs, saluted us with a bottle of wine as we bucketed past her house trailing a clattering snarl of wire, wood, and vines.

In slow motion, I reached for the buckle on my seat belt, wondering which would hurt more—a bullet or a fall from a speeding car.

He hit the horn again. We parted the aluminum-armored ranks of the Knights of Perpetual Mildew Marching and Slumgullion Society; they fell to the sidewalks, clanking together like empty pop cans in a supermarket cart as we executed a two-wheeled turn onto Sin Street. Ahead I saw the Coast Road and Greg Erdman, arms out at shoulder level, halting traffic. I let go of the buckle release and switched the tape recorder to my right hand.

"They're not going to get me!" Deeds quick-stepped from brake to gas to brake, jerking the wheel to the left, fishtailing into the turn.

Greg Erdman thrust his whistle between his lips and blasted it as he jumped out of the intersection. "Slow down!"

"Catch!" I shrieked and hurled the tape recorder. "Deeds killed Grabowski! It's all there!"

Blam.

The bullet hissed past my elbow and crunched into the door.

"Stop!" Greg yelled. "Stop right now!"

"You're dead, Molly." Deeds floored the gas and aimed for the narrow gap between marchers and sidewalk-bound spectators lining the Coast Road. A kaleidoscope of color swirled past, a collage of faces: Adam and Claire, Henri and a man in a purple jumpsuit, Prudence Deeds hovering beside Joe Benton.

"I love you," Deeds howled in her direction. The speedometer needle leaped to thirty-five, to forty.

The last of the Musty Melody Makers scattered. The color guard mini-devils dropped their banner and leaped for safety as we roared onto the bridge. Beyond it a patrol car sat broadside in the road and I caught a flash of polished metal as a deputy swung a gun to his shoulder.

Would he hit a tire? Or would the shot go high? Would we slam into the guard rail before or after we flipped over? My mind closed down to a dark vortex of fear.

The speedometer needle jumped to forty-five.

I had to do something.

Anything.

I braced my feet against the floor, leaned forward, and snaked my left hand under the seat. My fingers touched a metal bar.

The speedometer ticked up to fifty.

I pressed the seat belt release, and then wrapped my fingers around the seat adjustment bar, yanked as hard as I could, and shoved with my feet. The seat slid back.

"Wha—???"

Deeds' feet left the pedals. His hand flew from the wheel. The car swerved toward the Come On 'n' Get It. I grabbed for the gun with both hands, wrapped my fingers around the barrel.

"Let go!" Deeds hammered my shoulder with the side of his right fist.

"Never." Sinking my teeth into his wrist, I clamped my jaw. He writhed like an eel. My frigid fingers slid along the cold metal.

The car hit the curb, jolted into the potholed parking lot, and careened toward the store.

"I'll shoot!" Deeds shrieked in my ear.

I channeled every ounce of strength into my hands, my arms, my teeth. Deeds grunted and cursed. By inches, I levered the gun away from my face.

"Hold on, Molly!" a man's voice called. The car clanged into the metal trash can at the edge of the parking lot. "I'm coming."

I got one knee up on the seat, unclamped my teeth, and butted my head under Deeds' chin.

With a shattering cascade of safety glass, the car smashed through the front window of the convenience store and plowed into the snack rack. Corn chips and cheese curls fell like salted hail. A woman screamed. We whiplashed into the wheel, then back against the seat, but I kept my grip on the gun. The car crumpled into the beer cooler against the far wall, releasing a geyser of golden spume. The engine coughed itself to death. I planted my knee in the layer of lard over Deeds' groin and head-butted him again.

"You can't stop me." He elbowed me in the ribs.

I flinched. The gun swung back toward my face.

"I got it Molly!" A hand reached across Deeds' shoulder.

Too late. Deeds' finger twitched on the trigger. I closed my eyes.

Blam.

The explosion rammed through my ears, hammering the inside of my skull. The acrid smell of gunpowder scorched my nose and the recoil numbed my fingers. I didn't know if I'd been hit, but I knew I couldn't let go.

"Agghhh!" someone grunted.

A woman screamed again. A thin, distant, tearing sound punctuated by a sob.

"Let go!" Deeds slammed his elbow into my stomach. I gasped. My grip loosened. The gun barrel swung toward my face until it was all I could see.

"If you hurt her I'll rip your face off."

251

Deeds elbowed my sternum. A wave of black nausea swept over me.

"Let go!" Deeds snarled and ripped the gun from my grip. "You're dead, Molly."

A bloody hand gripped Deeds' wrist and twisted.

"Get down, Molly!"

The barrel jerked toward Deeds' chest. I slid to the floor. Blam.

TWENTY FIVE

"**I** know you're tired and upset, Molly," Mike Donovan called through the bedroom door. "And I know you're mad at me on top of all that. But it's not going to help to hide in your room."

He cocked his head, right ear against the panel; he heard nothing.

"Molly, honey. You showered four times but you haven't eaten a thing. Should I make you some soup? Or a sandwich? Grilled cheese, maybe?"

He touched the knob, then drew his hand back, torn between concern and respect for her privacy.

"Molly, I just want to know that you're okay. Tell me that you're okay."

He leaned against the door again, but heard nothing.

"Molly, I'm coming in." He gripped the knob, turned it and inched the door open. In the dim light that filtered through the yellowed shade he saw her curled beneath the sheet, one arm cradling her head like she'd ducked and taken cover. Her eyes were shut. He smiled. Sleep was a good sign. Maybe she needed that more than food.

He tiptoed to the bed and lowered himself beside her. Molly slept hard; the creaking jostle of the bed springs wouldn't disturb her. And her oblivion gave him a chance to say what he couldn't seem to manage while they were eye-to-eye.

"Molly," he whispered, "I'm sorry I always say the wrong thing at the wrong time." He touched her damp hair. "Like tell you that you should have waited until the parade was over to confront Deeds. And saying Jeff saved your life. I didn't mean that you didn't handle things fine on your own." He twirled a strand of her hair in his fingers. "But, Molly, I was so damn frightened that I'd almost lost you . . . I couldn't think straight."

He sighed and looked at a silver-framed photograph on Molly's dresser: Helen, with a crown of flowers on her head, smiling from a long-ago meadow.

"I love you so much, honey, and I'm so proud of you. For being a fine reporter. For figuring out that Brighton Deeds was the killer. For knowing what to do to stop the bleeding after he got shot. And for believing in me." He plucked up a corner of the sheet and wiped his eyes.

"And I'm sorry I wouldn't tell you what Vince Grabowski and I argued about. But that secret is going with me to my grave. It was just more of his bullshit, anyway."

He leaned forward, putting his weight on the balls of his feet and sliding one hand to the small of his back. "I love you. Like it or not, you'll always be my little girl, Molly, darling."

He stood gingerly, favoring his left leg, and started for the door. Molly sighed and shifted. He turned to gaze at her, then retraced his steps, tucked the sheet around her shoulders, and bent to place his lips against her forehead.

"Ohmigod." Jennifer Daley squealed loudly. "It's me! I'm her!"

She stuck out her tongue at the other princesses and ran toward Chuck Yamamoto who'd been drafted as master of ceremonies. Snatching the salmon whirligig crown from his hands she jammed it onto her head and paraded across the narrow scrap-lumber stage she and Bart had assembled Friday night and trimmed with the only bunting they could find: threadbare red and green cloth left from a not-too-recent Christmas pageant. Six Musty Melody Makers—the only ones not injured during the parade—struck up an off-key rendition of "Copacabana."

"Thank you, thank you." Jennifer windmilled her arms, grinning at her subjects, most of whom were either congratulating Mike Donovan, or sucking up the appetizers Maybelline and LaDonna had concocted in what Bart described as a "seriously twisted giggling fit." Beyond the buffet table, Shelley and Icky danced to a tune only they could hear, bodies and lips melded together, eyes closed. Henri and a man in purple held hands and swayed to the music, eyes on each other.

Bart and her parents applauded, prompting most of the others to do the same. With a wave, she delivered the first lines of the speech she'd memorized. "Thank you all for this great honor. I will do my best as ambassador from Devil's Harbor to the world."

Her parents clapped again, her father casting one eye toward Gus Custer who Jennifer saw had tilted a jug over the punch bowl and was drizzling a clear liquid into the non-alcoholic mix. Bart jerked his thumb toward the other contestants, prompting her to finish.

"I just wish we could *all* have been chosen to wear the crown." She turned and gave the losers the smile that said, "But of course I deserve it more." Traci snarled and made a very unladylike gesture and the princesses huffed off the platform.

Jealousy is not pretty, Jennifer thought, as Chuck struggled to pin on the sash proclaiming her "Miss Whirligig." And this day was so not like it was supposed to be. With Vince

Grabowski dead, Mayor Deeds in the hospital, and the man who beat Big Billy Bohannon missing, she'd have to dance with Bart's father. And Molly wasn't here to take her picture for the paper. What a rip-off!

The double doors to the gym crashed open and a hooded man festooned in orange bounded through, trailing a velvet cape. "I am the Mango Marauder," he bellowed. "I demand a dance with the Whirligig Queen!"

Jennifer giggled and waved. "That's me! I'm her!" She jumped from the stage wondering how this guy out-bucked Big Billy. He didn't have a bulging gut. Was he an imposter?

Who cared? She sashayed to the center of the dance floor. Everyone was watching her. That's what mattered.

"Shall we share a cup of that punch Gus Custer created?" Henri put an arm around his friend's shoulders. Such nice shoulders. Muscular, but smooth. Strong, but sensitive. "It won't match the chardonnay I left chilling, but it will relax every muscle in your body."

"*Every* muscle?"

Henri clapped his hands. "Oh, sweet bluebird of happiness, I hope not." He led his friend past dancers trying to move to a mangled medley of Beatles tunes.

The doors crashed open. "Where ish he?"

Everyone froze as Elspeth Hunsaker stalked across the floor, the soles of her shoes squeaking on the polished wood. "You schnake in the grass."

She stabbed Henri's chest with a stiff forefinger. "I schuppose you sink I don't know you tried to make a schow of my mockery." She hiccupped, then corrected herself. "A mockery of my schow."

Henri stepped back. Her breath smelled like paint thinner. "Er . . . "

"Well I did." The forefinger struck again. "I noon it all long. Hic." She covered her mouth, eyes rolling. "You fried to make a tool, I mean a foul, out of me. In fron of my listless lobsters. "She tore at her tangled hair. "Loyal lisseners."

Elspeth drunk? Henri couldn't believe his ears or his nose. "*Moi?*"

"Don't lie to me." Elspeth balled up her fists and struck his chest. "You, you Judas!"

"Now, Elspeth." Henri clamped his hands around her wrists and looked around for help. No one, not the Mango Marauder, not even his purple-clad companion, stepped forward. Well, he couldn't blame them. Who wanted to be part of a spectacle? "Just calm down and—"

"I will nod clam down. Hic. I'm mad as hell. Mad as heck, hic. Those men schut down my schtayshun."

"What? KYMR is off the air?"

"Thanksch to you. Telling thoshe men no one lissens to my show. Hic. Telling them I don't scherve the commonity. I do scho. Hic." Fat tears rolled down her face and she collapsed against Henri's chest.

Henri shrugged and then patted her back. "I didn't know they'd do that. They asked me about Devil's Harbor and news and information and I answered honestly. Why, I looked forward to your show. I listened every day."

"Really?" Elspeth blotted her eyes on the flowing sleeve of Henri's embroidered linen shirt.

"Really. I was a big fan." Henri told himself it was almost the truth. He dug a crisp white handkerchief from his back pocket and pressed it into her hand. "If there's anything I can do to help, I will."

But really, he thought as he cast a wink at his companion, what could be done at this point? The plug had been pulled.

"Thash wonderful," Elspeth blew her nose, wadded the handkerchief, and stuck it into his shirt pocket. "Because thosh men tole me about public accessh televidshun. All I need ish a video camera anna photogerapher and I can reach thousands of people."

Henri blinked. Surely, he must have misunderstood her. "Television?"

"That's right." She spun on one rubber heel and started for the door, tucking her hair into a bun. "We'll start Monday morning at sunrise, up on the headland."

Henri noted that her drunken slur had dissolved into her usual self-righteous tone. He'd been played for a fool.

"Pick me up at five-thirty," she called over her shoulder. "And don't be late!"

I cracked open the door and surveyed the gym. A few couples staggered around the floor to a tune that might possibly be "Put Your Head On My Shoulder," or perhaps "If I Had A Hammer." Henri and Gus, glasses raised, serenaded a group by the punch bowl. Nearby, LaDonna and Maybelline, with Adam and Claire assisting, squirted whipped cream on brownies. Others sprawled, snoring, across a platoon of folding chairs in the far corner.

"There you are." My father snagged a glass of punch and hurried toward me. "I'm glad you came, honey. Try some of this stuff Gus mixed."

I accepted the glass, sipped, choked, swallowed, coughed and drank again. "Smooth," I rasped. Like drinking a mix of gasoline and broken glass.

He hugged me and turned toward the group at the dessert table. "Look, everyone. Molly's here!"

"Good golly, Miss Molly," Henri roared. He raised his glass. "Let's drink to Molly."

The band squealed into silence. Everyone scrambled for glasses and raised them. My face grew hot with embarrassment.

"To Molly," my father said.

"To Molly," the crowd responded, clinking glasses.

I gulped the rest of my drink. It hit my stomach like a flamethrower. The Musty Melody Makers struck up something that might have been "Moonlight In Vermont," or possibly a half-speed version of "Let's Go To The Hop."

"How about a dance with your old man?" My father took my glass and set it with his on the edge of the dessert table.

"There's nothing I'd like more."

We edged onto the floor, Dad attempting what I guessed was a fox-trot, and me relying on quick reflexes to keep my feet out from under his. Princesses swirled by us in their fluffy dresses and boys competed to see who could look more bored.

"Just one dance, Dad, and then I'm going home. I'm wrung out. And I've got to be up early to deliver *The Flotsam*. I just came because . . ." Because I hadn't been asleep. Because I'd heard every word he'd said but had still been too angry at him to accept his apology. "I wanted to tell you . . ." The words caught in my throat and I pressed my face against his shoulder.

"I know," he stroked my hair. "It's okay, Molly. We've both had a hard week. But we're family; I know what's in your heart. I'm sorry I said those things. I'm an old chauvinist pig and sometimes I treat you like you're still a kid. You were right to be mad."

I blinked. A to-my-face apology? Who was this man impersonating my father? "No, Dad, I wasn't."

"You were."

Apology merged into argument. We were back on familiar ground. "No. I should have waited and confronted Deeds later. I was just so anxious to get you out of that jail—"

"Enough arguing!" he laughed. "I'm out. That's all that matters. And I'm so proud that Portland paper wants to hire you to cover the coast. Monday we'll put your house in New Mexico on the market. Then we'll get your truck to the repair shop, find a bigger desk, rearrange the living room and—"

"Dad!" I abandoned my indoor voice, ignoring the staring princesses.

He widened his eyes. "What?"

"I haven't taken the job yet."

"Of course you'll take—" He flushed and bit his lip. "You'll do what's right for you. And I'll butt out. See," he beamed, "I can learn. I can change."

"May I cut in?" The voice came from behind me.

"Why not?" Dad grinned. "When you dance with the prettiest girl you can't expect to keep her to yourself." He released me to the muscular arms of a masked man draped in orange satin.

As he swept me around the floor, I peered through the holes in the mask at a pair of eyes sparkling with amusement. "You must be the Mango Marauder."

"That's right, Miss Molly." He swung me into a quick two-step as the band picked up the pace with a tune that vaguely resembled "California Girls." "I'm the man who sent Big Billy Bohannon packing."

"I heard you had a British accent. The one you're using now sounds like a cut-rate John Wayne knock-off."

He twirled me and added a deep dip. I clutched his shoulder; the muscle was like rock. "You don't think I sound like the Duke, ma'am?"

"I think you sound like you have a mouthful of cow pie."

The eyes twinkled as he brought me out of the dip, his muscles rippling beneath my fingers. "They warned me about your sharp tongue, little lady."

I thought of all the risks he'd taken, swallowed hard, and took one of my own. "And they warned me that what I've been searching for everywhere else might be right in front of me."

The eyes narrowed.

Queasy humiliation chilled my gut. *Did I blow it? Was I too late?*

"I don't get your drift, ma'am."

Not too late. Too vague. Time to connect the dots.

"Then let's try this drift." I tugged up the bottom of the hood and traced his lips with my fingers. "Let's drift over to your place. I'll swallow my pride and admit that I just might be just a bit competitive. You'll tell me what Prudence Deeds said when she got off the boat. Then you'll whip me up a soufflé."

"Hmmm." He twirled me again and the hood fell back into place. "I thought you didn't care much for soufflé."

I gave him a wicked wink I'd never used before in my life. "Maybe that's because the soufflés I've had in the past collapsed too soon."

A tide of red swept up the bit of neck I could see. "My soufflés have great staying power," he said in a husky whisper.

I smiled and checked my watch. "I've got the rest of my life to see if that claim is accurate."

Epilogue

The massive bull sea lion cranked his head back and glared at the camera-clicking tourists on the rim of Neptune's Grotto. Ever since that thing floated in with the kelp, he'd had no peace. They were up there from dawn until dark, annoying him with their shouts and squeals. Between that, driving off young bulls, and trying to keep the cows from slipping off the low ledges for snacks, he was exhausted.

And mating season didn't end until late July. Seven weeks before he got his mouth around a mess of squid and hauled out on an isolated rock for a long nap.

He rearranged his ton of muscle, bone, and fat and turned his nose into the wind, sniffing the odor of—

Whale!

He gronked out a warning and beat his flippers against his barnacle-encrusted favorite rock. Orcas would treat his harem like a smorgasbord.

The cows hronked at him and shifted about, but moved no higher on the ledges.

Panting, he paused to gather the energy to drive them to safety and heard—

Singing?

The bull cocked his head and picked up the wailing-hum of whale talk. Humpbacks. Lots of humpbacks.

Remembering that humpbacks ate krill, not sea lions, he gronked to the cows to never mind his previous order, trundled to the edge of the outcropping, and peered into the water. Something bobbed on the surface. It was too small to be a whale, but it was singing whale songs. As he studied it, a humpback surfaced a few feet away.

Braaappp—uh—whap—braappp.

The water around the whale erupted in a halo of bubbles.

An updraft assaulted the bull's nostrils and he gronked out a protest.

A cluster of hronking cows scrambled for higher ground. He torqued his neck to watch them and noticed tourists shouting and staggering away from the railing. In a moment they were all gone. And the cows were up on the high ledges where they belonged. Quiet. For once.

With a contented sigh, he turned back to the cove and spotted the flatulent fluked visitor surging toward the inlet, following the ebbing tide and that singing thing.

The bull shook his head. Blubber boy sure stunk up the grotto, but that had its good points. He gronked out an invitation to hang around.

One of the whale's huge eyes swiveled and the lid drooped in a wink. Then it arched its back and, with a slap of its fluke, dove toward the open ocean.

The bull raised a flipper in farewell. He understood how it was. Sometimes you just had to go with the flow.

About the authors

Carolyn J. Rose grew up in New York's Catskill Mountains, graduated from the University of Arizona, logged two years in Arkansas with Volunteers in Service to America, and spent 25 years as a television news researcher, writer, producer, and assignment editor in Arkansas, New Mexico, Oregon, and Washington. Her hobbies are reading, gardening, and not cooking.

Mike Nettleton grew up in Bandon and Grants pass, Oregon. A stint at a college station in Ashland led to a multi-state radio odyssey with on-air gigs in Oregon, California, and New Mexico under the air name Mike Phillips. He's been with KEX in Portland since 1994. His hobbies are golf, pool, Texas hold-em poker, and book collecting.

Carolyn and Mike have authored a number of mysteries. They can be found at their website: www.deadlyduomysteries.com

LaVergne, TN USA
06 November 2009
163310LV00001B/1/P